THE
NORFOLK
BEACH
MURDERS

An absolutely gripping crime thriller

JUDI DAYKIN

DS Sara Hirst Book 5

D1614509

Joffe Books, London
www.joffebooks.com

First published in Great Britain in 2023

Cover art by Dee Dee Book Covers

ISBN: 978-1-80405-859-6

The miserable have no other medicine
But only hope:
I hope to live, and am prepared to die.

William Shakespeare, *Measure for Measure*

AUTHOR'S NOTE

It has been my great delight to call Norfolk my home for the last forty years. As with all regions, we have our own way of doing and saying things here. The accent is lyrical and open, just like the countryside and skies. If you would like to pronounce some of the real place names in this book like a local, the following may help:

> Happisburgh = Haze-bruh
> Wymondham = Wind-am
> Norwich hides its 'w'.

The derelict World War Two gun emplacement at Happisburgh is still there (at the time of writing). Urban Explorers took photos of the underground areas several years ago, circumventing the infill the local council had put in place earlier. It is one of several such batteries along this part of the coast, some of which are in better condition than the one at Happisburgh. So far as I am aware, it isn't possible to go underground at any of them. Cliff collapses occur almost every winter, and the emplacement moves closer to the edge each time.

Seal colonies thrive at various places around the north Norfolk coast. Some are more easily accessible than others. If you visit, please respect the seals' privacy or you might cause a mother to abandon her pup, or you could get bitten.

For the benefit of my readers who might not know:

RSPCA = Royal Society for the Prevention of Cruelty to Animals. They run a seal sanctuary in Norfolk and are experts at helping injured seals.

Secret Santa = an office tradition. Involves the random selection of a colleague's name from a lottery. You purchase a present for the colleague up to a set value but don't reveal who you have bought for. Occasionally used to play naughty jokes on the recipients!

Ordinance Survey maps = OS have been mapping Britain since 1791. They are considered the gold standard of map makers. You can buy their maps for leisure, business or via satellite on an app with varying degrees of detail.

PROLOGUE

Childhood memories had led Mu here. No one else seemed to have used it or stayed long if they had. Mu snuggled down into her sleeping bag and roll of blankets. With luck, the cardboard would keep the dampness from rising under her during the night. Pulling Roger close to her, she tucked the edge of the blanket around him. It would help keep them both warm. She wound an arm around him and dropped a light kiss on his grizzled canine head. Part lurcher, part other unspecified breeds, the dog was about the size of a Labrador, though sleeker in build and mostly dark grey in colour. Roger huffed his pleasure in reply.

The place was abandoned and, despite the tatty security signs nailed on the gate, Mu doubted if anyone would disturb them. Certainly not on a night like this so close to Christmas. The wind was getting up. It whistled through the broken skylight in the reception room and rattled the outer door to the admin block for the old caravan site. This second room must have been the office, its windows now boarded with plywood. Once, they would have looked out across the rows of caravans standing ready for the holidaymakers that Mu remembered. The caravans had long since been removed or broken up, only the wrecked concrete pads where they once stood remained. The remnants of gravel paths wandered through the encroaching scrub to the office building.

Mu and Roger had arrived in the late afternoon. A violent red sunset had bloodied the clouds gathering over the North Sea. It had taken six days of walking, hiding, bin diving and sleeping in hedges to reach here from Norwich. The weather had not been kind. They'd slipped unobserved down the footpath by the side of the pub only to find that the caravan park was no longer there. Their luck had held out when Mu found the door to the abandoned breeze-block admin office jammed open. The old toilet block next door was still there too. Vandals had trashed both buildings but, to her delight, Mu had found that the water was still on. Expert at staying off people's radar, Mu and Roger settled into the corner of the office for the night. No one knew they were there, so they would be able to sleep in peace.

The full moon rode fitfully from behind the stormy clouds and shone through a gap between the plywood boarding and the top of the window, letting in enough light for Mu to open a tin of dog food to give to Roger. She unwrapped the pack of out-of-date sandwiches she'd pulled from the bin outside the tiny supermarket in Marlham and ate them. She had no idea what the time was. There was nothing else to be done tonight, so the pair bedded down.

Violence and fear had driven them out of London, where the begging was often good. Better than rural Norfolk anyway. They had especially enjoyed Saturday teatimes when one of the gurdwaras arrived with their van to hand out delicious curries, naans, hot drinks and sweets to the homeless community that gathered in anticipation in the alleys off the Strand. Mark's death had put an end to all that. Mu had taken Roger, and the pair had left the city.

The memory of those curries was making Mu hungry. Perhaps Roger was hungry too, as he vibrated under the blanket. Maybe he was cold.

'What's up, boy?' she whispered. 'I'll get us some more food tomorrow, I promise.'

She pulled at the blankets to wrap an extra layer over the elderly dog. His head rose, ears pricked, and he slowly scanned from side to side, trying to locate something. He began to grumble. Mu patted him gently, wishing fervently that what he was hearing wasn't rats. She hated rats.

Rain spattered and shattered on the office roof and drummed against the plywood in short bursts. She strained to listen for whatever Roger had heard.

A flash of fear ran through her. A light was skittering across the roof. It had to be a torch. Praying it was just a late dog walker, Mu pulled Roger closer and shushed him as quietly as she could. His grumbling stopped, but his scanning didn't. He shook off her protective arm and padded to the windows. He snuffed at the boarding, then turned to look at Mu quizzically.

'Who is it?' Mu stood up, pulling a blanket around her shoulders for warmth. The torch beam flashed again. She put a hand on the dog's collar. 'Let's keep it quiet, shall we, eh?'

The wind dropped momentarily, and they heard a man's voice call out. It was cut off suddenly. A babble of voices followed, speaking a language Mu couldn't recognise. A low guttural voice spoke sharply across the others, and silence fell again.

Mu clipped on Roger's lead and cautiously crept to the outer door. It opened inwards, and despite her best efforts, she had not been able to fully close it when they had settled for the night. Now she hid behind it, peering across the park through the gap between the door and its frame. Roger began to huff again, warning her that he felt threatened.

'Good boy,' she murmured and rubbed his hackles fondly.

The wind moved the clouds, and the moon reappeared, blazing its full, clear light across the derelict site. A group of people were standing on the cliff edge. If memory served, an old wooden staircase led up to the park from the beach below. It was quite the climb, and if the steps were as derelict as the site, they would be very dangerous, especially in this weather. It seemed they'd risked it as the last of the group appeared to rise from below the cliff. Whatever was going on could hardly be legal. If anyone knew that Mu was watching, she and Roger would be dead meat.

Two men — at least, Mu assumed these were all men — were arguing. Their voices reached her as faint echoes and their shapes were clearly defined in the moonlight. The group suddenly scattered when the larger man waved what looked like a gun. Mu stuffed her hand into her mouth to prevent herself from making any noise as the pair began to fight. Roger looked at her with silent concern.

It wasn't much of a match. The gunman was much larger. Arm raised, and with the butt of the gun in his hand, he delivered several blows to the other's head. The smaller man staggered sideways.

It was all over in a second. Whether the wind caught him or he was dizzy from the attack, the man stepped out into the void and vanished over the edge of the cliff.

CHAPTER 1

Some days, living so far from work seemed a penance rather than a pleasure. For Detective Sergeant Sara Hirst, this was one of those days. Still dark when she switched off her alarm, the urge to stay in her warm bed snuggling with Tilly, her cat, was huge. Of course, she was used to shift work. It went with the job. The prospect of the tortuous hour-long drive across the county on dark, crowded A roads palled sometimes.

'Must be getting soft,' she muttered. 'It's all your fault. I said you weren't going to sleep in the bed with me, didn't I? Fat chance, eh?'

She petted the cat, which lay stretched out at her side under the duvet, head on the pillow as if she were human. Tilly yawned and blinked at Sara, unmoved and unwilling to leave the warmth. There was no point in trying to lay down the law with Tilly — the feline always won. Leaving the elegant Siamese in bed, Sara climbed from under the duvet and headed for the kitchen.

In the back garden, the wind was shaking the trees and bushes. Rain splashed from the gutters on the bathroom extension, something she meant to have mended but had yet to arrange. She propped her mobile on the window ledge to give it the best chance of finding a signal and filled the kettle.

Christmas was imminent, Sara's second in this cottage in the coastal village of Happisburgh. When she'd inherited it from her late father, Sara hadn't known what to do. Having moved to Norfolk from Tower Hamlets, the thought of living in such a rural spot had never crossed her mind. At first, she had found Norwich quaint in comparison to vibrant London. Living even further away from the nightlife available 'up the city', as the locals said of Norwich, was unappealing. However, the pleasure of moving into the home of her East End dad had prevailed. It was the only adult connection she had with him. Here Sara was two years and eight seasons round, still learning to love the country life. Now when she went down to London to visit her mother, she sometimes felt that the streets were too crowded, the people were in too much of a rush and she found the constant noise draining.

Not that she had been to London since August. After years of living together, her mother, Tegan, and her partner, Javid, had finally tied the knot. It had been the Jamaican wedding to end all weddings. Not a morsel of traditional food or a Bob Marley song from the DJ had been left out. The Tower Hamlets African and Caribbean Social Club had pulled out all the stops for the couple, and it had been a delight — until one of Javid's sisters, too many glasses of bubbly under her belt, had spent part of the evening trying to persuade Sara to return to London.

'That Met Police would be glad to have you back,' she'd promised. 'You could sell this cottage thing and come home to us.'

Sara knew she had no desire to go back to London. Norfolk was where she loved to be, and this cottage was her home. She brewed a coffee and then, flicking on the Christmas tree lights and the television, she settled on the sofa to drink it. She'd get moving when it woke her up. The local news was warning her of problems on the roads. Maybe it was time to consider changing her small car for something beefy. A thought she'd had many times before.

She was in the shower when her mobile rang. Shivering in a damp towel, Sara tiptoed across the cold pamment tiles to grab it from its perch. The missed call was from her team boss, DCI Hayley Hudson.

The man Sara still thought of as her real boss, DI Edwards, had taken the arrival of a DCI in the spring rather badly. Things had settled down for the team over the summer, but Sara remained suspicious of the woman from Hampshire via Wiltshire. In theory, having a female career boss should have been a bonus for Sara. The DCI had suggested that Sara take her inspector exams, which was a logical step. But Sara remained dubious about Hudson's motives, wondering if she was the kind of woman who didn't like other women working for her. Nor did Sara want to leave the Norfolk force, and promotion might well mean having to do that.

The screen blinked a text notification. *What do you know about seals? Call me asap. HH.*

Seals? What sort of seals? The sea mammals that occupied various beaches along the north Norfolk coast? Or the kind made of wax that sat at the bottom of old official documents? With a grunt, Sara placed the phone on the table, knowing it wouldn't find a signal, and went back to finish her shower.

The sun was rising in a washed-out grey sky by the time she was dried. Sara dressed warmly and fed Tilly. She dialled the DCI's mobile from the bedroom, where a fitful signal could often be found.

'At last,' said Hudson. Sara couldn't decide if her tone was sarcastic or just plain tired. 'Have you left home yet?'

'No, ma'am, just about to set off. What kind of seals?'

'Winterton seals.' Hudson sounded cautious. 'The sort that need friends.'

'Ah, those kinds. Grey seals, I think. They use the beaches to have their pups over winter.'

'And the friends?'

'Local people patrol the beaches trying to prevent idiots from poking the poor things with sticks or letting their dogs attack the babies.'

'Would that be dangerous?'

'Probably,' said Sara. She thought of the annual local news reports of people throwing stones at the seals or standing their five-year-old child next to a seal giving birth and then complaining that the child had been bitten. Altercations with the rangers were not unknown. The seals themselves were more likely to be the danger. You wouldn't appreciate being attacked by one of them. They were much bigger than people realised until they got close to them. 'Why?'

'One of these *friends* called 999 to say they think they've found a body. A human one, I mean.'

'*Think* they've found?'

'It's right on the shoreline, apparently. In the middle of the herd, if that's what it's called. They don't want to go near it.'

'Has anyone gone out to look?'

'A couple of local uniforms are on their way.'

'Well, they'd better hurry,' said Sara. 'If it's on the shoreline, the tide could take it away, depending on which way it's going.'

'This is near to you, isn't it?'

'Yes, ma'am. A few miles down the coast.'

'Then I want you to go there and assess the situation. Let me know if we need the circus or if it's just a piece of junk like a shop mannequin.'

'On my way, ma'am,' said Sara.

At least she wouldn't be in the office much today, which meant she didn't have to avoid the attention of DC Adebayo of the Drugs team. People had been trying to pair them off for months, especially the Serious Crimes Unit's own admin, Aggie Hewett. Adebayo might be handsome and well built, but sharing a skin colour didn't mean they should be a couple — a fact that seemed to have escaped everyone, including Dante Adebayo. Sara was off boyfriends since her last relationship had ended, and she was running out of excuses to not go out for a drink with him.

Grabbing the expensive waterproof jacket she had recently treated herself to, Sara reversed her car out of the parking space at the front of the cottage. 'If it is a body, let's hope the tide is going out and not in.'

CHAPTER 2

Mu was rigid with shock after what she had witnessed. The attacker briefly looked over the cliff to watch the falling man, but made no attempt to go to help. The group quickly vanished from Mu's view, walking along the cliff path towards Walton. She sat shaking with fear, whimpering around the fist stuffed in her mouth. She and Roger might well be seen if they tried to leave the old office block now.

Furthermore, poor Roger was knackered. He licked his paws as he lay down beside her in the doorway. With a sigh, he rested his head on his stretched-out front legs, watching her with soulful eyes. They would have to wait.

A quick recce of the reception area provided Mu with a large shard of broken glass. In the office where they were sleeping, she unearthed a metal window bar with a shattered and ragged end, which could cause quite a bit of damage if used as a weapon. She wrapped Roger up in a blanket, pulling him close to her where she sat, leaning against the wall behind the office door. If anyone came in she would be hidden and have the element of surprise.

Mu opened the sleeping bag and lay it across her, leaving her legs free in case she had to move quickly. Roger was soon fast asleep.

The long, dark minutes stretched into hours. The rain steadily drummed on the roof. The wind began to drop, and clouds obscured the moon. This was proper dark. There were no street lamps in the village and no traffic on the tiny coastal road. Mu sat guard over the dog, the glass shard lying next to one hand and the spikey metal bar beside the other. Fear kept her vigilant for a while, but there were no more random beams from torches or voices carried on the wind. Eventually she dozed until a grey, dirty light crept in through the gap above the boarding on the windows.

Mu was younger than her road-stained appearance suggested. She had run away from home and her mother at eighteen, just four years ago. Since then, she'd acclimatised to homelessness. Short and thin, she was vulnerable in many ways. Weeks of walking, carrying her rucksack and lifting Roger over obstacles had left her more muscular than she looked. Her mind was quick and toughened with four years of street survival. The lack of regular washing facilities had left her clothes ingrained with dirt. Her skin was stained and grubby. Her hair fell in long, blonde dreadlocks, unwashed for two years.

Along the way, Mu had collected a handful of possessions, which she carried with her in a large, old rucksack. Apart from a few clothes, her sleeping bag and a roll of blankets, there were practical items like metal plates and mugs or plastic cutlery, and a much-loved find of a single-burner camping stove, which allowed her to boil a billy can of water when a gas canister could be found or stolen. She had no watch, mobile or other items of value in the usual sense of the word. Roger was her prize possession. His companionship since Mighty Mark had died was all Mu needed. That and her rucksack.

Food for herself could often be found in bins or charity feeding points at night. Any money she begged went firstly on dog food and then on looking after her other bodily needs. Hunger would sometimes stave off periods, but the tell-tale ache in her lower back this morning warned her that this wouldn't be one of those months. She would need to find more sanitary products to supplement the small box of tampons wrapped in an old plastic bag in one of the rucksack's pockets.

Flexing her cramped limbs, Mu went to the outside door and looked carefully around the derelict campsite. There was little sign of life except the occasional seagull coasting on the blustery breeze. It was no longer raining. Roger also had a good stretch and sat up, blinking.

'At least one of us had a good kip, mate,' she said with a smile. Attaching his lead, she cautiously opened the door and stepped onto the gravel path outside. The office was up against a small, sheer bank of sandy soil. Above it was the car park and backyard of the Hall House pub, which the coastal footpath ran past. It crossed the abandoned site to the clifftop, where it wandered in and out of the farmer's fields, heading both north and south. Poor Roger was limping, though the need to find somewhere to cock his leg was greater. He dropped his head over a puddle and began to lap.

'I can get us some fresh water from the tap in the toilet block,' said Mu. Roger obediently followed the gentle tug at his lead. Crossing the site, they reached the cliff edge where the men had been. The ground was trampled into muddy nonsense, so it was impossible to be sure where the men had actually fought. The old steps up from the beach were indeed still there. Erosion had removed sections of the cliff from behind it, and now the steps stood like a tower with a short bridge leading from the stairs to the land. It looked like one of those daredevil rides at the funfair. Mu would not have risked climbing up or down them. Tape and chains lay in a heap attached to one side of the entrance. They'd obviously been torn down at some point, making it easier for the group to get through last night.

Edging as close as she could, Mu peered over the side. There was nothing. The wooden sea breaks Mu remembered from her youth had been replaced by a wide band of giant grey rocks.

'What on earth were they even doing on the beach?' she murmured.

Roger whimpered in reply. He was shivering in the cold wind.

'Come on, Rog. I think there's a bit of gas left in that bottle. Let's have a brew.'

She kept her promise and brought him fresh water from the tap. She poured the minimum amount of water into the billy can over the tiny camping burner and made a cup of tea with last night's teabag. Scraping the last remnants of dog food from the tin, she crumbled two of her own cheap biscuits onto the plate with it and gave them to Roger.

'At least it's warm in here,' she said. 'I wonder if that old village shop is still there?'

Mu asked him for a paw when Roger had finished his meagre breakfast. Checking each one, she saw that he had a couple of incipient sores, which must be giving him trouble. He needed some rest. So did she. Her intention had been to hide up here over the Christmas holiday. She had assumed that the caravan park would still be there, and had imagined being able to break into one of the more hidden vans and keep a sufficiently low profile to stay until at least New Year.

Now she was unsure. Not only was the camp no longer there, but what would happen if those men came back? Where had they been heading? Whatever was going on, it didn't look good to Mu. The problem was that having gone this far away from the city, they would be too remote for homeless people's services. The bits left in the carrier bag had been from a food bank four days ago. Her last set of tampons had come from the library in Norwich, where there was a 'help yourself in need' shelf. Neither she nor Roger was well enough to walk back to the city to get help. She just had to hope that the men she had seen last night were now miles away.

'It's too far to walk to Walton,' she said to the dog.

He cocked his head as if he were joining the debate.

'Do you think you can manage a short walk round the village?'

Footsteps sloshed along the wet path past the pub. They waited, listening to an early dog walker letting his pet off the lead and throwing a ball. After a few minutes, their noise disappeared along the coastal path. Although the track didn't pass too close to the office, they had to be careful. Obviously, the locals used the area to exercise their own pets.

'It must be breakfast time, then,' she reasoned. 'Let's go and see if the village shop has survived.'

CHAPTER 3

The coast around Norfolk and down the eastern seaboard was subject to frequent bouts of erosion. On stormy days, the pounding of the sea would send great gouts of earth crashing from the sandy cliffs onto the beaches below. Between the village of Happisburgh, where Sara's cottage crept ever closer to the land's edge, and Winterton-on-Sea, where she was now headed, the cliffs reduced in size and were replaced by extensive sand dunes. It was these dunes that encouraged the seals to come ashore and use them as a nursery. Winterton didn't escape the erosion, and a couple of years ago, the wooden beach café and its car park had tumbled over the twenty-foot drop onto the beach. Both had been demolished, and the sea had moved inexorably closer to the village's main street and church.

Sara found the patrol car parked on a sandy track by the road which led to the beach. She pulled in behind it, only to receive a dirty look from a dog walker passing by. Parking was notoriously a sore point for the residents. The road to the beach was tarmacked but hidden beneath a layer of sand. The stuff drifted everywhere, catching in the blustery wind to whirl in spirals aiming straight for an unwary walker's eyes. Scrunching up her eyelids, Sara walked down to the beach.

Part of the hardstanding where the café had been remained at the end of the road. Sara stood on its edge to try and locate the officers, and it creaked ominously. A group of four people appeared to be talking about two hundred yards away on top of the dunes.

'I wouldn't stand too close to the edge if I were you,' said a man's voice behind her. The tone was friendly, and as Sara turned round a tall, blond, thickset man in an RSPCA uniform smiled at her. He held out a hand to help her down to the road, which she ignored.

'DS Sara Hirst.' She reached in her pocket to bring out her warrant card.

'No need—' he waved it away — 'I guessed. I'm Dave Wise. RSPCA welfare officer.'

'I've had a call about a possible body.' Sara pointed along the sand dunes. 'I assume those are the people who reported it.'

'Likewise,' said Dave. 'They thought you might need help with the seal colony. It'll be easier to walk along the dunes than on the beach.'

He led Sara along a winding path beside some old black huts. It dipped into sandy hollows, where the marram grass kept the shifting beach stable for a while, and the sea momentarily vanished. They climbed a bank and Dave led her along the top of the dune until they reached the group. The two uniformed officers seemed relieved to have reinforcements when Sara produced her warrant card. The other pair were a man and woman. They introduced themselves as Harry and Dilys, and each shook Sara's hand. They clearly knew Dave Wise already.

'Dilys and I were just doing our morning rounds,' Harry said, indicating an area behind him. In another hollow stood a rugged four-wheel all-terrain vehicle. 'We have a rota. To check on the seals. That isn't a seal.'

A pair of high-spec binoculars swung around his neck as Harry pointed across the broad, clean beach, just one of the many that made Norfolk such a good family holiday destination. The body, if that's what it was, lay close to the lowest point of the strand where the hungry waves were breaking.

Dozens of female grey seals lay scattered across the beach. Their cream-coloured pups seemed to be randomly distributed among them, though doubtless they knew which baby was theirs. Some were feeding, others sleeping. Several had raised their heads and were looking towards the people on the top of the dune.

'Can I borrow your binoculars?' Sara asked.

Harry handed them to her and showed Sara how to focus them. It took her a moment to scan through the mothers and pups to find the object the couple had spotted. It was difficult to tell, even with the focus pulled up sharply. The shape indicated a body in length. The upper end was bright orange, and the lower was dark blue. Sara's heart sank. That might be a head at the top.

'Best go and have a look,' she said. 'How do I avoid upsetting the seals?'

'Thank you for asking.' Harry nodded in approval. 'That's why I asked Dave to be here. He helps us sometimes when we can't sort out a problem or an ill or injured seal needs to go to the sanctuary.'

'We need to go outside the group and stay as far away from the animals as possible,' Dave said. 'If we get too close, we can cause the mother to abandon her young. Or she might attack us.'

'Great.' Sara sighed. She eyed the ATV. 'Can we take that?'

Harry and Dave both rolled their eyes. Dave conceded, 'If we have to.'

'I'd rather get this done quickly.'

Harry gave Dave a walkie-talkie, and while Dilys showed Dave which channel to use, he scrambled down into the hollow to the ATV. Engine revving, he made it climb through the clumps of grass to the top of the bank, where it balanced precariously. The two uniformed officers stood back, watching without comment, as Sara shuffled onto the spare front seat. There were no doors on the cab. The rear was an open metal cage, presumably ready to carry injured seals or equipment. Dave pulled himself onto the back and clung to the rim of the cage as he stood behind them.

'Hang on,' called Harry. He swung the ATV down the dune, bumping and sliding down the soft sand. Sara grabbed a handle above the hole where a car door would normally be. Maybe the instruction had been for her, not for Dave, who was balancing unperturbed.

The suspension groaned as the ATV righted itself on the beach. Harry headed in a long arc past the last seals on the Winterton side before turning back along the water's edge. Keeping his speed down, one set of wheels were battered by waves. The inside ones sprayed water-logged sand all over the vehicle, Sara and Dave. Her jeans leg looked as if it had been sand-blasted.

As they approached the form, Sara felt sure that this was no shop dummy or piece of detritus. Harry pulled onto firmer sand about ten yards above the body. A large female seal lay a few feet away. She regarded them dolefully before rolling onto her front and flopping away. A pup further up the beach watched her sleepily. The mother seal gave a bark, and the baby followed her.

'That was lucky,' said Dave. He climbed out of the back and dropped onto the sand. 'She would have been too close for comfort otherwise.'

'Can you wait here, Harry?' asked Sara.

'Happy to.' The man nodded, his eyes wide with anxiety. He clearly didn't want to leave the cab.

'Come on then,' said Dave. As they walked the few remaining yards, he fell into step next to Sara. The sand was soggy. It squelched under her boots.

'Is this quicksand?' she suddenly asked. The sodden sand closed over the top of her boot.

'Possibly.' Dave bent swiftly over and patted the sand's surface. 'I think it's just really soaked. The storm would have stirred up the margins and made it loose.'

Sara stared at the body, which didn't seem to be sinking. 'Let's keep going.'

It took just a dozen or so more steps before they stood beside the man. He lay on his front, head turned towards the sea, arms by his side. His legs were splayed out behind him. The eyes were open, and his lips pulled back in a rictus grin. He was fully dressed in dark clothes, which were ripped and shredded. The orange colour so visible through the binoculars was some sort of life jacket. It hadn't done its job.

'North African at a guess,' murmured Sara.

Dave pulled off his hat in a gesture of respect. 'There are plenty of rocks just beyond the shoreline. They could tear up his clothes like that.'

'How would he end up here?'

'Washed ashore in the storm? Or down the coast from that direction.' Dave pointed along the beach towards Happisburgh.

'One thing's for sure, we're going to need the circus.' Sara sighed and pulled out her mobile.

'Well, they'd better get a move on,' said Dave. 'I checked the tides before I came out. It's on its way out at the moment. It won't be long before it turns, and he'll be washed back out to sea.'

CHAPTER 4

Danni Jordan rang the video-entry bell outside Lisa London's beautiful Ealing home. Ten foot high and several inches thick, a pair of wooden gates stood in an even higher wall surrounding the house and garden. Above that, a steel grid topped by razor wire made the wall difficult to scale, while tucked under the grid, just out of sight, an electric intruder wire ran along the top of the fence. The video panel was embedded in the brick pillar holding the right-hand gate. The housekeeper's face appeared on the screen.

'Good morning, Mrs Strong.' Danni took care to look directly at the little camera at the top of the panel so that her identity could be confirmed.

'Good morning, Danni.'

There was a buzz followed by a click from the small door in the main gate. Danni pushed it open and stepped over the bar beneath. As usual, Striker was standing in the glass porch of the large, detached Modernist house, watching to ensure that Danni wasn't being followed or coerced. She closed the door firmly and stood to one side, allowing Striker to see that it was properly shut. He opened the front door with a nod, and Danni strode along the gravel drive, Armani handbag and briefcase in hand. It was their morning ritual at exactly five minutes to nine every day apart from Sunday.

Her cheery greeting to Striker was met with a grunt and a glare. Sometimes she wondered how much English the man actually spoke. In recent months Lisa London had tended to talk to him more often in Italian, which Danni was beginning to learn courtesy of a language app she'd downloaded. She hadn't told any of them that she could understand some of their conversations these days. Safer not to admit to it.

It was almost two years since Danni had first come into contact with the London family. It made her smile now to think of what she was like back in those days. A council-estate gutter rat with a drug-peddling boyfriend, who had been forced into being a drug mule for a county line into Norfolk's remote and rural county. Once there, fate had given her an opportunity to help Lisa London and her not-so-bright younger brother, Gary. Her reward had been a job as the mafia queen's personal assistant.

After all this time, it still seemed Striker didn't altogether trust her. Mrs Strong, on the other hand, had unbent towards her as much as the old housekeeper was willing to go. Danni had barely put her bags on the elegant vintage desk in the small office, which was the centre of her life these days, before the woman appeared with a tray.

The coffee set she carried on it was Clarice Cliff Bizarre Ware, worth £1,000 and Danni's favourite crockery. She followed her boss in almost everything, including collecting small Art Deco items, like china tea services. The pot would contain dark Java roast, her flavour of preference. When Danni had been on that estate with her loser boyfriend, who knew such luxurious choices could be made for a simple cup of coffee.

Tucking a loose strand of her precision-cut bob behind her ear, Danni thanked Mrs Strong and lifted the lid on her expensive laptop to sign in.

The housekeeper managed a half-smile and a nod as she put down the tray. 'Is Ms London busy today?'

Lisa London usually left the dirty work of running her empire to well-paid minions. She spent more time meeting with other organisers and businessmen to smooth the wheels of their secret and illegal empires. And it was mostly men. London was a rare female presence in those dangerous domains. However, she was thorough to the point of obsession and didn't like loose ends. She was not above sorting out problems on the ground. She also possessed a streak of violence that was legendary. Danni was proud to work for her. She accompanied London to meetings in expensive restaurants, rendezvous at art exhibitions, or visits to disgustingly dirty old warehouses in the back of run-down industrial estates all over the city.

'Lunch at Number Thirty-Five,' she confirmed.

Mrs Strong raised an eyebrow.

'Booked late last night. Striker to drive. Called for eleven. Nothing in the diary for tonight.'

Of course, that didn't mean London was having a free evening. Lounging around in pyjamas and binge-watching a box set wasn't the woman's style. Once upon a time, it had represented the perfect evening for Danni. It still did if she had an evening off. The difference was that now she would relax by watching news broadcasts from all over the world, so she could stay aware of likely problems wherever they might crop up, or doing online courses to educate herself and improve her language skills. Whatever might happen to her in the future, Danni was taking advantage of everything that Lisa London offered to ensure she would never sink back to that disgusting council flat life ever again. She also modelled herself on her boss in other ways, from the chic clothes and immaculate make-up to the obsessive completion of every task.

Armed with likely meal requirements, Mrs Strong returned to the kitchen. Danni sipped her coffee as she flicked through her emails. Her inbox only contained missives from legitimate businesses like restaurants, art galleries and auction houses. Confirmations of table bookings, invitations to view some newly available rare Art Deco item of the sort that London was obsessed with, or trawlers from artists hoping for a visit from the known collector with deep pockets. She couldn't access Lisa London's emails and didn't want to. There was nothing from Gary, London's brother.

Danni had been instrumental in getting Gary to the airport as he had fled a UK police summons for a lesser drug-dealing offence. Once in Italy, Gary had been swept up by his Nonna and the di Maletesti clan, the largest of the Neapolitan Camorra families. Despite only being together for a few days, Gary still regarded Danni as his girlfriend and emailed her almost daily with tales of his new life. These messages often ended in a plea for her to visit him or move out to live with him. Danni gently encouraged him without ever giving any definite promises. It was a fine line to walk with Lisa who, Danni assumed, knew what the pair talked about.

Over the months, the emails had become more grown up and less chatty. When they Zoom-called, Danni saw that Gary was maturing, becoming more independent. She wondered if he really was taking a more active role in the clan's Naples enterprises, as he sometimes hinted. Danni had reinvented herself. It appeared that Gary had too.

What worried Danni was that the emails had suddenly stopped. At first, she hadn't taken Gary's warning that he was 'doing something for the family' very seriously. The last time he'd said this, he'd escorted Nonna to Sicily for a family wedding. The silence had stretched out for days, and Danni didn't dare ask his sister about it.

Her coffee finished, Danni checked her lipstick in a hand mirror. Gathering her desk diary, notepad and an elegant antique fountain pen, she walked calmly to the living room. London would be having her coffee there, and they would go through the schedule for the next few days. She knocked politely and went straight in. London would be expecting her.

Her boss was on the phone, looking out the window with her back to Danni. She held a weary hand to her forehead. To Danni's surprise, it was trembling. 'All right, Zio, don't go on about it. I'll call this morning as I've got some news.'

CHAPTER 5

The village of Winterton was almost an hour's drive from the police HQ. When Sara had explained what she'd found, and with the urgency of the tide turning soon, the office must have emptied in double-quick time. She had barely had time to help the uniformed officers close the beach road and co-opt Dilys to keep walkers up on the dunes before the Serious Crime Unit's entire complement had gathered where the old beach café used to stand. DCI Hayley Hudson stood shivering next to DI Edwards, her face pinched.

'Good job you were near,' said Edwards to Sara. 'Otherwise, he might have been swept back out to sea again.'

'Then he'd be someone else's Christmas present,' muttered Hudson.

Edwards glanced at the DCI with one eyebrow raised. Sara turned away to hide a smile. Hudson buried her hands deep into her coat pockets. Her nose was already turning bright red with cold.

'If he washed up in Suffolk or Essex, yes,' snorted DC Mike Bowen. 'The Netherlands, even.' He pulled his waterproof jacket tighter around his dad-bod tummy and eased the zip shut.

'Could a body go that far?' asked DC Ian Noble in surprise. He scrunched up his eyes against the flying grains of sand.

Bowen sniffed the air and checked the clouds, which scudded vigorously across the wide Norfolk skies. 'Unlikely in this weather. The wind is driving the tide down the coast, not out to sea.'

Dr Stephen Taylor, the forensic pathologist, and his team were only minutes behind the detectives, although they had been beaten by a car full of RSPCA officers. More Uniform reinforcements soon rocked up, eager to be in on whatever action might be available. In fact, there were soon so many people that Sara was glad to stand back and allow DCI Hudson to organise the chaos.

'We're famous already,' said Dr Taylor to Sara as he passed below on the beach. The forensic investigation team followed him, with the three RSPCA officers at the front carrying boards. They tramped along the shoreline towards the body. The RSPCA men spread out as they approached the seals, holding the boards vertically to discourage the curious seals from approaching the team.

Sara glanced along the dunes to where a small crowd of onlookers had gathered. Half of them held their mobile phones out, videoing the proceedings. She pursed her lips in frustration. Not only were they filming the team, who might prefer to be anonymous, but they couldn't even give the poor victim a bit of privacy.

'Should we move that lot on?' she said to Hudson.

The DCI looked to the cluster of voyeurs. 'Yes. Take Bowen and Noble with you.' Hudson nodded to the two DCs, then at a pair of uniformed officers standing behind. 'And you two. Let's get this place shut down as best we can.'

'Jesus, my legs are going to ache after this lot,' moaned Bowen. The soft sand slipped under his feet as they clambered along the dune tops. 'My bloody thighs!'

'You should get more exercise,' replied Sara. 'Then you'd look slimmer in your wedding pictures. And fitter.'

'Ha!' snorted Bowen. 'Listen to the pot calling the kettle black.' He pulled up suddenly and blushed. 'God, sorry. I didn't mean it like that.'

'I know.' She hid her grimace of exasperation. She kept moving.

'Right, right.' He scrambled to catch up.

Sara patted her midriff. 'Besides, you're not wrong. How long have I been saying I need to start hiking or something?'

'Er, a couple of years?' suggested Noble. He glanced down at his trim, very tall figure with a grin. Sara sometimes thought he could empty an all-you-can-eat buffet at a restaurant without it touching the sides. Lucky bugger.

'Have you organised a photographer for the wedding?'

Bowen winced. 'No. Look, it's not going to be a big affair. Not at our age. We don't need a photographer.'

'That's a shame.' Sara raised her voice as they reached the onlookers. 'I'm sure someone here could do it for you. All right, ladies and gentlemen, the show's over. Cameras off, please, and no streaming on social media, thank you.'

'Off you all go,' shouted Bowen. 'Come on. Give us some privacy to do our jobs.'

'You can't stop us,' called a young man from the back of the group. He held his mobile above his head and pointed it at Bowen. 'This is a public place.'

Unfortunately, they knew he was right. Noble weaved through the group to reach the young man, who stood his ground.

'We know,' he conceded quietly. Then he raised his voice a little. 'No doubt you can make a few quid selling this to the local news or something. But leave that poor soul some dignity, can't you? Who knows how he got there, and what if his family saw this before we could let them know?'

'Illegal immigrant,' called a belligerent voice from the back of the group. 'Fell off one of them rubber boat thingies, no doubt. Coming here, taking our benefits . . .'

Bowen moved more swiftly than his bulk might have suggested he was capable of. 'That's an interesting point of view. A contentious statement, in my opinion. In fact, likely to encourage or create a disturbance, wouldn't you say, DS Hirst?'

'You're all disturbing the seals,' wailed Dilys from the back of the group. She waved her arms in a shooing gesture. 'Please just go away if you can't keep the noise down.'

'All right, all right,' said Sara, shouting above the ensuing complaints. 'I'm having this area closed off until the investigation is completed.'

Sara could hear Noble still talking to the young man with the mobile. She waved the two uniformed officers over, and they began to cordon off the top of the dunes, ineffectually tying the lengths of barrier tape between tall clumps of marram grass. It would soon be flapping in the wind. Another pair arrived to help them move the crowd on.

'I suppose,' the man said finally. He fiddled with the mobile before shoving the screen towards DC Noble. 'That okay?'

Noble watched the tiny screen intently for a few moments, then nodded. 'Thank you for your cooperation. If you wouldn't mind going down the dunes to the footpath below, that would be really helpful.'

The young man trudged down the back of the dune to follow the rest of the group. Dilys slumped down onto her bottom with a heartfelt sigh. Sand puffed up as she hit the dune, and she gazed across the beach to where her husband still sat in the ATV. Dave Wise had joined the other RSPCA team to help keep the seals away.

'I guess he's waiting to see if he can help,' she said resignedly.

'You can go home if you would prefer,' suggested Sara. 'Do you live in Winterton?'

'Yes, we do.' Dilys looked up, her face brightening. 'I could make some hot drinks and bring them down in flasks. Do you think your people would like that?'

'I don't know about them,' said Sara. 'But I'd be grateful. Can one of us help you?'

With a nod, Bowen accompanied Dilys. He could get her back inside the cordon when she was ready.

Sara turned to DC Noble. 'Well done,' she said. 'You handled that really well.'

Noble ducked his head with a blush. 'I don't think the local television news would show it if you could see the body. Too gruesome for them. Are we in for a long morning?'

'Possibly.' Sara looked to where the forensic team were working, partly shielded by the RSPCA's animal baffle boards. The sea had retreated some yards further out from the ATV. She checked her mobile for the time. 'Dave Wise said the tide would turn about now. I reckon they only have about an hour before they have to move him.'

CHAPTER 6

The wind was bitter. It cut through all the layers Mu was wearing as she stepped out of the office door. Mu promised herself she would rip up something to make a coat for Roger if it still seemed safe when they returned. She'd decided to take the calculated risk of leaving all her worldly possessions behind with the door closed. The weather wouldn't encourage the local youths, who obviously vandalised the place when they were bored. Mu wasn't sure if they would have finished school yet, though the holidays must be imminent. Christmas Eve was only two days away. She hadn't seen anyone since that dog walker earlier this morning, though she'd heard bottles being emptied into a bin at one point and assumed this was the cleaner at the pub. With luck, she might find some food for herself in one of the bins later on.

She had less than four pounds in bits of change in her pocket. It was the last of her begging money from the three nights she had slept on the streets of Norwich. Allowing Roger to set the pace, she guided him past the pub and down the hill to the village's main street.

To be honest, it wasn't much of a main street. The infants' school was still there. It looked closed, and the children's playground was beyond it. A couple of hardy mothers were pushing toddlers on the swings, all of them wrapped up like arctic explorers. One had a dog, who heard Mu and turned to investigate. It barked in a desultory way at Roger, who gazed back vaguely. Neither animal seemed to have the energy to be interested in the other. The dog's owner looked at Mu and turned to her friend, pointing in Mu's direction. The pair wrinkled their noses and watched Mu with suspicion as she walked on.

The shop had survived. Partly, it seemed, by turning half of what had once been the small supermarket into a tiny coffee shop with five tables. The other half of the store still contained shelves of food — expensive stuff for the most part. Local artisan producers of cottage garden honey, posh chocolate and flavoured gin jostled one another for space. All cleverly designed to be trendy for holiday visitors. The shop had been gentrified, wasn't that the phrase? Mu knew she couldn't begin to afford any of it. She pressed closely against the window on the food side and looked up and down the displays. About halfway back, there was a long rack full of holiday souvenirs. Behind it, there seemed to be a few more shelves that might actually contain useful stuff.

Mu tied Roger to a 'dog parking' space on the gravel outside, next to a couple of picnic tables. She gave him a reassuring pat. 'I won't be long.'

An old-fashioned bell tinkled as she opened the door. The woman behind the counter glanced at Mu before allowing a nakedly disapproving frown to form. She folded her arms and glanced at a small television screen to indicate a CCTV feed.

Mu knew what she looked like, that the years of living rough or in hostels had taken their toll. There was little opportunity to keep her body clean, let alone her clothes. She knew she must smell bad like homeless people often did. But there wasn't much she could do about it. She needed dog food, not to mention some tampons if she could afford them.

There was a tinkle of a glass jar being placed into a wire basket from the back of the shop. Mu shrugged at the woman. Passing the posh food, she turned the corner by the Norfolk-dialect tea towels to find the remnants of the old minimart.

Three small aisles of shelving held a selection of basic goods. A grandmotherly figure was loading a bag of flour into her basket.

Mu's aroma arrived before the woman became aware of her. She felt deeply embarrassed when the grandmother looked up and around until she spotted Mu standing for-lornly in front of the small selection of pet food. It was nasty, cheap quality and £1 a tin. Hesitantly, Mu headed for the two shelves in the farthest corner, which held the sum total of likely medical needs. A tiny pack of tampons was £2.50. That only left her enough for one tin of dog food. Mu pulled the change from her pocket and counted it more accurately. The tampons would have to wait. God only knew how. There was a shelf with a few reduced-price items, where she collected a stale-looking loaf to tide her over.

The grandmother was still putting things into her basket as Mu headed for the till. The grumpy woman picked up the tins Mu had handled with extended fingers as if she was picking up dog shit, though there was no hesitation in how she scooped up Mu's coins from the counter. Checking the amount was enough, she nodded to Mu and flicked her head towards the door. 'Don't come back without money,' she said. 'We don't like your type here. Don't you try begging in front of my shop or my husband will sort you out. And keep that dirty, flea-ridden creature away from my lovely dog.' Her voice could have brought down walls it was so severe.

Collecting Roger, Mu stuffed the tins into her pockets. He stood to greet her with a wag of his tail. Behind her, she heard the two mothers from the playground strolling past, toddlers in pushchairs. Their dog pulled against its lead and let out a volley of barks at Roger. He grumbled in return. The dog got a yank on its collar for its audacity.

'Stupid creature,' said the first mother. She glowered at Mu and Roger.

'Look, Mummy,' said the child of the second mother. 'Doggy.'

'Look, Annabelle,' said the mother to her friend. 'Tramp.'

They both laughed and strolled on along the pavement.

'I'm sorry, Roger,' whispered Mu. Tears were beginning to form. She was tired after her vigil, and the enormity of being so far away from help hit her hard. 'I've made a terrible mistake bringing us up here. If we're not inside somewhere by Christmas Eve, we're buggered.'

She bent down and hugged the dog. He returned her affection by pushing into her shoulder and licking her ear.

'I think you left your bag behind,' said a woman's voice.

Wiping her face, Mu looked up at the grandmother who had been in the shop with her. She had one of those wheeled shopping bags. It was jammed so full the lid was straining over her purchases.

'I don't think so,' said Mu. The carrier looked full, and it was tempting to accept someone else's shopping and run. But she hadn't sunk that low yet. That was stealing.

'Oh yes, I'm sure it's yours.' The woman smiled, making her eyes sparkle in the winter sun. She pushed the carrier towards Mu. 'Please take it.'

'Thank you.' Mu's tears returned.

Inside were two packs of tampons, several tins of dog food and two of baked beans, a pack of sliced ham, some cheese and a wrap of chocolate digestives. It was more generosity than Mu's heart could take, and she sat down on the picnic table bench crying. The grandmother handed her a small pack of tissues.

'Where are you sleeping?' she asked gently. 'Have you somewhere safe?'

Mu nodded. She blew her nose and wiped her face. 'It's dry at least.'

'You take care of yourself and your lovely fella here.' The grandmother pointed to Roger. 'Can I pat him?'

Mu fondled Roger's ears as the woman held her hand out for the dog to take her scent, and then they both stroked his head.

'If you need more food, you can find some items in the church,' said the woman. She pointed across the street and up the hill. 'We have a food bank donation basket by the door. I'm sure the vicar won't mind you helping yourself if you're in need.'

Mu wasn't sure the vicar would be as generous as this old lady. In her experience, vicars came in two types — the genuinely Christian, who handed out charity on the streets at night, and the ones who worried far more about what their parishioners or bishop would say if they allowed a smelly vagrant to pollute the pews of their church.

'He keeps the door open all day. Hardly anyone goes in, I'm afraid, so you should be safe.'

'Thank you.'

'My name's Gilly, by the way. What's yours?'

'Mu,' said Mu. 'This is Roger.'

'Pleased to meet you both.' Gilly suddenly looked puzzled. 'Mu?'

'It's short for Muriel.'

'Muriel?' Gilly examined Mu's features closely. 'Don't I know you?'

CHAPTER 7

Lisa London rarely looked as upset as she did this morning. The woman was usually an ice queen, even when personally handing out punishments to those who crossed her. The first thing London had forced Danni to witness had been her boss tormenting a small-time Norfolk drug dealer as they'd worked to get Gary out of the country. Danni had understood the lesson and ensured that anything she did was entirely supportive of the di Maletesti clan's business. In return, Lisa London provided her with an executive flat in a secure gated community and paid her handsomely.

London was breathing heavily as she ended her call. She sat down quickly in the nearest armchair and contained her anger with visible effort. 'Good morning, Danni. Did you make the booking I asked for?'

'Yes, Miss London. Twelve thirty at Number Thirty-Five.'

It was an exclusive restaurant on Jermyn Street. The table was for two. Danni would be left to make her own arrangements. She favoured a small café on a side street a couple of hundred yards away — easily in reach if she was required and no booking necessary. She didn't know who London was meeting, which suited her fine. The booking was in Danni's name, but all the places they used for such business lunches were quietly aware of who she worked for.

London flicked through the pages of her handmade diary and glanced at today's page. 'We'll be going earlier than I thought. I want to call at the 3Js first.'

The 3Js was the original Italian coffee shop in Soho, famous for starting the whole 1950s scene that blossomed into the UK's teenage pop subculture. It had belonged to the di Maletesti family from the start, and London's uncle was the current owner. Elderly and infirm these days, he still lived on the two floors above the shop as he had done most of his life. It was where Lisa London had been brought up.

Danni waited. London flicked angrily through the following few pages. 'OK. Cancel all appointments for the next two days. Then book me into that hotel in Norwich until Christmas Eve. Striker and yourself as well. You will need the full emergency kit. You have half an hour.'

Danni was careful to keep any surprise from her face. With a nod, she headed to the kitchen to update Mrs Strong.

Just over an hour later, Striker was guiding their bullet-proof car with its tinted windows down Frith Street. A suitcase of Lisa London's clothes sat in the boot, Striker's bag beside it. It didn't worry Danni that there had been no time to pack any clothes for herself. Once London was lunching, she could shop for new clothes on Regent Street. Eager to learn and please, she styled herself on London's elegance, using the same exclusive shops her boss favoured when she could afford them and high-end fashion brands for the rest. The days of Danni being grateful for a trip to a low-budget chain store were long gone.

Lunch was still two hours away when Striker pulled the car up outside the 3Js, its period facade gleaming. The current manager was a handsome, tall Italian man in his mid-thirties. Danni recognised him as he nodded a greeting to her boss.

'*Buongiorno*, Alessandro,' said London as she weaved her way through the small metal tables. The manager lifted the staff hatch so London could get behind the bar. She pointed to Danni. '*Tavolo per uno.*'

She opened a door behind the bar and vanished through it. The place was crowded, and there was a queue of customers waiting. Alessandro politely hustled a young couple from a table at the back of the café and cleaned it before seating Danni.

'What can I get for you?'

Danni ordered an espresso.

'Would you like a cake? The lemon ricotta is fresh today. *Molto bene.*'

Alessandro's accent was strong. He looked well muscled. Like all the men associated with the di Maletesti clan, he obviously worked out in case his services were required away from the café. Danni didn't doubt that he was a family member if he managed the place. She was unusual in not being related to them. Even Striker was a distant relative. Of the close staff, only she and the Strongs were outsiders. Mr and Mrs Strong were considered family by virtue of their long and loyal service.

'Thank you.' She smiled and balanced her handbag on the spare chair, where it would be difficult to reach for any potential snatchers. As instructed, she'd packed the full emergency kit. Pulling up the internal base of the bag, she had filled the hidden void below. Now it held a set of false IDs and passports, several thousand pounds worth of sterling and euro notes and two brand-new burner phones. A third unused burner phone was tucked in a low pouch for Danni's use. Her own purse and personal items were nestling on top, just as they usually would.

She signed into the Wi-Fi and got on with cancelling the appointments she hadn't been able to deal with before leaving the house.

'You are Miss Jordan,' said Alessandro when he returned with her order. 'You've been here before, I think?'

'I am.' Danni stuffed the diary into her handbag to make room for the cake plate. 'The personal assistant.'

Alessandro bent down, pretending to clean a spot on the tabletop. It brought his face closer to her. 'You are being followed this morning.'

Danni knew better than to look surprised. Or to doubt the observation. She glanced at Alessandro in confirmation.

'At the back of the queue for takeaways,' he murmured. 'Man. Late forties. Going bald. You know him?'

Danni inspected the sugar sachets, selecting two to empty into her cup. 'Can I have a glass of water with this?'

'Of course.' She watched Alessandro go back behind the counter. Keeping her gaze as vague as possible, she let it slide past the man in the queue. It almost made her smile. After two years working for London, she knew what she was looking at. His clothing, his stance, his whole demeanour screamed plainclothes copper. She looked down at her plate and took a forkful of cake. Danni couldn't be sure with such a brief glance, but she thought she recognised him.

When Alessandro brought the water, she smiled up at him. '*Grazie. Ben notato.*'

'*Piacere mio,*' replied Alessandro. 'My pleasure. *Parle italiano?*'

'Not really,' replied Danni. 'Just enough for a holiday, perhaps.'

'Napoli is very fine in the spring,' he suggested.

'I'm sure it is.'

He went back behind the counter and left Danni to her snack. She took the burner mobile from its pocket. Between forkfuls of cake, she typed a text and hit send.

Being followed. Plainclothes. Will watch.

They all knew that London's house was under surveillance. Sometimes a car was parked down the road from the gate. Usually, they just kept track of the car's movements on the traffic cameras. Whether by luck or payola, some of London's business lunches were watched by 'diners' at another table.

It had been a while since the police had directly followed them. That meant that some new information had come to light, and Danni would have to be very careful.

CHAPTER 8

Despite the flasks of hot drinks provided by Dilys, the bitterness of the wind had driven the cold right through to Sara's bones. Dave, the RSPCA officer, had been right about the tides, and Dr Taylor arranged for the body to be removed within an hour of arriving. They brought the poor man off the beach in a black body bag. Harry followed in the ATV, his face drawn and white. The couple had gone home afterwards in a state of quiet shock.

'I can't see much to be gained from where we found him,' Taylor said to DCI Hudson, and the SCU team gathered around her. 'He's been in the water for a few hours at least. Although it's not impossible that he was killed here, I strongly doubt that. I'll call when I have more.'

'Let's run checks just in case,' said Hudson. She looked along the line of dunes to where a group of large sheds stood in defiance of the erosion. 'What are those?'

'Fishermen's sheds,' said Bowen. 'Inshore fishing for crabs or lobsters, that kind of thing.'

'What about up here?' Hudson asked DI Edwards as she pointed to the beach road. 'We passed some places as we came down, didn't we?'

He nodded. 'There are a few bungalows and cottages further up. Beyond the dune systems. Wouldn't fancy it myself. Too close to the sea for my liking.'

'Bowen and Noble, I want you to do a quick door-to-door on the approach road. Check if any vehicles came down here at odd times in the night.'

'Ma'am,' said Noble. Bowen looked grumpily at the sky, where gathering clouds suggested more rain was imminent. The pair walked off up the beach road.

'DS Hirst,' snapped Hudson. She was still in organising mode. 'Find a couple of the forensic team and look around those sheds. You never know.'

Sara would have preferred to get back to the office to warm up. 'Yes, ma'am.'

'The rest of the officers can go,' the DCI said to Edwards. 'Thank them for me, will you?'

She strode to Edwards's vehicle, her arms wrapped tightly around her body for warmth.

The forensic team were back at their vans, pulling off their overalls and wellington boots. Sara found the team leader and passed on DCI Hudson's order, although she phrased it as more of a request. Grumpily, he asked for a couple of volunteers. After a bit of horse-trading, two men agreed to stay behind to conduct a quick search.

It was after lunchtime now, and Sara's stomach grumbled as they followed the sandy track. Each shed was about the size of a detached garage, with double doors at the front but no windows. Standing in two rows, there were eight of them. Some were in better condition than others. All of them had once been painted black. A couple must have been recently repainted. The rest were various shades of weather-beaten.

The forensic investigators walked between the huts, slowly and methodically examining the ground. Just one of the huts had its doors open, and Sara headed for it. There was a small boat on a trailer inside. Lobster pots were stacked against the walls, along with plastic crates and buckets. Sara peered past the boat into the dark at the rear of the shed.

The daylight was bright enough to make it difficult for her eyes to adjust.

A clank of something metal being dumped on a wooden bench was followed by a man's voice asking, 'Can I help you?'

'I hope so.' Sara pulled out her warrant card and gave her name. 'You may be aware there's been an issue here on the beach this morning.'

'That poor bloke they're all talking about?' The man pushed past a pile of lobster pots into the daylight. He was dressed in navy-blue paint-spattered overalls. Although he carried a good-sized beer belly, Sara estimated that he was only in his forties. A bright red spotty bandana was wrapped around his head, which was either bald or shaved. She glimpsed a heavy-metal band T-shirt under the overalls. He looked more like a biker than a fisherman. He held out a hand for Sara to shake. 'Call me Dodge.'

'Thank you. Yes, it's about the man on the beach.'

'Drowned, I'm guessing.' The man's accent was local. 'He gone now?'

'They've taken him to the mortuary. I wondered if you saw or heard anything unusual last night or early this morning.'

Dodge paused to consider his words. 'Came down here early this morning with the dog for a walk.'

'Was it possible the body was there then?' asked Sara.

'Maybe. I don't take the dog on the beach when the seals are here.'

'What about last night?'

'That's a different matter.' Dodge chewed his lip for a moment, his eyes holding a faraway look. 'I went to the pub, you see.'

'So, you didn't come down here last night?'

'Yes, I did. Brought the dog for a walk, last thing.'

Sara waited for Dodge to continue. Her stomach grumbled loudly.

'That you?'

'Sorry. Missed my lunch.'

'Decent chip shop in the village. Might still be open for lunch.'

Sara nodded. 'Thank you for the information. You were saying about last night?'

'I was a bit pissed, weren't I?'

'That's not a crime if you weren't driving over the limit,' she said.

'I was in the Heron's Head in Marlham. My mate brought me back.' Dodge sounded defensive. 'I can't be sure. That's the thing.'

'Of what?'

'I brought the dog to the end of the lane for a late-night pee.'

'And?'

'There were some lights out at sea.'

'What sort of time would that have been?'

'About midnight, I guess.' Dodge turned his attention fully to Sara. 'But they was in the wrong place. Even though the weather was rough.'

'What do you mean by that?'

'You can see them container ships if it's clear.' Dodge waved an arm behind him. 'They come in closer to shore if the weather be bad. Can't come that close, though.'

'This one was close?'

'Close as.' Sara had to work through the accent to realise he meant 'far too close'. 'Too small to be out in that weather.'

'Too small?'

'Not a fishing boat either. No self-respecting inshore fisherman would be out in that sea or that late at night.' Dodge frowned. 'It were a cruiser. A holiday job. Shouldn't have been out of the marina.'

CHAPTER 9

Mu thanked Gilly again as she hastily uncoupled Roger's lead from the ring in the wall. Clutching the carrier bag the woman had given her, she encouraged Roger to a moderate pace back the way she had come. When they reached the turning for the pub, Mu paused to look behind her. Gilly was watching her. Having realised Mu was checking, Gilly pulled at her shopping trolley and walked off in the opposite direction. Roger sat panting while Mu waited until she thought no one was looking and it was safe to head up the little hill.

Halfway up, a lane branched off towards the church, while the hill road ended outside the pub. There were several cars in the pub car park. The front door stood open, and the sound of activity drifted out. She could see tables of diners and drinkers enjoying their Christmas celebrations through the windows.

Roger was struggling. His head drooped, and Mu couldn't encourage him up the last small climb. Despite his size and weight, she picked Roger up and tried to carry him down the path to the old rickety gate outside the abandoned caravan park. Fearfully watching the pub in case any of the customers spotted her, she struggled down the gravel slope.

Steam drifted out from the back door of the pub, carrying smells of cooking that made her stomach clutch with hunger. A man dressed in chef's whites wandered out carrying a packet of cigarettes. He headed towards a sheltered area near the bins at the edge of the yard above the derelict office in the old site below.

Roger chose that moment to whimper and give Mu a slobbery lick. It made her jump in surprise. The noise was sufficient to attract the man's attention. He paused to look at them.

'Nothing down there,' he called. Scratching at his dark beard, the man watched them curiously.

'Just taking him for a quick walk.'

'Right.' The man turned the cigarette packet over in his hand, his gaze still fixed on Mu.

She turned her back on him and forced her way through a small gap between the gate and its post. The tins in her carrier banged and clattered. It was too late to hope for secrecy. The man knew where they were heading.

Fear gnawed at her belly, along with the hunger pangs. Now what should she do? That man might easily figure out why they were here. Where the hell else could she go?

Roger lay unresisting in her arms. They were both tired and hungry. She had to risk it. Reaching the level ground, Mu looked up at the back of the pub. There was no sign of the man.

The old site stretched open in front of them, the bitter and blustery wind whipping across it. The sea in the distance looked as grey and angry as the sky. To the right, a band of trees cut off the view. To the left, muddy farmland stretched above the crumbling cliffs. In the distance, Mu could see the village of Walton.

The remains of an old Second World War gun emplacement stood about half a mile along the field, three walls and a rotten roof above a concrete pad where once two giant guns had been trained out to sea in case of invasion. She remembered it being out of bounds back in the old days. Erosion had moved it much closer to the top of the cliff. By common consent, the public footpath had been diverted to the rear of the remains. Mu checked carefully in all directions, and although the path followed the top of the cliffs directly between the two villages, there was no sign of anyone.

They reached the door of the old office. Mu stood Roger on the ground. Checking a final time, she opened the door, and the pair slipped inside.

She paused to listen. There was only the sound of the wind battering against the plywood window boards. The inner door was still closed. Her bags, blankets and worldly goods were exactly where she'd left them.

Mu closed both doors as best as she could and sank onto the floor gratefully. What a goddamn morning. Roger dropped down flat onto the blanket next to her and whimpered. His eyes began to glaze with sleep. She waited, ears straining for any noise outside that might suggest they had been seen or followed. None came. Her breathing recovered.

Mu forked out a helping of the new dog food onto Roger's tin plate. He looked too tired to move, so she put it by his head where he could smell it. She was grateful that Roger sat up after a few sniffs and began eating. Wiping her hands on her already filthy jeans, Mu ripped open the packet of ham. Stuffing a single slice between two pieces of nearly stale bread, she tore at it with her teeth, pulling it in great lumps into her mouth and barely chewing the rubbery mess before swallowing. Gratitude to Gilly flooded her as she ripped into a second sandwich.

'Not too much at once,' she whispered to Roger, although the instruction was as much to herself as him. Her stomach ached for more. Mu wrapped Roger up in a blanket as he lay down to sleep. Then, after opening the packet of biscuits and taking two out, she did the same for herself. Muffled under the blankets, she thought how wonderful it would be to have a cuppa to go with this. But Mu had used her last teabag, and there was no milk. Nor did she want to venture out of the old office again until after dark.

Lulled by the wind, Mu's mind wandered over the morning. The two snobby mothers in the playground and the attitude of the woman in the shop were pretty much what she was used to. No one ever stopped to wonder why Mu was where she was. They all assumed that she was a junkie and/ or a sex worker. They all thought her unclean in so many ways. They didn't know her at all. The charity shown to her by Gilly was unusual. Especially in an out-of-the-way place like this tiny seaside village.

Don't I know you? That had induced panic. Surely this grandmotherly type couldn't recognise Mu. She had still been in junior school when her mother had stolen them away from here in the middle of the night.

Exhaustion pulled Mu into a half-sleep where her ears were still consciously functioning, but her eyes were tightly shut. Her mind slowed as it searched the archives of her brief life. Surely no one would remember her. Why would they? Apart from that teacher, no one would have seen Mu often enough to have retained an impression of her. Gilly hadn't sounded like a teacher. The tone was all wrong.

As she slipped onto her side, Mu's memories came up trumps. A clear image of someone who could be Gilly. Dressed in her Brownies' leader uniform, with a warm smile and a kind laugh. Hadn't Gilly been their Brown Owl, for the handful of weeks Mu had been a member of the Brownie pack?

CHAPTER 10

Striker collected Lisa London and Danni and drove them less than a mile to Jermyn Street. The congestion charges were somehow always avoided, perhaps by someone on the payroll at TfL. London never walked far, and if Danni didn't know the secret, she would wonder how her boss kept so slim. The truth lay in London's iron discipline and will. The restaurant of choice today was one of those fashionably low-key places. A salad here was three strips of lettuce with half a spoon of some dressed grains, two mouthfuls of some organic meat or fish or a rare variety of avocado, and a tiny drizzle of extremely old balsamic vinegar. London wouldn't finish this on principle. Nor would she drink alcohol. Even so, Danni had noticed that London looked to have gained some weight in the last few weeks.

London's lunch guest was familiar to Danni. Middle-aged, balding and paunchy, his suit looked tight in all the wrong places. Not a member of the extended family, but certainly a business associate. Which area the man belonged to of the many dubious interests Lisa London ran didn't concern Danni. The same couldn't be said of the man, who looked distinctly uncomfortable when he sat at the table. His face was red, and his attitude was full of anxious bluster.

'Mr Smith,' said London with a nod. That was hardly going to be his real name, Danni knew. London was wearing her ice-queen poker face, making it impossible for the man to tell how much trouble he might be in. He didn't look confident that this lunch would turn out well.

Danni ensured her boss was settled with her lunch visitor and then left the restaurant. Usually, Mrs Strong's husband acted as their chauffeur when they went out and Striker as their bodyguard. Danni assumed the change today was due to their journey to Norwich later. Turning down Jermyn Street, she was unsurprised to see Striker walking rapidly back towards the restaurant, having parked their vehicle somewhere it wouldn't be disturbed. Comfortable that London would now have protection, Danni cut through Princes Arcade to reach Piccadilly and the boutiques she knew were in the area. With luck, she had at least a couple of hours to shop for clothes and grab something to eat.

She worked methodically and quickly through the half-dozen favoured boutiques. To the dismay of the elegant assistants, she didn't bother to try anything on, just paying for the items that appealed. Cutting back through the Burlington Arcade, Danni purchased a modest-sized suitcase on wheels. She hung her various bags over the handle and headed to her favourite café on Babmaes Street. It was busy, but a handsome young waiter spotted her and, with a grin, deftly guided her to her chosen table in the window. She rewarded him with a smile and an order.

A small ledge ran along the edge of the window at knee height. Danni balanced the case on it and unzipped the top. She had stuffed her various purchases inside by the time the waiter returned with her herbal tea and her Buddha bowl salad. Rather more substantial than the one she knew London would be toying with, Danni ate the food in genteel forkfuls until the bowl was clean.

'Can I get you anything else?' asked the waiter, whose grin made it obvious that he found her attractive. Danni wondered how long it would take him to get around to asking for her number. She ordered more herbal tea.

The small café was wedged between the Three Crowns pub and a shop selling handmade men's shoes, which stood on the corner of Jermyn Street. Her window seat gave her a good view, and as she glanced between her mobile and outside, she saw that the plainclothes officer from the 3Js was gazing at the shoe shop display. It had taken him over an hour to find them again, but there he was.

Raising her phone to a discreet height, Danni snapped a picture of him. The camera in this latest, expensive model was pin sharp. Swiping the screen, she could see his profile clearly. Danni gazed at the enlarged image with a gnawing sense of familiarity. She definitely knew this man. But how?

Placing her mobile on the table, she stared across the narrow side street. At exactly the same time, the man turned and looked straight at her. Their eyes locked for a moment, and Danni was sure this was no accident. She also remembered who he was.

Detective Sergeant Mead. He had been one of two detectives who had interviewed Lisa London at Norwich Airport the day they had helped Gary escape to Naples. The pair had unsuccessfully tried to arrest London that day. No doubt the failure still rankled. Was he following her or Lisa London? It was no secret who Danni worked for, so if he was following her, why now? Something must have changed, and the di Maletesti clan didn't do coincidences.

'Don't know how you can drink this stuff, if I'm honest,' said the waiter. He plonked a teapot and clean cup and saucer on her table.

Danni jumped. She glanced at the young man, then back out of the window.

'Are you all right?'

Her concern must have shown on her face. 'Not really,' she replied. When she checked again, DS Mead hadn't moved. He was still watching her.

The waiter looked out of the window. 'What is it?'

'You see that man over there?' Danni waved her fingers vaguely towards the shoe shop window.

'The middle-aged dude with the checked shirt?'

'Yes. Please don't make yourself obvious.' Danni sighed inwardly. People could be so unsubtle sometimes.

The waiter sat on the spare seat opposite Danni. 'Is he bothering you?'

She nodded, her eyes gazing demurely downwards, and dropped her voice to a whisper. 'He's been following me all day. I think my father sent him.'

The waiter whistled gently. 'You don't look like an underage runaway.'

'Oh, I'm not,' Danni assured him. She added a tearful wobble to her voice. 'My father is arranging a marriage for me, and I don't want to do it.'

'Arranged marriage?' The young man sounded outraged, and then he looked at her more closely.

Danni knew she was as white and English as it was possible to be but felt her pallor was deeply unfashionable. Which was why she kept up the levels of her fake tan for that sun-bronzed look, and her highlights were regularly topped up. If an observer wanted to believe it, she might have a mixed English/Arabic heritage, and her carefully and expensively curated wardrobe could suggest a dual-continent lifestyle. Danni allowed a single tear to escape from her eye. The waiter could see her distress even if he didn't buy her look.

'He's just waiting for me to leave.' Danni looked up and down Babmaes Street furtively. 'There will be a car somewhere.'

She almost wanted to laugh aloud when the waiter fell for it. 'There's an alley at the back of the café. It goes past the back of the shops and comes out on Duke of York Street. Is that enough of a start?'

Danni nodded. She tapped her suitcase with her foot. 'I need my things, though. He'll see me take them.'

'There's a toilet at the back,' said the waiter. He was chewing his lip in excitement. 'Take your handbag and go that way. Wait inside the kitchen. I'll bring your suitcase in a minute.'

He got up and handed her the bill. She nodded, then theatrically pointed into the café interior. Following her lead, the waiter gave her instructions. Hoping the dumb show worked, Danni picked up her handbag and walked off.

The kitchen door was a simple two-way affair with a window to prevent collisions. She stepped through it, pulling out the burner phone to text her boss.

Still being followed. Recognise him.

There was no one else in the kitchen, although a back door stood propped open. The smell of cigarette smoke explained the absence of a cook. Just a few seconds passed before her handsome waiter pushed through the door, carrying a tray of dirty crockery at shoulder height with one hand and her suitcase with the other. He dumped the tray with a loud crash.

'This way,' he hissed and strode through the small kitchen. The cook stood in the tiny yard to the rear, cigarette in hand and a surprised expression on his face, as the waiter steered Danni outside. A high brick wall with a tall wooden gate led to the back alley. She soon found herself out there among the rubbish bags and bins.

The waiter dropped a quick kiss on her mouth. It was a small enough payment. 'Good luck.' He pointed along the alley, ducked back inside the yard and slammed the gate shut.

Danni's mobile rang.

'You can explain later,' said Lisa London. 'Where are you?'

Danni picked up the case so the wheels didn't make any noise, dodging between the rubbish until she reached a point where the alley widened slightly into a tiny lane. Glancing up at the side of a building, she said, 'Apple Tree Yard. Comes out on Duke of York Street.'

'We've finished here,' said London. 'Wait there until we come for you.'

The call clicked off. Danni walked to the end of the short road and waited for no more than two minutes until a car pulled up on the bigger street. It wasn't Lisa London's car.

CHAPTER 11

The fish shop was as good as Dodge had suggested. Replete with chips and a battered sausage, Sara berated herself for giving in to temptation all the way back to the Police HQ in Wymondham. There would be cake waiting; there always was. Aggie, their civilian admin, made sure of that with an endless rotation of cake tins stuffed with goodies. Sara felt certain it was one of the things that had attracted DC Mike Bowen to Aggie, their recent engagement sealing his access to a lifetime of home-baked goodies — unlike herself, Billy No-Mates as the locals would say, with no boyfriend and only a cat to love, and little social life apart from the occasional drink with DS Ellie James from the drug squad. Unless she gave in to Aggie's matchmaking and went on a date with DC Adebayo. Not on your life! She'd had enough of boyfriends.

One thing Sara had come to admire about Aggie and Mike Bowen was how they managed to keep their personal life together out of the office. Despite a very public marriage proposal in front of the team earlier in the year, the actual wedding still hadn't happened. Sara suspected that Mike Bowen's desire for it to be a small affair meant that they would simply vanish for a few days' holiday and arrive back with the deed done. In many ways, she hoped so, because if there was a reception, Sara would be there on her own. Again.

There was a buzz about the office when she arrived. Grateful to be warm again after a cold day in the biting coastal wind, Sara peeled off her jacket and slumped in front of her computer. DC Noble was putting street maps and tide information up on the whiteboard while Aggie fussed at the coffee percolator. DCI Hudson was in her office, her head bowed next to DI Edwards as they examined something on the computer. Bowen was on the phone.

The evening was already drawing in, the sky rapidly darkening outside the office windows. Sara couldn't help wondering how they would cope with working on Christmas Day if that became necessary. Like many other officers, Sara had worked on 25 December in the past. But in all her years as a detective in the Met and in the Norfolk Police, she was lucky enough to have never been on a murder case over the holiday. Given that Sara had intended to spend the day at home with Tilly, lounging in front of the television, the prospect of working didn't seem so bad.

Hudson emerged from her office. 'Let's see what we've got so far,' she called.

The team gathered around the whiteboard, Sara scooting her office chair over on its wheels. Hudson glanced at her with a frown. 'Long day?'

Sara shrugged and gave a half-smile. Hudson turned to Noble. 'Anything of interest on the door-to-door?'

Noble consulted his notes. 'Between the dunes and the church, there are about twenty houses, mostly bungalows. We only found two with people in. One was an older chap who said he slept heavily and wouldn't have heard anything. The other — well, that lady was a bit odd.'

'Odd?'

Noble glanced at Bowen, who had put down the phone.

'Eccentric, I suppose you might say.' Bowen snorted in amusement. 'Weird hippy clothes, dyed purple hair, skinny as anything. Anyway, claimed she had been out at her boyfriend's last night. Seventy if she was a day. I doubt she saw anything, probably just wanted to chat.'

Edwards opened the cake tin and peered inside. 'I'll organise local Uniform to go and pick up the rest of the door-to-door. Mmm, brownies.'

Their boss had a gluten intolerance and disliked the team's cake addiction unless she had her own special helping. Hudson's disapproval showed until Aggie produced a smaller plastic box containing a separate brownie, which she passed to the DCI. 'What else, Bowen?' she said after a bite.

'I just spoke to Dr Taylor,' he said. 'They've got the victim back in the lab. Says preliminary inspection shows a lot of surface bruising, cuts and abrasions. The body is bloated, suggesting he was in the water for a while. He's going to open the fella up and let us know first thing in the morning.'

'Nothing to identify him in his clothes?'

'No such luck,' replied Bowen. 'They've been ripped to shreds, although Taylor says he was well wrapped up when he fell in. Jacket, thick jumper, heavy boots. That won't have helped his chances of survival.'

'Especially in that weather,' agreed Sara. 'It got pretty wild up at the coast last night. The sea was very rough.'

Hudson turned to her. 'Any luck at the sheds?'

'There was a fisherman called Dodge in one of them. The rest were locked up. Of course, we need to get a full statement, but he did say one very interesting thing.' She explained about the leisure cruiser that Dodge thought he'd seen. 'Said it was heading down the coast towards Great Yarmouth.'

'Caught out and trying to make a safe haven in the river there?' Edwards sounded interested. Pushing aside the cake tin and coffee cups, he unfolded a map of the coast on the desk. 'Mike? You know about this sort of thing better than I do.'

'Ooh, nice detail.' Bowen peered at the map. It was a scale Ordnance Survey map, showing the land and some sea features.

'Picked it up on the way here,' said Edwards. 'You never know what might help.'

'Our man drifted to shore here.' Bowen pointed to Winterton. 'The coastline turns south, and the North Sea gets pinched between here and the continent, so you get strong tidal currents. With last night's wind, they would have been going south, so the boat followed the flow. There's a spring tide due in the next couple of days.'

'Spring?' Hudson sounded surprised. 'It's December!'

'Doesn't mean the season,' said Edwards. 'It means it will spring up, and the tide will be exceptionally high.'

'Why?'

'Something to do with the gravitational pull from the moon,' said Bowen. His chest puffed out a little as he enjoyed educating a non-local. Sara didn't know either, but she kept quiet about that, as she had learned to do over the last couple of years. If you let Bowen ramble on, he often said something decidedly useful. 'It's only a problem for us when the wind is particularly strong from the north. Then you get a storm surge, and we have to close down the coastal villages. You must have heard of the floods in 1953?'

Hudson shook her head. 'Before my time. What else?'

Bowen subsided with a grumble. Sara studied the map and found her own village. 'And the body would also have to follow this tidal flow?'

'Depends where he went in. I'd say the tides are more likely to have driven him into the shore.' Bowen frowned. 'The body could have drifted some distance before reaching the beach.'

'Look at all these features.' Sara pointed to grey marks in the blue sea area. 'What are those?'

'They're the sea defences. Those huge piles of rocks like the ones you have near you.'

'The body could have got caught on those.'

'Or damaged by them,' suggested Noble.

'Why didn't it just sink?' asked Hudson. 'Was there a life jacket of some sort?'

'Yes, there was,' said Sara.

'Right.' Hudson stretched up. 'This can wait for the morning. Let's see if there are any lists of people lost at sea. One for you, Aggie, I feel. Sara, get on to Yarmouth and find out if this leisure craft got into the harbour, just in case they lost anyone. It's getting late.'

Sara glanced at the wall clock. It was after six, which didn't seem that late to her. Perhaps Hudson had a hot date. Sara had a date with a hot chocolate.

'We can't do much more until we get the post-mortem,' concluded Hudson. 'It sounds like an unfortunate accident to me. Let's go home.'

CHAPTER 12

The pair were so tired that neither Mu nor Roger realised they had a visitor until someone was banging on the outside door. Roger shot to his feet, barking furiously. Heart pounding with shock, Mu scrabbled out of her blanket cocoon and reached for the dog with his bristling hackles. It was dark now, though Mu could see enough to catch at his collar.

'Good boy,' she crooned. Roger resisted her attempt to pull the dog into a hug and stalked to the office door, grumbling a strong warning.

The loud knocking came again. The derelict door rattled. Roger replied with a couple of sharp barks.

Pulling a blanket round her shoulders for warmth, Mu clipped the lead to Roger's collar and opened the office door a few inches to look and listen. She was in deep shit if this was any of the men from last night. A torch beam shone through the gap where Mu hadn't been able to close the knackered door properly. She heard heavy breathing.

'I can hear the dog,' said a male voice. 'I don't mean you any harm.' The tone was carefully neutral, and the accent suggested that English was a second language.

'Go away,' Mu called. 'We're not doing anything wrong.'

'I know,' said the man. 'Not a great place to be staying, though.'

Mu didn't reply. There was no point in arguing.

'Look, I'm not going to report you or anything. I bring some food, if you want it.'

A waft of roast dinner and gravy reached Mu. Her stomach rumbled. Roger grumbled again. If the dog wasn't keen, then neither was Mu. They looked after each other.

'If I leave it outside, it will get cold. It's a dinner for you and some meat scraps for your old friend.'

'Just leave it inside that door, then,' she called. Hunger overcame safety objections. She hadn't had a roast dinner since the night shelter in London.

The door scraped open, and there was a clink of crockery. The shadow of a man stepped inside, and torchlight swung around the interior of the office. 'Amazing this place still has a roof. I work in the kitchen at the pub. I promise I'm no threat.'

Mu still didn't say anything. Roger was vibrating with aggression.

'I'll go back there now. When you've finished, can you bring the plates back to the kitchen for me? I'll make you a warm drink.'

'All right,' agreed Mu.

The bottom of the door scratched noisily as the visitor tried to pull it shut. Mu waited for his footsteps to recede on the gravel path before she opened the office door wider. Roger tugged away from her hand and trotted to where the man had left the plates on the broken reception desk. He tried to stand on his hind legs to sniff the nearest bowl. With a sigh of exasperation, he couldn't manage it and turned to look at Mu. She followed, lifting off the silver foil to inspect the offering. One was a shallow bowl filled with meat scraps and covered in gravy. The other was a plate with a large roast beef dinner, complete with a Yorkshire pudding. Another bundle of foil contained a small plastic pot of gravy and some cutlery. Momentarily Mu wondered if this was really just generosity. What if this man was one of those bastards who loved to taunt homeless people? What if he'd spat on the food? What if he'd put something that might hurt Roger in the dog's bowl?

As if life wasn't bad enough, homeless people often suffered harassment, especially on Friday or Saturday nights. Like the night she'd watched Mighty Mark fight three drunk twenty-somethings after they'd discovered them sleeping in a doorway around the back of a theatre in the West End. The drunks had posh accents, expensive clothes and half-finished bottles of booze in their hands. One had thought it such a laugh to unzip his flies and piss on Mark in his sleeping bag. The men had laughed and jeered, made rude gestures and screamed abuse. Mu shuddered at the memory.

Roger's whine brought her back to the present. She forked up a mouthful of the leftover meat, tapping it to her tongue and sniffing it before putting it in her mouth. There was no suspect smell or buzzing on her taste buds. Encouraged, she put the bowl down. Roger was a wise old street dog and sniffed carefully before deciding it was okay. Then he ate hungrily. Mu took her own plate to the door and examined it in the moonlight. It looked and smelled fine. She stuck a dirty finger into the little gravy container, which tasted like it should. Then Mu poured it over the meal and ate rapidly, standing at the derelict reception desk.

Her hunger sated, Mu realised she had something else she now had to do. The ache in her back had changed to that heavy feeling behind her bladder and the tell-tale trickling sensation. She extracted a tampon from the bag the old lady at the shop had given her, and temporarily shutting Roger in the office, she carefully checked outside. There were fewer clouds tonight and more moonlight, although it was still very blustery. She seemed to be alone, so the man must have kept his word and gone back to the pub kitchen. She went to the toilet block and came back to get Roger and the used crockery.

Roger was unwilling to follow Mu when she clipped on his lead. She picked up the dirty plates and clicked her tongue at him. 'Come on, Rog,' she murmured. 'The man gave us a fair feed. We ought to take the plates back.'

If a dog could roll its eyes, Roger would have managed it as he stood up to follow Mu. She allowed him to take his time on the path outside as they climbed the hill to the back of the pub. The kitchen door was wide open. A dishwasher rumbled, and pans clattered inside the room. Bright electric light and the noise of the pub's customers filtered out into the night. Mu knocked politely on the door.

As Mu hesitated to knock again, the man she had seen earlier smoking in the backyard came to the door. She proffered the dirty plates, which he accepted with a nod. He was tall and well built. His dark beard was neatly trimmed, his long hair tucked under a chef's protective hat.

'Tea?'

'Oh yes, please.'

The man looked her up and down, then glanced at Roger. 'He can't come in, sorry. If you go over behind the bins, there are a couple of chairs by the wall. I bring the tea out.'

Mu told him how she liked her tea, and he turned back to the kitchen. A cheap plastic roof protected the area where the plastic chairs were. By the number of cigarette butts on the floor, it was obviously the staff's unofficial smoking place. She sat down to wait. Roger lowered himself beside her, facing out so he could see anyone approaching.

'Why are people here being so kind?' she muttered to the dog. He lifted one ear to listen to her. 'Those bitches at the playground are what I expected. Or that snotbag in the shop. Not the old lady or this.' It seemed too good to be true. The years of homelessness had made Mu necessarily cynical and wary.

The man crossed the yard and ducked behind the bins. He handed Mu a mug of tea and sat next to her.

'Thank you,' she said. The tea was good. 'You've been very kind.'

She half-expected the man to look embarrassed, as donors sometimes did when thanked. The man just shrugged. 'Nearly Christmas.'

Mu sipped her tea again, gently fondling Roger's head. The man watched her as he sipped his own drink.

'You don't sound local,' she tried, feeling she ought to at least try to have a conversation with him.

'No. Nor do you.'

'Don't I? It must have worn off. I lived here as a child.'

The man raised an eyebrow. 'No shit?'

'Until I was eleven,' said Mu with a nod. 'I'm Mu, by the way.'

'Paolo,' said the man.

'That definitely doesn't sound local. Where are you from?'

'It's Italian.' Paolo dusted some imagined speck of dust from the jeans that tightly wrapped his thighs. 'I'm from Napoli.'

CHAPTER 13

Sara had just shut her front door when there was a knock. It had been a long, cold and frustrating day, and she wasn't in the mood for visitors. Dragging off her coat, she threw it onto the sofa. Tilly weaved between her legs, talking in the chittering way that only a Siamese cat can manage. Her mew was hoarse and croaky. Whoever it was, it had better be important.

'Evening, my dear. I'm sorry to bother you this late.' Gilly Barker was the only other permanent resident in this row of five terraced cottages that stood on the edge of Happisburgh village. The other three were holiday lets.

'Is it important?'

'I'm not sure, but I'm worried.' Gilly frowned.

Sara looked at the older woman, accepting she wouldn't have come here after dark unless it was significant. Tilly let out a mew of complaint, edged out the door and wound around Gilly's legs instead. She knew their neighbour well as Gilly often popped round to feed the cat when Sara was working late.

Gilly bent down and scooped Tilly up in her arms. The cat headbutted her affectionately in return. Sara told herself off in her mind for being less than welcoming. She opened the front door wide and Gilly carried the chittering cat inside.

'Sorry, I've only just got in,' said Sara. 'I'll get the fire lit. Have a seat.'

'I'll feed Tilly,' replied the neighbour and carried the ecstatic cat to the kitchen. She spooned food into the cat's dish without being asked and put on the kettle.

It was almost like having a second mum, Sara reflected as the fire began to crackle. She flicked on the Christmas tree lights and slumped onto the sofa. Gilly soon reappeared with mugs of tea.

'So, what brings you out this late?' asked Sara.

'I had a strange encounter this morning,' said Gilly. 'At the village shop.'

'Someone was rude to you?'

'No, nothing like that.' Gilly settled on the sofa, and Sara realised she was in for a bit of a story. 'There was this young woman with a dog. I think she's homeless. What she's doing all the way out here, I don't know.'

'Unusual for a woman, at least,' agreed Sara.

'Poor thing hadn't much money, and you know how Marge at the shop can sometimes be.'

Sara knew and nodded in agreement. Marge had been rude to her when she'd first moved into the village, presumably based on her skin colour. Not these days, now she'd been a regular customer for two years.

'I bought her a few bits and pieces,' said Gilly. 'She'd been looking at dog food and tampons as if she could only have one or the other, poor thing. It's not something I'd ever thought about if you're a homeless woman. I got some of both for her.'

'That was kind.'

'She seemed to think so too. Although I didn't intend to patronise her. I hope she didn't think that.' Gilly looked up at Sara, her expression clearly saying she had only just realised that.

'I don't think she would have. Not if she thanked you.'

'She did. Got a bit upset, actually. Anyway, I asked about the dog, and we chatted a bit. She said her name was Mu.'

'Moo? Like a cow?'

Gilly smiled. 'Short for Muriel. It's ever so old-fashioned, isn't it? Girls in my generation got called Muriel, but not these days. And that made me think that the girl looked familiar.'

'How so?' Sara was intrigued, despite herself. Gilly didn't say these things randomly.

'You remember I told you I used to be Brown Owl for the local Brownie pack back in the day?' Sara nodded as Gilly continued. 'I did it for fifteen years and had lots of girls join us over the years. We had a Muriel with us at one time. When this woman told me her name, it came back to me in a flash. She was only there for a few weeks.'

'Did it look like the same person?'

'Yes. And the more I think about it, the more I'm sure it was.'

'Did she remember you?'

'I don't think so. She pretty quickly made her excuses and walked off. I watched where she went because I was worried about her.'

'Do you have any idea where she's staying, then?'

'She turned up the lane past the pub.'

There weren't many possible destinations up there. The pub itself. Happisburgh church. The derelict holiday caravan site with the coastal path running through it. Sara listed them out loud.

'And the gun emplacement,' suggested Gilly.

'That's just three walls and a tumble-down roof.'

'Better than sleeping in a hedge.'

'I suppose.'

'Besides, I believe you can still get into the cellars of the place if you know how to.'

'Really?'

'My grandson showed me something on his tablet last time he was here. Someone had gone down there and taken pictures. Pretty grim, but there are still some old metal bed-frames from the war and stuff like that.'

'Ah! I think that's called *urbexing*,' said Sara. 'Urban exploring. A somewhat dangerous hobby. Breaking into derelict spaces or buildings and taking photos to post online.'

Gilly put her mug down on the coffee table. 'Somewhere a homeless woman could hide? The thing is, there was something strange about Mu and how she left the village.'

'Back in your Brownie days?'

'Yes. They never could afford the uniform, and I had collected some second-hand bits for her. Of course, I knew their address from my records, so I popped round with them so the poor child wouldn't feel left out at the next meeting.' Gilly's expression grew solemn at her memories. 'Her parents were having some sort of row. The girl was shrieking and crying. It sounded violent. I didn't dare knock. I took the clothes back with me, thinking I could give them to her next time I saw her.'

'And did you?'

'No, I never saw her again. When she didn't turn up, I tried the house. The dad was there but wouldn't say where they'd gone. Told me to bugger off. So, I spoke to the school. She hadn't been in for days.'

'She just vanished?'

'With the mother. The father apparently left a few weeks later, claiming he was off for a job in Felixstowe.'

'They ran away from him, then?'

'It seemed so.' Gilly nodded. 'I was glad. I'd noticed that Mu had bruises on her arms that looked like finger marks as if someone had grabbed her too hard.'

'You think she was being abused?'

'I wasn't alone. The teacher at the school told me that they were trying to get social services involved.'

'What had she noticed?'

Gilly drew a deep breath. 'The teacher said that Mu had refused to get changed for outdoor games one afternoon. She wondered if the poor mite had started her periods, although she would have been a little young. The teacher took her to the sick room just in case. The child broke down in tears and lifted her skirt.'

Sara realised she was holding her breath.

'There were bruises where no child should have them. On the insides of both of her thighs.'

CHAPTER 14

The car belonged to Mr Smith. Danni said nothing as she climbed onto the back seat next to the sweating business-man. Lunch couldn't have gone well for him. Lisa London was sitting in the front and, as ever, Striker was driving. The windows were, of course, tinted. Danni didn't bother to ask what had happened to the Range Rover they had set out in. Mr Strong would be picking it up in due course. Presumably, their bags were in the boot.

'Mr Smith was kind enough to lend us his car,' said London with a small smile. They would be travelling to Norfolk in a car not associated with Lisa London. Clever. Striker drove sedately down Jermyn Street.

'That's the one,' said Danni as they passed the end of Babmaes Street. She pointed to the detective, who seemed to have just realised she was no longer in the café and was striding towards the front door with his back to them. 'He was at Norwich airport two years ago, if you recall.'

London glanced at the man but didn't reply. Mr Smith looked out of the window in the opposite direction with a deliberate lack of curiosity.

Danni settled in for the drive. The car was a top-of-the-range black Mercedes, but it wasn't nearly as spacious as their usual vehicles. Even so, it had the level of comfort Danni had become accustomed to. By the time they were purring up the M11, she was slipping in and out of a doze, which nicely shortened the journey to Norwich.

It was dark when they reached the boutique hotel that her boss had chosen. It was next to one of the city's two large cathedrals, and the rooms looked out over a long sunken garden. Both were artistically lit as landmarks. They went inside the hotel, and Danni took in the tasteful Christmas decorations around reception. She hadn't booked a room for Mr Smith, as she hadn't known he would be with them. The receptionist told them the place was full, and Danni wondered what would happen to him now. By the look on his face, so did Mr Smith. Sharing a room with Striker wasn't an enticing prospect, but London wouldn't want him out of her sight.

'Be back here in half an hour,' said London. 'Dress for the outdoors.'

Just enough time to get ready. Once in her room, Danni sorted out the clothes she had bought. Among other items were a pair of designer jeans, trendy and practical, a pair of low-heeled boots and a warm jumper in navy. The visit might be a mystery, but past experience warned her that it would involve a practical element, and Danni's memories of Norfolk were that it could be cold in winter.

She was ready and waiting in the foyer by seven o'clock. Lisa London appeared in a completely black outfit. Jeans, top, jacket and a warm hat. She looked Danni up and down and then handed her a similar pull-down hat with a nod. Striker was outside in the Mercedes, with Mr Smith sitting grumpily in the back. Danni watched the brightly lit streets of Norwich slide by, realising with a jolt that she recognised some of them. It was no surprise when they drove past the airport. The darkness enclosed them after that. The roads, then the lanes, got ever narrower and darker.

Directed by Mr Smith, eventually Striker guided the unsuitable car down a rutted dirt track. Well-built the vehicle might be, but the Range Rover would have coped better. He parked behind a huge pile of dirty straw, much to Mr Smith's annoyance. Danni suspected this wasn't how he had expected his day to pan out.

She gagged at the reek of ammonia and stench of cattle dung that came off the waste heap when they got out. Her eyes watered, and she fished a tissue from her pocket to cover her nose. London clamped a hand to her mouth, stifling a gagging sound that suggested she might vomit.

Danni's heart began to race. Unless she was mistaken, she could hear the sea. A sound that she usually loved. The wind was whipping the waves tonight, which were crashing against an unseen shore. It sounded frighteningly angry rather than soothing and pleasant. Occasionally, the wind buffeted her so hard that she found it difficult to keep her balance on the stinking mud.

There was some light from the moon. Danni could work out that they were on top of a cliff. In fact, she began to wonder if she recognised the view. Striker turned on a large torch, keeping the beam carefully trained to the floor. Mud clinging to her brand-new boots, she stepped cautiously behind London and Mr Smith as they headed towards the cliff edge.

As they approached the pile of animal manure, two figures walked from behind it. Obviously male, dressed head to toe in black, this pair were also wearing balaclavas to cover their faces. Striker swung the torch up to inspect their faces anyway.

'Evening, boss,' said one to Mr Smith. Their party had obviously been expected. They looked better equipped than prison guards. Each man carried a riot baton attached to his belt. Cable ties, walkie-talkies and handcuffs dangled, ready for use.

'Well, this is a bit of a bugger,' said Mr Smith.

The man shrugged. 'Just picked up the cargo like you instructed.'

'You didn't think to check them as they got on board?' asked London. Her tone was edgy, a sure sign that these guys were in real trouble.

The man shook his head.

With a sigh of exasperation, Lisa looked around. 'Let's get on, then. We need to sort this out. Is that it?' She pointed to a square, single-storey concrete ruin. It must have once been a building.

'They're under there,' said the guard. 'Best way in is over here.'

He led them all behind the muck pile, where an old red van was parked. The man leaned inside the cab and flicked on the headlights. Just in front of the bumper, a large steel manhole cover winked in the beam. From the amount of dirty bedding around it, Danni suspected the cover was normally buried under the waste heap and had been recently cleared.

The man pushed under the edge of the cover with a metal bar and lifted the lid with a grunt of effort. Striker shone his torch down the hole. Rusty rungs were attached to the wall, forming a corroded ladder that descended vertically underground.

'You first,' Striker said to Mr Smith. He pushed the businessman towards the drain. The other man's hand strayed to his belt to finger the baton.

'Never mind.' Mr Smith held up a hand to prevent further action. He nodded at Lisa London. 'We're business partners here to solve an issue. Let's see exactly what the problem is.'

The two men pulled torches from their belts to light the descent and went underground first.

'You wait here,' said London to Danni. 'Shout immediately if you see any vehicles. Stop any nosey walkers from getting too close. Move them on if you have to.'

Striker went down next. London followed him, leaving Danni alone and without a torch. God only knew what was down there. Danni's nose wrinkled in disgust at the smell rising from the hole, a stench that was definitely more human than animal. The sound of the party's footsteps was muffled in the vague sucking of sludge on the tunnel floor. They soon vanished.

Scanning around to ensure they were still alone, Danni risked looking into the top of the drain. The moonlight reached the bottom of the short concrete-and-brick shaft and highlighted four or five feet of tunnel. Comparing it to what she could see aboveground, the tunnel seemed to be heading towards the old derelict building and the cliff.

Another figure stood on the edge of the light, dressed like the other guards. He stared up at Danni and pulled up his balaclava to reveal his face. He grinned as Danni recognised him with a gasp. Raising a finger to his lips in a shushing gesture, he blew her a kiss. It was Gary, Lisa London's younger brother. He pulled down the mask again, then paced away down the stinking corridor.

Danni's heart pounded with adrenaline. What the actual? What was Gary doing in the country, let alone in this place? Why was he down there, pretending to be a guard? How the hell had he got here?

She shivered. Grey, heavy clouds raced over the front of the moon. Pulling the hat London had given her tightly over her ears, Danni stared in confusion out to sea as drops of rain began to hit her back. The rain grew heavier, and her feet grew colder.

Suddenly the sound of angry voices came up the tunnel. Danni quickly checked the fields and clifftop for people or cars. They were still alone. With a yelp, Mr Smith climbed clumsily out of the drain cover. He might have been going to make a dash for it until Striker's hand grabbed his ankle and felled him to the floor. Moving at speed, Striker emerged from the drain and launched himself at the winded man. London followed more delicately, while one guard appeared more slowly, only emerging to chest height before pausing to assess the situation.

Striker and Mr Smith struggled on the concrete pad, rolling around in the farmyard stink and straw. Striker soon had him kneeling among the crap, arms locked up his back, blade to his throat. Danni glanced at the guard. He was balanced on the ladder, half in and half out of the drain cover.

If he joined in, there was no way she could take him out by force. Something silver flicked towards her, and Danni instinctively caught it. London had thrown her an old-fashioned switchblade. Her boss didn't normally expect her to be directly involved in these things. Her usual role was to be a witness.

Things were going wrong, weren't they? Because Gary was here. Did Lisa London know that he was?

Danni's mind ran furiously as she tested the trigger. Her ex-boyfriend had been fond of these things. Could she remember?

The blade sprung open. Danni advanced towards the man in the drain, holding the handle tightly. He shrugged and held up his hands. Danni waited.

Mr Smith's chest was heaving with effort. London stepped forward and, bending over him, raised a blade of her own towards the man's eye.

'So, tell me, Mr Smith,' she snarled. The blade took a nick out of the man's face, millimetres from his eye socket. 'How come my cargo is down five workers and up one pregnant fucking woman?'

CHAPTER 15

Paolo wasn't very chatty. Mu failed to find out much about him other than he had been working at the pub as their chef since the summer. He wasn't forthcoming about how he had ended up there, although he did say he had been a cook in Naples. In return, he hadn't asked Mu many probing questions either. He lounged in the old plastic garden chair and eyed her speculatively. Mu wondered if the food and cup of tea would have to be paid for with favours. She should have known there would be a catch.

'You really come from here?' Paolo hadn't sounded convinced about this piece of information. Mu knew that the local accent was strong and distinctive. 'Not sound like it.'

'Until I was eleven,' she said. 'Then I moved away with my mum.'

'Why you come back?'

Why indeed, pondered Mu. It hadn't been her best decision. She'd been homeless for long enough and had suddenly felt the pull of childhood memories. Was it just nostalgia, then? It was a lonely life. Roger was all she had, and he was getting old. She stroked the dog's head, which lay on her knee, eyes watching Paolo warily.

When she didn't reply, Paolo sat up straight. 'Listen to me,' he said. Leaning forward, his face came close to hers. Mu kept eye contact as she waited for him to start kissing her. Instead, he took her chin in one strong hand, gripping it gently. 'Not safe down there. That place will fall down soon.'

Mu pulled her head away, and Paolo let it go. 'I know. But it's Christmas soon. Where else can I go?'

'Hostel? In big town? I could take you.' Paolo pointed to a small car parked in the backyard.

'Norwich is the only one,' she said with a shrug. 'It's always full, and they won't take Roger.'

Paolo pulled back a little as he seemed to ponder what else they could do. 'Big storm coming,' he finally said. 'It say on the news. You should be indoors. I keep dog.'

'Not a chance.' Mu's hand strayed to Roger's collar. No way was she being separated from her companion.

'That place might fall on you both.' Paolo gestured over the back wall. 'Or burn down.'

Clouds were gathering and drops of rain spattered on the plastic roof of the bin shelter where they were hiding. It was becoming much windier. Mu thought if it kept raining like this, the place was more likely to collapse from being too wet than from fire.

'Tomorrow, you go.' Paolo was becoming more forceful. 'Not safe here. I give you breakfast, then you go.'

'I have some food,' said Mu. She suddenly felt reluctant to be in this handsome Italian man's debt any more than she already was.

'Paolo! Where the hell are you?' shouted a man's voice from the kitchen door.

Paolo rolled his eyes. 'Tim. My boss. I go. You wait a little, and I give you takeaway drink. Don't let him see you.'

Mu nodded. Paolo collected the mugs and walked round the rubbish bins. She heard the landlord grumbling as Paolo returned to the kitchen. He wasn't gone for more than ten minutes when he returned with a thermal takeaway cup of tea. Thrusting it into Mu's hand, he gestured for her to leave quickly and said, 'Go tomorrow. You not safe down there.'

Clicking her tongue to Roger, they went back down to the old office as fast as he could manage. It was raining hard now, the gusts driving the water in all directions. Neither of them wanted to be out in this. The old office roof wasn't coping very well — Paolo was right about that. Water trickled in through unseen gaps, turning the dust and dirt underfoot into slimy mud. The interior office where they were sleeping was in better shape.

She wrapped Roger up. He quickly fell asleep, his hunger satisfied for once. Mu made a cocoon of her sleeping bag and several blankets. The wind was battering at the windows now. The plywood on the outside rattled and creaked. The moonlight came and went, lighting the inside of the room through the tiny spaces around the window coverings. She treated herself to a couple of biscuits to go with the tea. Full of food herself, Mu began to drowse.

Perhaps Paolo was right. If he drove her back to the city, she could find somewhere at least for Christmas. But what about Roger? No, she couldn't leave him alone. He wouldn't understand. She might not get him back. Why should she trust this stranger anyway? It was odd that people here were being so kind. The old lady was one thing. That sort of charity happened sometimes, thank God. There must be another reason for this chef to want her out of the derelict site.

A chill crept down Mu's back. Why was he so insistent?

The familiar low ache in her groin warned her that she needed to change her tampon before allowing herself to sleep. Mu had no idea how long she had been sitting there since she'd finished her drink. Unwrapping herself from her cocoon, she sorted out what she needed. Roger was snoring lightly, so she let him be. Closing the inner door carefully, Mu walked to the outside door. She yawned. Something was making her even more tired than usual. Perhaps it was the feeling of relative security or being so full of food. Maybe it was her long vigil last night. She wasn't going to deny herself sleep for long.

It seemed to be the middle of the night. The pub was in darkness apart from a light in an upstairs window and the kitchen door. The moon was still dodging behind banks of clouds. It had risen much higher than when she'd returned from the pub yard.

Natural caution made Mu pause to check outside before she went any further. Slipping behind the door, she looked out through the gap. It was a good job she did. Squeezing himself in by the rickety gate at the site entrance was Paolo.

He was dressed in dark, rainproof clothes. Though he hadn't bothered to cover his face, there was something clandestine about how he set off down the slope past the office. He kept checking to either side, ensuring no one else was there. Over his shoulder, he carried a heavy bag, the sort of thing that food delivery drivers used, although this one was dark and had no logos. It was clearly heavy, as it kept slipping off his shoulder, and he had to keep pulling it back up. At one point, he stopped to watch the office building. Seemingly satisfied that Mu and Roger were asleep, he carried on.

When he had gone beyond her sight, Mu waited for a count of sixty before pulling open the recalcitrant outer door wide enough for her to edge out sideways. It scraped on the floor, though it had eased a little over the last day or so. She waited inside for another count of sixty before squeezing out of the gap. Keeping her back against the derelict building wall, she crept to the edge of the building. It had been much darker last night. Cautiously, Mu peered round the edge of the building.

Paolo was evidently feeling more secure. He was down near the cliff, walking along the footpath in the direction of the next village. He trained a torch beam just in front of him. If Mu hadn't known what the indistinct and weird shape was, it would have looked like a nightmare creature.

Rain occasionally obscuring her view, she continued to watch him. Paolo followed the footpath towards the gun emplacement. Just beyond it, she saw a light flash on and off as if it were giving a signal. Paolo's torch flickered in response. He was distant and barely visible. Mu could only make out the pinprick beams of the torches.

Suddenly both vanished.

CHAPTER 16

Danni thought she had seen some odd things in her two years with Lisa London, but last night had certainly been one of the strangest. How had anyone known about that underground site or thought to use it to hide people? Why did they need guards to keep them there? It was in the middle of nowhere. The place obviously had some connection to Mr Smith. But why was her boss involved with it? What the fuck was Gary doing in the middle of it all and not safely home in Naples?

Mr Smith was deemed too smelly to be taken back to the hotel, having been rolled around in the muck more than Striker. He had been bundled into the red van with a pair of the guards from the gun emplacement. Danni wondered how many of them were still down there. Although the guards had kept their balaclavas pulled down, Danni was certain that the one hemming Mr Smith in on the passenger side of the cab had been Gary.

The manhole cover was put back into place, and despite the smell from his clothes, Striker had driven them back to the hotel. Strangest of all, Lisa London had appeared to be badly affected by the stink. She rode with the air conditioning on and the car window down all the way back to Norwich.

When they got back to the hotel, she looked pale and ill. What had happened to London's famously strong stomach?

'Get yourself something from room service,' she had murmured as she'd dismissed Danni to her room.

Danni had showered and scrubbed her boots until they were spotless and had ordered food before collapsing on the bed, wondering what they would do with a pregnant illegal immigrant. Because it didn't take much effort to put the evidence together and come up with the fact this was a people-smuggling racket. It just didn't seem like Lisa London's style. And that was another worry.

Her instructions were to be at breakfast no later than six, which Danni obeyed. The restaurant was only just opening. She and London were the first to take a table. The menu offered everything from bowls of 'luxury' muesli to full English breakfasts. London ordered a smoothie, and Danni settled for a croissant and coffee. She was buttering her first mouthful when she saw London glance at the door. Careful not to show concern, Danni listened to the soft tread of footsteps across the carpet. A figure loomed above them, and London looked up at Striker.

For the first time ever, Danni thought he looked strained and tired. It was in the greyness around his eyes. His shoulders sloped where they were usually broad and proud. He must have already been out somewhere this morning.

'*Cosa hai fatto con lui?*' asked London.

Danni struggled for a moment, then came up with, *What did you do with him?*

'*Alla casa sicura,*' replied Striker. Danni took a moment. *At the house something or other? Safe house?*

'*Hai mezz'ora.*' London dismissed Striker with a wave of her hand. He wasn't invited to have any breakfast. Danni gave up and sipped her coffee. It wasn't as nice as Mrs Strong's morning offering.

Striker was waiting for them by the reception at exactly six thirty. He had showered and changed clothes, but the dark pouches under his eyes remained. All of them were wearing serviceable trousers and boots. Danni had wrapped a croissant in a napkin. She handed it to Striker as they walked behind London to the car. He took it without a murmur, although he glanced at Danni with gratitude. It was probably the most human interaction she'd ever had with him.

The Mercedes, spattered with mud and animal dung, stood close to the front door. Striker stuffed the croissant into his mouth in big chunks, hurriedly brushing the crumbs from his dark jacket. London looked at both with distaste.

'Let's fetch Mr Smith first,' she said.

The journey wasn't long. With a jolt, Danni realised they were on the same estate she had stayed on the first day she'd worked as London's drugs mule. In fact, they were knocking on the door to the maisonette where she had stayed with a man called Nick until Gary had moved her on. She had nicknamed him Mr Chatty because the man too easily confided in her.

The slightly tubby, tousled writer answered the door. He was blinking with sleep. London pushed past him into the kitchen. With a flick of her head for instruction, Striker strode upstairs, leaving their host staring at Danni as she followed London inside. Memory stirred, and he suddenly smiled. 'Danni, isn't it?'

She nodded.

'I didn't recognise you in your smart clothes.'

She smiled. 'How are you? Did you finish your script?'

It was true that she'd had a serious upgrade since she'd last spent a night in Nick's spare bedroom.

'I did, eventually.' He sounded rueful. 'Still trying to sell it. Doing a novel now.'

Nick clattered around the kitchen, putting on the kettle and reaching down mugs. London ignored him and looked out of the window, waiting. He pulled clothes from a tumble dryer and pattered upstairs with them. When he returned, Danni declined a drink.

'Just had one,' she said. 'How is that other chap? The one with all the tattoos?'

'Tony? Haven't seen him in a while. He got done for hurting some actor in Cromer.'

Danni's eyes opened wide in surprise. She moved closer to Nick and lowered her voice. 'You still supplementing your income?'

'Not that way.' He glanced over Danni's shoulder at London. 'I'm a safe house these days.'

He was still Mr Chatty, then. Still talking too much. Danni wondered just how safe this house would be even in an emergency.

'Shut up,' said London. Her voice was neither anxious nor angry. In fact, she was in business mode. Danni recognised it.

There was a thump from upstairs. Presumably, Striker was getting Nick's visitor out of bed. Given Mr Chatty's easy-going nature, Danni was unsurprised when Mr Smith came down the stairs followed by Striker and the two guards from the gun emplacement.

Neither had their balaclavas on now. She didn't recognise the first one. The other was Gary. He looked her in the eye and ghosted a wink, which she didn't respond to. He shuffled his right hand by his side to draw her attention to it. A large sticking plaster was pulled tight between his forefinger and thumb, making the skin white with pressure.

Danni felt Nick shift uncomfortably at her side. He knew Gary from the old days, Danni remembered. When she glanced his way, the strain of pretending he didn't know stretched Nick's face tight with tension.

'I could have had this done at the hotel,' said Mr Smith. He grumpily indicated his crumpled clothes. He pointed at Striker. 'I could've used his room. He could have stayed here.'

'Hardly,' said London. She didn't acknowledge her brother as she surveyed the guards without comment. 'Time to get this disaster cleaned up. *Andiamo.*'

London strode out of Nick's home and along the concrete corridor to the stairs, the little entourage following obediently behind. Of course, London had known all along,

Danni realised. She must have been expecting Gary to be there at the gun emplacement before they'd set out. At some point, Striker must have been included in the secret. It was Danni who hadn't been informed.

She took time to whisper goodbye to Mr Chatty.

He dropped his hand lightly on her arm to restrain her for a moment. 'You do know who that is, don't you?'

Danni nodded. 'Of course.'

'Be careful,' said Nick. 'I have a bad feeling about this.'

'I still have your number.'

He nodded. 'Good. Anytime.'

The old red van was hidden behind the block of flats under a tree in the residents' car park. Mr Smith was allowed to join Danni in the back seat of the Mercedes.

Before she could climb in, London pulled her to one side. 'Have you got the emergency kit with you as I asked?'

'Of course, Ms London.'

'Get on your laptop and find us as many escape routes as you can. Family members only.'

Danni glanced at the party. Naturally, not the guard, but not Mr Smith either. Striker was family. Danni had his fake Italian passport in the bottom of her handbag. There was one for Gary and a choice of two for London. What about herself?

As if she could read Danni's mind, London asked, 'Did you bring yours?'

Danni nodded.

'Then the choice is yours.'

Slipping in the backseat beside Mr Smith, Danni made herself comfortable and fired up her laptop. Connecting through her mobile, she looked for flights. So long as she didn't lose the signal, it wouldn't take her long. Availability would be the only issue this close to Christmas.

With the red van in the lead, the two cars moved off. Their route took them back past the hotel. Striker hesitated in the rush hour stream of vehicles, and as they inched past the hotel gates, Danni glanced up.

She hadn't noticed the building across the road before. It was behind a wall with a tall hedge above it, with two sets of gates at either end of a semi-circular drive. One set of gates stood open, and she could see a few cars parked on the gravel. It looked like the sort of place that would house a firm of lawyers or accountants. What attracted Danni's attention was that one of the cars was directly facing them. It was black or dark blue, and two people sat inside. As Striker passed the gate, the other car's engine started.

Swivelling her head as they inched forward in the queue, Danni saw the car pull out into the traffic about three cars behind them. She put her laptop down on the backseat and whispered in London's ear.

'I think we're being followed again.'

CHAPTER 17

Sara was pleased that she'd been organised about Christmas this year. She had already bought her presents and written her cards. Knowing in advance that she was working on Christmas Eve, she had posted cards and presents to her mother the previous weekend. All she had left was to hand out her cards and Secret Santa to work colleagues. They sat in her handbag on the back seat of DI Edwards's car. She hadn't had time to give them out. At the morning meeting, DCI Hudson had suggested that Sara and DI Edwards head out to the Great Yarmouth Port Authority to ask about the stray cruiser Dodge had seen.

Edwards weaved through the busy town centre one-way system before heading down the spit of land that allowed the River Yare to enter the North Sea between Great Yarmouth on one side and the Edwardian seaside resort of Gorleston on the other. There was a new, purpose-built harbour on the seaward side and other vessels anchored in the river at the original docks. There seemed to be acres of derelict land covered in concrete that were now unused but hinted at greater activity levels in the past. Despite the clear blue sky and bright sunlight, the place had a run-down air. The North Sea wind buffeted the car as they drove by the old wharf buildings.

A handful of ships were moored in the river, though Sara couldn't see many crew on them. None of them appeared to be holiday cruisers. The Port Authority was run by a private company in an anonymous building on a piece of concrete wasteland. Constructed of metal panels painted in a bright blue-green, it looked like the only new building in the area.

'You'll need to speak to the harbour master. Ashley Peel.' The receptionist was polite and helpful. She dialled a number, and someone came down the stairs to meet them in seconds.

The man seemed too young to have so much responsibility. Sara doubted if he was more than thirty-five, although being blond and clean-shaven might have made him look more youthful. He was tall and well built. His handshake was extremely firm.

'We need to ask about any ship movements over the last few days, Mr Peel,' the DI explained.

Peel glanced at their warrant cards. 'You'd best come up to my office.'

The building was a square, modular-style affair and the harbour master's office was blandly efficient. There were three computers on a table near the window. Each one showed a different programme running in real time. A smaller desk with another computer stood to one side. Peel had clearly tried to make the space more interesting by fastening sea charts to the walls. Sara stopped in front of one of them to examine it. There were red blocks marked in groups out from the coast.

'Are you interested in maps and charts?' Peel smiled at Sara, obviously hoping that she was keen on that sort of thing.

Some people must be, she thought, as she pointed to one of the charts. 'It has never occurred to me that a sea map would be as complex as a land one,' she said. 'I suppose I've never had much to do with it, as I don't go boating.'

Peel nodded encouragingly and pointed to the charts. 'I don't actually need charts like this, not these days. You can get it all online, of course. I like the feel of having them there, though.'

'Quick to reference in an emergency,' suggested Edwards.

Peel turned to look at the DI amiably. 'Indeed,' he said. 'Not that we have many of those now. Most of the vessels we deal with have first-rate navigation systems and accurate weather forecasts. Please, have a seat.'

Edwards sat down. Peel waited politely, his hand held out towards a visitor's chair. Sara continued to examine the charts.

'What are these red blocks?' Sara pointed to the one she was still studying.

'Wind farm sites.' Peel stood next to Sara. 'It's a large part of our work here, constructing the farms and maintaining them afterwards. Big business for the town.'

'And these lines here?'

'Navigation routes.' Peel tapped at another chart, which showed the port itself and the sea lanes in and out. 'This is the whole port on a larger scale. The two ports are my main remit. Once a vessel leaves the harbour, in theory, it should join one of the shipping lanes until they are far enough away from the coast. That way, they avoid running into the turbines or one another.'

'In theory?' asked Edwards.

'We get the occasional rogue.' Peel shrugged. 'Taking a shorter route and getting among the turbines. Trying to save time.'

He moved to one of the three computers. Little squares with numbers in them moved slowly across a digital outline map. Peel pointed to one of the numbers. 'This is the unique code for a given vessel. The number tells us what sort of ship it is and its registration details. These smaller ones buzzing about are things like the rig supply boats.'

'Do all boats have these trackers?' Sara watched the screen as the numbers gently sailed on their journeys.

'Commercial ones do,' said Peel.

'Even fishermen?'

'Not the little ones, like the crab and lobster fishermen. They don't go beyond the inshore line.' Peel pointed to a hatched area on the screen. 'Trawlers have them.'

'How interesting.' Sara thanked him with a smile and sat in the other visitor's chair. 'What about pleasure cruisers?'

'If you mean cruise ships, then yes, they do.' He pointed to one blinking square. 'I like following the cruise ships, so I recognise their codes.'

Sara wondered how boring his job could get if he had time to track cruise ships. 'Privately owned small cruisers? Four or six people?'

'Not compulsory.' Peel settled in his own chair. 'Some of them have them voluntarily. Is that what you're trying to trace?'

Sara looked at Edwards, who nodded. 'We have an unsubstantiated report that a boat of that type may have been close to the shore on Monday night. Heading south from Winterton-on-Sea. We thought they may have been making for here as the nearest place they could get real shelter.'

'Blimey!' Peel looked surprised. 'It was a really bad night on Monday. Not a good time to be out. Especially in such a small craft. We had three emergency berths around teatime because the forecast was poor.'

'You mean vessels that weren't due to be with you but came in for safety?'

'Exactly.'

'This would have been around midnight or not long after,' said Sara. 'Would you have a log?'

'Of official berthing, yes.' Peel tapped on his computer keyboard. He scrolled until he found the screen he was looking for. Frowning with concentration, he reeled off a handful of names of ships and docking times. 'Sorry, nothing between our last, a Hull trawler that came in about seven in the evening, and the emergency overnighters leaving next morning.'

'So, you can't tell if something was out there later?'

'You would be better speaking to the Coastguard if you want to track something.' Peel reached for a notepad and scribbled down a name and number. 'May I ask why you want to know all this? Has the vessel been lost at sea?'

'We found a body on the beach at Winterton yesterday morning,' Edwards said. 'We're trying to trace where he may have come from and thought he may have been connected with this boat.'

'Ah.' Peel shuffled some of the papers on his desk before selecting one and reading it. 'Is your body male and black?'

'Yes,' said Sara.

'Then this Mayday report may be what you need. I'll print you out a copy.'

CHAPTER 18

A simple phone call separated the group's two vehicles. Striker inched through the ring-road traffic towards the airport while the red van turned towards the coast. Watching in the rear-view mirror, Striker confirmed that the suspect car was following them. They drove past the airport and along a dual carriageway. Without warning, Striker doubled back at a roundabout and headed towards the north coast. The car was still in view when Striker sped up a slip road over a pair of roundabouts on a flyover and hammered back past the airport. Danni gave up on her internet search as the car swung frantically about. Tyres squealing, Striker turned off at a lesser-used roundabout on to the Holt Road.

They flew through a busy commuter village before being surrounded by a small wood. Striker took a sharp turn and weaved through narrow, minor lanes at breathtaking speed. Mr Smith's face was a rictus of fear. He clung to the door handle to steady himself. *God help anyone coming the other way*, Danni thought.

After fifteen minutes and several heart-stopping bends, they turned down a side road that led to a tiny village. The place was delightfully old-fashioned, with red-brick cottages and houses built around a large green. A tall church surrounded by a knapped-flint wall occupied the fourth side. The red van was waiting in the parking space by the entrance gate. They pulled up beside it, obscuring it from view.

Gary was leaning nonchalantly against the far side of the van. The other guard sat in the driver's seat, legs swinging out of the open door. There was no sign of the car that had pulled out of the office in Norwich. Striker had lost it miles ago.

'Wait in the car,' London told Smith. He wound down the window and sucked in deep breaths of air. London paced off.

Danni followed her boss. She'd heard the phrase 'looking green' but hadn't actually ever seen anyone who fitted the description until now. London walked unsteadily along the edge of the village common. When she had got round the church corner, she propped herself with one hand on the wall and threw up. Danni felt queasy herself after Striker's driving antics. Returning to the car, she grabbed a water bottle from the side pocket and approached London carefully.

'This might help,' she said, offering the bottle. London held out her free hand but kept her head down. Danni knew she would be furious if anyone suspected she was becoming vulnerable. She resisted the urge to put a comforting arm around her boss. Retreating to the vehicles, Danni left London in peace.

Watched by Striker, the guard slumped out of his seat and opened the back of the van. He pulled down a panel in the side wall and extracted some tools, then lifted a floor panel to reveal a secret storage area. Striker flicked through half a dozen number plates before choosing a pair. The other guard nodded and began to change the van's registration plates. Striker picked a second pair.

It would take a few minutes to do, so Danni gazed around the village. There was a little craft shop and tearoom diagonally opposite. A woman was placing a chalkboard outside. Presumably, the place was about to open. Danni strolled over to investigate and bought some bottled soft drinks. The sweet fizz would help with car sickness.

When London reappeared, looking pale but clean, she gave Danni the half-empty water bottle. In return, Danni handed her a bottle of diet lemonade. London sipped at it as they watched the guard change the plates.

'We'll head across country,' decided London.

The guard nodded his acknowledgement.

'You can take as much time as you like. Turn back as often as you feel the need. I don't want to arrive together.'

They drove away from the pretty village several minutes after the van. Striker pulled off the road into an empty car park for a woodland walk. Taking a screwdriver, he also changed the number plates on their car. Now both vehicles were less traceable than before. For nearly an hour, they took a twisting, winding route through small villages and a tiny town before they found open, rolling countryside. Farmland stretched out on each side of the lane they were following. They passed few cars and even fewer people. Danni tried to keep working on her laptop, although the mobile signal came and went. She occasionally jotted a wobbly note in her diary. At a dip in the road, Striker turned down a cart track with high hedges on both sides. The bottom of the car ground into the dirt several times before reaching a high chain-link fence with barbed wire wound around the top.

A man dressed in black appeared and opened the padlocked gate to let them in. Three large, modern farm buildings surrounded a muddy yard, forming a square with the fence on the fourth side. They were joined up as though you could walk from one to the other without going outside. A broken tractor trailer, old pieces of agricultural machinery draped in ragged tarpaulins and piles of pallets stood in the yard.

The van was already parked next to a couple of other dirty-looking vehicles. Gary and the other guard were waiting for them. There was no other sign of life.

Striker yanked open the back door and pulled Mr Smith out. He stumbled onto the mud, caking the knees of his trousers. Striker lifted him up by the back of his jacket.

'Let's go,' snapped London.

'All right, no need for that.' Mr Smith brushed himself down, only managing to further smear his trousers with mud. With a heavy sigh, the businessman led the way.

There was just one small door on the side of the wall of the first building. It opened as they approached. The party filed in, with Danni bringing up the rear. Gary walked next to her, still playing the guard. His hand briefly touched the back of hers as they went inside. When Danni closed the door behind them, she heard it lock itself.

The first room looked like a staff break area. A narrow wooden bench acted as a reception desk, and an old telephone was screwed to the wall behind it. A broken-down sofa and a couple of armchairs stood against the wall. In the corner was a table with a kettle and dirty mugs, used tea bags, scattered sugar and empty plastic milk bottles. Danni screwed up her nose and mouth in disgust at the sight of it.

Two men in black jeans and well-worn black hoodies waited for them. The outfit looked exactly like the one worn by the men Danni had seen on the cliff last night. Striker pushed Mr Smith in the back, and the first man looked at him in surprise. His hand moved swiftly to a bottle of pepper spray dangling from his belt.

'You okay, boss?' he asked uncertainly.

'It's fine,' said Mr Smith. 'These are my associates. We're here to sort out our little problem.' He turned to Lisa London, holding out his hands in a gesture of display. 'Welcome to the facility.'

CHAPTER 19

It had become stormy during the night. The wind had rattled the window boards, and rain had dripped through the roof. Somehow, Mu had managed a rare decent night's sleep. Grey daylight filtered into the office as she rolled stiffly from lying down to a sitting position. Roger had shaken off his blankets and was already sitting up, head cocked to one side. The sound of footsteps crunching on the gravel path, followed by a whistle and a 'Here you go, boy,' warned them that a local dog walker was outside. It was a man's voice. Roger huffed once or twice until the footsteps and the skittering of the dog chasing his ball on the mud receded down the coastal path.

'I must have overslept,' Mu muttered to the dog. She clipped on his lead, found a change of tampon and led Roger cautiously outside.

Squalls of rain battered her, gusted by the wind. She looked for the dog walker, who had made it as far as the old gun emplacement. He looked well dressed for the weather, though he was beating his arms around himself as if he were freezing. Mu knew how he felt. She shivered as she allowed Roger a short walk to relieve himself. Checking for observers, she slipped into the old toilet block. Roger stood guard while she used it.

The roof of the block sagged alarmingly in places. It had fallen in at the far end, leaving space for the bad weather to force its way in. Mu used the least gross sink to wash her hands and splash her face. God knew she could use a long, hot shower.

Outside, she saw the man and his dog fussing around the old emplacement. It was a golden Labrador, and she smiled as the man tried to call the dog to him. Everyone knew Labs had minds of their own, and this one was on a mission. As she and Roger walked back to their office, no one else was in sight.

Now Mu had a decision to make. The place was hardly safe or weatherproof. However, it was the best shelter they had found in some days and wouldn't be too bad a place to wait out Christmas. She could have done with another canister for her tiny camping stove, as there was no access to hot drinks here apart from the pub or the little café-cum-shop with the angry woman at the till. It was the one thing you could almost always get a donation of in a city. Thanks to the old lady, she had food for herself and Roger, although it wouldn't last very long. Nor could she rely on Paolo being generous again.

The chef's insistence that she should move on was the most worrying. She couldn't trust him, despite his kindness. Where had he been going with that bag last night, and who had he met? It wasn't difficult to imagine that it might have something to do with the group of people who had appeared up the rickety steps two nights ago. He'd gone to that old gun emplacement with it. Surely there weren't people over there? How could you keep people there in this weather? Her derelict office was bad enough. Besides, it was open to the footpath, as the curious Labrador had proved.

Mu gave Roger his breakfast and made herself a sandwich. Then she checked Roger's paws, which seemed to be healing enough for a bit of a walk. She spent a few minutes folding and tearing at the most worn of her blankets until she had an oblong of fabric. Scrabbling on the floor, she dug up some bits of wire, which she poked through the ends of the cloth to form a simple clip. Mu draped it over Roger and fastened it down with her spare belt. He inspected it, then accepted it with a lick of Mu's hand. She tidied up her things in case they had to make a getaway, then encouraged the dog to follow her. She could think as she walked.

The wind was definitely getting stronger. Waves pounded noisily at the base of the cliff. The suck and roll of the water in the giant breakwater rocks echoed up at them. They kept well away from the edge as they headed along the footpath. Roger trotted over to inspect the old war building like the Labrador had done. Mu could see from where she stood that there was no one trying to shelter in the remnants of the place. Roger seemed most interested in one corner.

'What is it, boy?' asked Mu. 'What have you found?'

He was snuffling excitedly at the top of an old set of concrete steps in the furthest corner of the remaining three walls. They led underground. Whatever its function might once have been, the entrance was now collapsed. Bricks from the wall lining and concrete from a ceiling panel lay smashed on the lower steps. Large, random blocks of stone underpinned the rubble. Old grass, dirty straw and cobwebs formed a disgusting organic mat of debris that hung like a net over the rubbish. It clearly hadn't been touched in years. It was impassable.

'Come away.' Mu patted Roger.

He glanced at her but continued to whimper and sniff from the top of the steps.

Mu clipped on his lead and gave it a gentle tug. 'Don't get down in all that. You'll hurt yourself.'

Roger stuffed his nose in a tiny gap at the top of the mat. He scented deeply, then backed a couple of paces and barked. Mu tentatively stepped down the two clear steps to try and pick him up. The dog put a resisting paw on her outstretched arms and barked again.

'All right,' she sighed. 'Let me see.'

Holding on to the crumbling concrete edge of the stair-well, Mu stretched forwards. The matted debris felt disgusting under her fingers. She dragged her coat sleeve over her hand and poked it into the gap. Some of the rubbish dislodged, making the hole bigger. She peered into the space as Roger danced impatiently on the stairs, urging her on. Beyond the small gap, it was dark. All Mu could see was more rubbish and broken concrete.

'Nothing there, old fella,' she assured the dog.

He barked his dissatisfaction.

'All right.' Gritting her teeth, Mu dragged down more of the cobweb mat. It stuck to her sleeve, making her feel nauseous. The air in the void stank, which was hardly surprising, as the local farmer had dumped a load of dirty animal straw in a giant pile at the back. Even with all this blustering wind, the stench of the dung heap hung in the air.

Except, it wasn't animal shit, was it? Roger nudged under her arm to get another sniff at the air escaping up the ruined stairwell. Mu put her head next to his and tentatively sniffed again. She jerked back and gagged as it hit her. It was the same stink you got in old toilets. Human toilets that had been overused for years or had no ventilation. For a moment, Mu wondered if it was simply some walker who had been caught short and used the thing as a toilet. Surely, they would have disturbed some of this disgusting organic mat if that were the case. And the real trouble was, this stink was warm.

'What the hell are you doing?'

Mu screamed as the man's voice shocked her. She nearly tumbled into the old stairwell. Roger went rigid at her side, snarling angrily. It was Paolo.

CHAPTER 20

Ashley Peel gave them the address for the nearest Coastguard Agency office or 'nerve centre', as he called it. It was in Colchester. Edwards pulled a face at the idea of driving that far.

'They're the ones who can track your cruiser,' Peel said. 'Although I'm not sure how long they keep traffic movement recordings.'

It turned out to be seven days. Sara rang them while Edwards drove them back to Norwich. Sara wished they had visited the Coastguard's office, but he was the boss. They were queueing at a roundabout that led out of Great Yarmouth while she spoke to a friendly woman called Lizzie Hardaker, who declared herself to have been on the night shift on Monday.

'Rough night,' Lizzie agreed. 'Thought we might have more trouble than we did. You sure it was a seagoing leisure cruiser?'

Sara explained again about the sighting. 'Around midnight off Winterton-on-Sea.'

'Hold on.' For a couple of minutes, Sara could hear the woman breathing heavily as she tapped away on a keyboard. 'Okay, here we go.' She rattled off what sounded like coordinates, and muttered about there not being much to see before she stopped speaking altogether.

'You've found something?'

'Maybe. It's close to the shore but definitely moving. I'll fast-forward it a bit.' The woman called out to a colleague. 'Jack, do you see what I'm seeing?'

'What is it?' asked Sara.

There was a hurried conversation at the other end.

'I've picked up a small boat just north of Winterton at 23:42,' Lizzie explained. There were more muttered questions and the clicking of a computer mouse. 'It's going south. You'd think it would have been heading for Great Yarmouth. That's the nearest port.'

'It didn't go in there. We've checked.'

'Okay. There's something odd about this. Look, this is going to take time. Give me your details, and I'll get back to you.'

Biting back her frustration, Sara gave her number and email address, explaining that she was based in the Wymondham HQ building.

'This is a wild-goose chase, isn't it?' she said. 'Nothing to do with our body?'

Edwards sped along the Acle Straight. 'Could easily have been someone just trying to outrun the storm,' he replied. 'I don't think it's worth taking any more time over. Let's take that Mayday report to Dr Taylor. That's almost certainly the answer to this mystery.'

She hoped the DI was right. With luck, they would be able to resolve this before Christmas Eve, and everyone could have the holiday they had been planning on.

* * *

Dr Taylor was busy in the forensic suite. He had sent Sara and Edwards to the small viewing gallery above the room. It was intended for the police or student trainees to observe, though it was rarely used.

'Don't want you contaminating the proceedings,' he'd said gruffly. 'Bowen's up there already.'

Bowen was the official observer, and he greeted them with a nod. Sara never enjoyed attending post-mortems. None of them did. It was something you just had to get used to. At least up here, they were away from the smell. The victim was laid out on the metal examination table. Dr Taylor was at the grisly stage, extracting and examining the internal organs. Over the intercom, they could hear the squashy sound of the pathologist picking up, poking at and weighing body parts. 'Plenty of water in our chap's lungs,' he said.

'Life jacket didn't work, then,' said Bowen.

'I'm afraid not.' Taylor pointed to a workbench where the jacket and the remnants of the victim's clothes lay. 'All that did was ensure he floated into the beach. The sea was very rough. He couldn't have swum in it for very long.'

'What about all that damage?' asked Sara.

The victim's face was ripped open. Flaps of flesh hung from his cheeks, and his lower lip was missing. He would be hard to identify from his face alone.

Taylor pointed to the man's hands. 'You can see it here. It goes all the way up his arms, as well. I think he got caught on the breakwater rocks, which caused all this. I'm pretty sure he was dead before that.'

'Would he have died of exposure?' asked Sara. 'It must have been cold in the water.'

'No. Cause of death is drowning. I think the high waves got him before he got that cold.'

'Time of death?' asked Edwards.

'Between eleven and three at night,' said Taylor. 'Hard to be more exact with this much confusion.'

'Fits with this, then.' Edwards waved the printed report Ashley Peel had given them.

'What have you got?'

'A Mayday report,' Sara said. 'A man overboard filed by a container ship on Monday evening.'

'Poor bugger,' said Taylor. 'Go on, give me the rest.'

'The *Evergreen Voyager*,' read Sara. 'Left Felixstowe at 1800 hours, against advice. Heading for Denmark, they decided to hug the Suffolk and Norfolk coast for as long as possible.' She skimmed through the nautical details. 'About 2300 hours, they had a problem on deck. A deckhand got kitted up and attached to a safety rope and went to sort it out, despite the bad weather.'

Sara felt her skin begin to crawl. In her head, she could imagine the poor man struggling in the cold and wet as the long ship bucked in the heavy seas. 'Got swept overboard in the dark. Captain called a Mayday, and the lifeboat from Great Yarmouth was launched. They searched for a couple of hours but had no luck. Captain says he can't have fastened himself on properly.' She folded the paper with a sigh. 'Why didn't they go back for him?'

'Takes a while to slow those big buggers down, let alone turn them around.' Bowen shot her a sympathetic glance. 'The lifeboat was his best chance.'

'Do we have a name for our possible deckhand?' asked Taylor.

'Omar Rahman. Registered merchant seaman from Sudan.'

'Great.' The pathologist sighed. 'I'll get some DNA done to identify him while you try to contact the Sudanese authorities.'

Sara glanced at Edwards, who was smirking. Obviously, she was going to get landed with that one.

Taylor rinsed his hands. 'Someone will be missing him,' he said. 'You'd better come down and take these.' He went to the bench and held up a small bag. 'These were in a solid plastic credit card case in an inside pocket. It was trapped under the life jacket, which is how they survived when the man carrying them didn't. Three photos. I assume they are of his wife and children.'

CHAPTER 21

Back in the comfort of the Serious Crimes Unit office, Sara placed the man's family photos on her desk. An envelope with her name on it was propped against her screen. The place was empty apart from Aggie and herself, so she opened it while no one else could see.

It was a Christmas card from DC Adebayo signed, *Wishing you a Happy New Year, Dante xx.* Under the *xx*, he'd added, *Any chance of an Xmas Eve drink?*

Sara snapped the card shut and put it in her desk drawer, then walked around her colleague's desks, placing Christmas cards carefully on each.

Aggie looked up and smiled. 'Thank you,' she said and held out an envelope in return. She watched as Sara opened the card.

It wasn't what Sara had been expecting. A colourful square of card decorated by hand with champagne glasses and bunches of flowers invited her to Aggie and Mike Bowen's wedding on 7 February. 'We aren't having much of a do. Only a few friends and family.'

Sara checked out the details. The Norwich registry office in the morning, followed by a meal at a city restaurant. The 'plus one' jumped off the invitation at her, reminding her she had no one to bring along. Sara frowned. Well, unless it was Dante Adebayo.

'You will come, won't you?' asked Aggie. 'Mike particularly wants you to be there, and so do I.'

Sara fixed a smile on her face. 'Of course. I'd be delighted. Where's Hudson?'

'Gone upstairs to Personnel with the Christmas leave rota. Once you rang in and said you'd almost certainly identified our John Doe, she was willing to get everyone signed off for a few days.'

'It's been a long year,' agreed Sara. 'One thing left to do, if you can help me with it?' She picked up the photos and showed them to Aggie.

'Poor family,' Aggie said.

'Indeed. If it is the same chap, he's Sudanese. Registered merchant seaman.' She passed a copy of the Mayday report to Aggie. 'Any suggestions?'

Aggie turned to her computer, and her fingers began to fly on the keyboard. Her lips pursed as she scrolled the screens. 'There's an international register. Leave it with me.'

'Dr Taylor needs a copy of that too.'

Aggie nodded absent-mindedly, already focused on something she had found. As she reached for the phone, Sara went for water to fill the coffee machine.

When she returned, all the team had come back. Bowen and Noble sat relaxed in their chairs. Hudson was in her office with Edwards, the door closed. Aggie had finished her call and produced a cake tin.

'That was a narrow escape,' said Bowen. 'Thought we might be in for a working holiday.'

'Going to my girlfriend's parents on the day,' said Noble.

They looked at him. This was the first time he had mentioned any details about his relationship, although they all knew he had a girlfriend.

'Be a bit tricky if I couldn't turn up,' he added.

Aggie handed the photographs back to Sara. 'I've spoken to the seamen's registrar,' she said. 'They'll email the local agent, and he can go round in person. I said we would prefer that. He would like copies of the pictures. I've scanned them for him.'

Sara looked at the family in one of the photos. The proud wife smiling at the camera, presumably held by her husband. She had a hand on the two children's shoulders, one boy and one girl. They were all smartly dressed. The house they stood in front of looked brand new.

'Just remind them to be cautious,' she said. 'We need a DNA sample to be sure. Let's not put the family through all that, only for it to be another man.'

Aggie nodded. 'I'll remind them in the email.'

Edwards and Hudson emerged from the office. Both looked as happy as they ever allowed themselves to look.

'Updates?' asked Hudson. Aggie handed her a Tupperware box with her own gluten-free cake in it. Hudson smiled. 'Thank you.'

'The Mayday report seems fairly conclusive,' said Sara. She explained about the local agent and the DNA samples. 'However, it's unlikely that we will have a resolution to this before the holidays.'

'I agree,' said Hudson. 'I've signed off all your holiday requests and given them to Personnel. It doesn't look like this is a murder, just a tragic accident. So, I see no reason for anyone to be in after tomorrow for a couple of days.'

There was a general murmur of happy agreement.

'Let's just tidy up the paperwork on this,' Hudson continued. 'Then tomorrow is Secret Santa day.'

The happy murmur turned grumbly. While everyone participated in the anonymous present-giving, they all worried about being paired with a joker. Sara had pulled Aggie from the hat and was confident that her gift would be acceptable.

Her phone rang. 'Good morning,' she said, hoping she sounded efficient. Her mouth was full of Aggie's seasonal cake offering.

'DS Hirst?' asked a female voice. 'Lizzie Hardaker here. Coastguard.'

Sara had almost forgotten about the random late-night cruiser. It didn't have any bearing on their unfortunate man.

'I thought I'd better let you know.' Hardaker sounded anxious. 'We tracked that private cruiser.'

'It's not good news, is it?' asked Sara. Hardaker's tone was enough to have fired up Sara's detective's instincts.

'No, I'm afraid not. I tracked it on the monitor recordings. It didn't put into Yarmouth. It didn't get that far. It was abandoned just off North Denes. It's been drifting outwards near the wind farms. If you hadn't alerted us, it would probably have sunk before we'd realised we should be looking for it.'

'What happens now?'

'We have a boat out there, fixing a tow to it. We'll bring it back into Yarmouth Outer Harbour. But there's more.'

'Go on . . .' said Sara.

'Our vessel's captain says he thinks there's a problem on board.' Hardaker hesitated, then spoke rapidly. 'To be specific, they've found a body. They put a man over to check the engines, and he found him. The poor sod is definitely dead.'

'When will it get in?' Sara sighed and raised a warning hand to the rest of the team. The happy chatter and clinking of coffee cups ground to a halt.

'Give us an hour,' said Hardaker. 'But there's even more.'

'How come?'

'You should speak to Great Yarmouth Police and confirm what they've told us — they've found an abandoned rigid inflatable boat on the beach in the dunes at North Denes.'

'We'll meet you there as soon as possible,' said Sara.

'I'll be at the harbour.' Hardaker rang off.

Sara looked at the team, who were watching her closely. 'Sorry guys, Christmas may be cancelled after all.'

CHAPTER 22

'Wait, wait,' called Paolo. 'You fall. I'm sorry. *Adesso. Uno momento.*'

He walked quickly across the dirty floor of the derelict emplacement and reached out to grab Mu's hand. Roger barked warningly, bouncing up and down and winding himself up to attack if necessary.

'*Andiamo,*' said Paolo, giving Mu a hefty tug. She stumbled up the concrete steps, bouncing off Paolo's body. Keeping his grip on her hand, he deftly manoeuvred her outside. Roger bounced around them, huffing and barking, unsure what to make of it.

Paolo let go a few steps along the footpath, and Mu staggered to a halt. She swung round angrily to face him. His hand was already raised as if to hit her. Mu cowered, arms over her head as Roger launched himself at Paolo. When the hand made contact, it roughly brushed away the cobweb mat from her arm and back. But it was too late to stop Roger's assumption that Paolo was attacking Mu. After all, it wasn't the first time he had seen this. The dog jumped, and his jaws locked on Paolo's arm. Gravity pulled the ball of fury to the floor. Snarling, he began to shake and tug at Paolo. The man turned on the dog, and Mu feared the worst.

'*Calmo, calmo,*' said Paolo. He allowed Roger to continue tugging without resisting. There was a ripping noise from Paolo's jacket. '*Va tutto bene.*'

'Roger!' shouted Mu. 'Roger, stop it.'

Roger let go. Panting, his head flicked between the two people, trying to understand what was happening. Mu dashed forward and hurriedly clipped on his lead. If Roger was confused, Mu was equally so. She dragged him several paces away before turning back to face Paolo. 'What did you do that for?'

Paolo shrugged. 'I frightened you, and you fell. Very dangerous that place.'

'Were you following me?' Mu retreated a few more steps along the path.

'I bring you some food.' Paolo frowned.

Mu wasn't buying his 'misunderstood good guy' act. Too many nights on the streets had made her cynical. 'Where is it, then?'

'Where you sleep.'

Mu was horrified. 'You went in where my stuff is?'

'I knocked,' said Paolo. He pulled his jacket straight and wiped at the dog slobber on his arm. 'You not there. Then I see you over here, with *il cane*. I came to tell you.'

Mu swayed indecisively. The food last night had been welcome. It didn't seem to have been tampered with, and there had been plenty of it. She patted Roger gently. 'Did he hurt you?'

With a smile, Paolo inspected the tear in the sleeve of his jacket. 'Don't think so.'

There might be bruises later, Mu guessed, but the dog's worn and elderly teeth hadn't got through the fabric to break the skin. Roger slumped to the floor, exhausted by his bravery.

'What is it?'

'*Scusi?*'

'The food, what is it?'

'Bacon sandwich.' Paolo pointed at Roger. 'Tin for him.'

'That's very kind.'

'You come away now,' said Paolo. 'Before you get hurt.' He turned and began to walk away.

Hurt? By what? Or by who? Mu watched the chef stride back towards the pub. She let him get a decent distance away before deciding what to do next. The old office no longer felt at all safe. Not only had she witnessed something she would have preferred not to see, but Paolo had been inside. It felt like a violation. What the hell was she going to do now?

The footpath that ran behind the old gun emplacement split in two. One path headed along the clifftop towards Walton. The other followed a farm track for a few hundred yards until it met the old road into the village. This tiny lane went left and sharply up the small rise, past a house, and the church stood at the most prominent point. It made a circular route.

'Fancy a walk, fella?' she asked. To her relief, Roger rose immediately, tail wagging. She let him off the lead again and aimed towards the church. Roger busied himself, checking out clumps of grass and lumps of dung from the giant heap.

'Don't you dare roll in that shit,' Mu called. 'I've only just made you that coat. I'll put your lead back on.'

Roger ignored her and vanished behind the pile. With a sigh, Mu followed him. Luckily, he showed more interest in a random manhole cover than the scattered animal manure.

'Enough now.' Mu pulled on his collar. 'There's my brave fella. Come on. Let's go and get some fresh air.'

Roger followed her reluctantly. The wind whipped across the fields, buffeting the pair as they walked to the lane. Raindrops battered them in sudden squalls, which stopped after a few seconds. The sky was full of rolling grey clouds. The weather was certainly getting worse.

Mu put Roger's lead on for safety when they reached the lane. The hedge that lined the road offered a decent amount of shelter, which they were grateful for. When they got to the solitary house, Mu saw a sign that said, *The Vicarage*. Of course, that made sense. The church was the next building, and the pub was about a hundred yards beyond that. Surrounded by a high hedge, the 1930s-looking house had a large garden. It was obviously in use. There were lights on inside the house, and the gravel drive held two small cars.

The church was enormous. Built of flint and stone, the ancient structure boasted a huge, four-storey, square bell tower. It was surrounded by a large graveyard with hundreds of headstones. A short grass path led from the lane to the church porch. Mu halted and surveyed the impressive building.

'I wonder if the old lady meant it,' she said to Roger. The dog looked up at her, tongue lolling from his open mouth. 'Do you think there might be some free food in there?'

'There should be,' said a man's voice behind her.

Mu nearly screamed again. She wasn't sure if her system could take many more shocks this morning. Turning swiftly, she confronted whoever it was.

The tall, middle-aged man was wearing a black suit with a vicar's collar. He had short-trimmed hair and his neat goatee beard flashed with silver. He was smiling in a friendly, deliberately non-confrontational way. A cheerful golden Labrador was tugging excitedly at his lead by the man's side.

'Steady on, Terry,' he said. The dog ignored him, wagging his tail furiously at Roger.

'Did I see you this morning, walking your dog?' asked Mu. Roger had frozen close to her side, not yet prepared to be friends with this new canine.

'Earlier on?' The man nodded. 'Terry was particularly interested in those old sheds this morning.'

'Gun emplacement,' said Mu.

'Yes, indeed. Second World War. Don't know what got into him. He doesn't normally pay any attention. I'm Theo, by the way. Theo Collins. Shall we go and see if there is anything you would like?'

The vicar opened the gate and set off up the path.

CHAPTER 23

The tension was palpable to Danni. The suspicious guard looked between Mr Smith and Striker, still unsure what was happening.

'Let's get this over with,' growled Mr Smith to the guard, who punched a code, opened the single inner door and led them inside. The second man stayed on duty in the outer room.

The next room was larger and very different. Two more men in black outfits sat watching a bank of monitors. Their backs suddenly became more upright as the party entered, making themselves look more attentive.

London approached the men and inspected the screens. Mr Smith hovered next to her, anxiously watching for her approval. Gary, Striker and the guard stood back from the rest. Waiting behind London, Danni looked curiously along the various screens.

Some covered CCTV stations in the yard. The next section showed more outside views, presumably other approaches to the buildings. There was little to see except waving greenery and the area of scrubland that separated the buildings from a high hedge. There was a glimpse of farm fields beyond that. The biggest set of monitors were trained inside the building, and what they showed confirmed Danni's suspicions about the function of the place.

'This is your brother's land, I take it.' London pointed to a view of the hedge.

'Yes,' agreed Mr Smith. 'All the fields around the immediate area are under cultivation. My brother always looks after those fields himself.'

'Rights of way? Walkers?'

'None.'

'I do hope your brother is pleased with the level of my investment,' said London. Her tone was saccharine. Danni heard the warning in it but doubted Mr Smith did.

'He is, yes. So am I,' the man blustered.

'Two years and a substantial amount of *my* money,' London continued.

'We're both very grateful. Glad to be in partnership with you.'

If this was a partnership, Danni knew it would be an unequal one. London was always in charge. She regarded Mr Smith with a sharp, cold gaze. Mr Smith looked away at the screens, blushing with embarrassment. After surveying him for several long seconds, London looked back at the cameras.

The next set showed a large cannabis-growing room with daylight-simulation lamps blazing. There were long rows of metal frames with ranks of plants in large pots standing on them. Along one row, the plants appeared to have been to a party. Instead of being tied to their hydroponic system, they staggered drunkenly or lay on the floor. Four workers were rescuing plants and reconnecting them to the system one by one, closely watched by a pair of guards. Another worker was sweeping the floor clean of debris. The air was steamy, and the room would be hot.

The next set of cameras showed an area with what looked like manufacturing equipment and packing tables. There were more men here. Some were working on a production line. A man at the end of the line was counting and packing little plastic packets into larger bags. Others were tidying up piles of damaged boxes, their contents scattered all over the floor near some storage shelves. Someone had already swept what looked like powder into piles. Next to this, a worker in a mask was scooping up the stuff and trying to pour it into empty plastic bottles. Another man was crumpling dead bottles before loading them into bin bags.

'We recycle what we can.' Mr Smith waved in the direction of the man collecting the empty bottles.

London looked at him quizzically. 'Are you insane? You bring chemicals here, use them to make street food and then take the empty bottles to the recycling depot?'

Mr Smith huffed. 'Well, it seemed the least we could do.'

'God help us,' said London with an exaggerated sigh. 'Fucking amateurs.'

The final monitors showed a canteen area with a kitchen and a dormitory with shower rooms. This area looked to be in the best shape. A worker was mopping the floors and a second was preparing food. It was obvious that no part of these workers' lives wasn't overseen. All areas were closely monitored by the black-clothed guards. Some wore sunglasses despite being indoors. Every guard had a baton, while some also seemed to have spray cans attached to their belts. Pepper spray, no doubt. They were all tall and well-muscled, clearly chosen to be as intimidating as possible.

It was the last two monitors that made Danni pause. One camera was looking down a narrow, well-lit corridor. There was no mistaking that the man who stood there was on guard duty. There were two doors, both closed. He stood rigidly in front of the furthest door, almost at attention. Another camera was trained into a locked room. It contained two men but no facilities apart from a bucket in one corner. One man lay flat on his front on the floor, asleep or unconscious. The other man sat leaning against the wall. He rested one hand on his companion's limp arm.

'These are the ringleaders, I assume?' asked London.

'I'm afraid so,' replied Mr Smith.

'Is that one just sleeping?' London pointed to the prone man on the monitor.

Mr Smith winced. 'I think one of the guards got a bit carried away. Might need a doctor.'

Danni looked more carefully at the picture. Now she could see that there was a dark patch under the man. It could be a dirty floor. Or a pool of blood.

'What I simply don't understand,' said London, 'is how such heavily armed men, sufficiently well paid and in such good numbers, allowed a riot to start in the first place.'

Mr Smith shuffled uncomfortably until his usual blustering demeanour came to his rescue. 'Those immigrant buggers had it planned and jumped them. My men got caught out.'

'They're not going to be the only ones,' replied London.

Danni heard Gary stifle a giggle.

CHAPTER 24

Even DCI Hudson joined the team as they drove at speed to North Denes, a suburb north of Great Yarmouth sandwiched between the River Bure and the North Sea, where a wide bank of dunes protected the homes, the racecourse and a golf course from the worst of the high tides. Following instructions from the local police, Bowen and Sara pulled up into the nearest car park next to the newly restored Venetian Waterways. Edwards and Hudson had gone directly to the Outer Harbour.

Led by a couple of local uniformed officers, they tramped along a path between the dunes and the waterways. After a few minutes, they turned towards the sea. The grey-green waves grew tall some distance from shore and angrily battered onto the sand, the spray covering everyone with salty droplets. Sand grains whirled in the blustering wind, catching Sara's face.

They halted among the last of the dunes. In a depression, two forensic investigators were combing over a rigid inflatable boat. It was smaller than Sara had imagined. She'd been expecting something large, black and dynamic, like something the SAS would use or the ones that took tourists on river trips on the Thames. This one was orange with a black band running around it. She doubted you would get more than half a dozen people in it.

She introduced herself and Bowen. 'What can you tell me about this?'

'I doubt we'll be able to identify which boat it came from,' said one of the forensic investigators. He pulled himself up from where he was running his fingertips around a seam inside the rib. 'These things are pretty common. You can buy them from the internet, for goodness' sake.'

'So how do we know this is important?' she asked. 'Why are we here?'

'It's unusual, sarge,' said the older of the two uniformed officers. 'These things are usually kept by small cruisers as a method of escape in extreme circumstances.'

'And you can easily buy them?' asked Bowen. 'How much are they?'

'Four or five hundred pounds,' said the officer. 'It's an entry-level jobbie.'

Sara looked at the officer. 'Disposable in a way? Like buying a cheap tent and leaving it behind at a festival?'

The officer nodded. 'That's one way of looking at it.'

'Is there any way of identifying where it came from or who used it?'

'Only if there's something forensic, like fingerprints.'

'Which is what we're doing here,' said the investigator. He beckoned Sara over. 'Under here.'

He ran a cotton bud where the bottom of the boat met the inflated, circular sidewall. When he extracted it, there was a red-brown deposit. He dropped the bud into a plastic tube.

'And there's this.' The man pointed to a fragment of fabric. The RIB had two plank seats attached above the sidewall by a pair of metal rails. The fragment was plastered underneath the front plank. It was also stained red-brown. 'Might be from the same person. Might not. Either way, someone hurt themselves getting on board, and their clothes snagged on here.'

Sara nodded and handed the man her card. 'Let me have the results when you can.'

'All this sand is making things more difficult,' he said. He tucked the card into his trouser pocket under his protective suit.

Sara looked inside the RIB again. There was sand on the floor, and the outside of the boat was covered in the stuff. The dunes had been soaked with the rain and the waves over the last couple of days. But the wind was so strong it must be drying the top layer. The stuff was everywhere. Sara could even feel some getting into her mouth as she spoke. Stretching up to get her bearings, she looked at the beach and the dunes below her. 'Would this thing have been washed up here?'

The uniformed officer shook his head. 'In my experience, I'd say no. Normally, if it had been washed up, it would have been stranded on the beach.'

'Someone dragged it up here on purpose?' Sara sounded sceptical. If this RIB was connected to the cruiser, why would they leave it behind when it could provide evidence?

'I said *normally*.' The officer sounded cautious. 'The storm two nights ago wasn't normal, even for this coast. The tide was exceptionally high. This might seem like the shoreline if you didn't know the coast.'

'Two nights ago? Why two?'

The officer looked at his boots, pausing to scrape some of the sand from the upper of one. Sara waited until he looked at her again. 'It wasn't my decision.'

'I understand that.'

'The RIB was here yesterday,' he sighed. 'That's when it was first reported. I came down to have a look. It was lying upside down, and I thought it had just been washed up during the storm. I told my station boss, and he told me to inform the council to come and collect it as rubbish.'

'What made you change your mind?'

'When I thought about it, I wondered if it was something to do with drugs.' He shrugged. 'I mean, why hide it? Why was it the wrong way up? It just rankled me. So, I came back this morning and had another look.'

'Do you get a lot of drugs coming in this way?'

112

The officer nodded. 'They run up on to the beaches with big bags of the stuff. Offload it to someone waiting with a van and are back out to sea in minutes. We work with the NCA on it sometimes.'

Collaborations like that weren't unusual. The Special Combat Unit team had been involved in a joint county lines investigation with the National Crime Agency earlier in the year. The quiet East Anglia coast, with its wide, shelving beaches and empty roads, would make an easy drop-off point in the winter.

'I talked to the boss again,' said the officer. 'He authorised a forensic team visit just in case.'

'Why are we involved here, then?' asked Sara.

The officer looked at her in surprise. 'The cruiser. The one the Coastguard are bringing in. It's the talk of the station that there's a body on it. What if this RIB was how the killer got off?'

CHAPTER 25

DC Bowen parked his car next to DI Edwards's vehicle on a piece of waste ground by the Outer Harbour. There were also two Forensics vans and a Coastguard off-roader. Sara zipped up her jacket against the bitter wind and tried to get her bearings. They were south of the tourist promenade with its seaside attractions. The River Yare joined the sea immediately beyond the harbour. The blue-green office of the Port Authority, which they had left just a few hours previously, was across the road.

DCI Hudson was deep in conversation with a woman in Coastguard uniform, which Sara assumed was Lizzie Hardaker. Binoculars hung on a leather strap round her neck. Wrapped in a splashdown jacket, the woman looked quite chubby. Her blonde hair stuck out from under a beanie, and her lined face suggested that she was well into her fifties. That could be deceptive, of course. The outdoor life many locals led often weathered their features. Sara went across and introduced herself.

'Pleased to meet you.' Lizzie Hardaker turned a beaming smile on Sara. 'Call me Lizzie. Any luck with the RIB?'

'Could be interesting. There are some samples that might give us DNA information, if it's not too degraded. The boat was there for two nights.'

Hudson pursed her lips. 'No one spotted it yesterday?'

'Yes, ma'am,' replied Sara. 'At first, they thought it was just flotsam. Changed their minds this morning and are doing a forensic check.'

'Give us a break,' muttered Hudson. Her lips curled in derision. 'Local plodders.' She gazed out to sea.

Sara and Lizzie shared an eye-roll moment.

'They're only a few minutes out,' said the Coastguard. 'They'll have to bring her into the Outer Harbour. The river berths are full.'

She led Sara around the harbour, which also seemed busy with a mixture of rig supply ships and wind farm vessels. The latter had four huge gantries on their decks. Lizzie explained that they strapped the turbine blades, engine housings and pillar sections to them. 'Then they ferry them out to the construction site. With this weather, they're all in port today.'

'Bad forecast again?'

'Indeed. In fact, if this keeps up, we may get a full storm surge tomorrow. Currently rated at a sixty per cent chance.'

It was difficult to face the wind. The sheer strength of it made Sara's eyes water. Even on the concrete hard standing around the small port, sand whipped into tiny razor-sharp showers.

When they reached the end of the working area, Lizzie put the binoculars to her eyes and scanned the horizon. 'That's them,' she said. Unhooking the strap from her neck, she handed the binoculars to Sara.

They were a far more complex and expensive-looking pair than the ones she had borrowed from the seal watchers at Winterton beach. She peered through them until she found the white Coastguard boat. Bristling with antennae and radar dishes, it dwarfed the pleasure cruiser, which followed it on a tight towrope, twitching and bucking in the waves as if it were still trying to escape. She returned the binoculars.

Lizzie viewed the approaching boats again. She pressed a button on her radio. 'Control, this is Hardaker 509. Come in.'

The radio crackled in reply. 'Receiving, Hardaker 509. What message?'

'Vessel search on a Broom New Yorker 311. Designation *Empire State.*'

The voice on the radio indicated that it would get back to her. The lead boat cut speed and carefully steered into the harbour basin, the cruiser bobbing close enough to knock into the stern. Sara watched one crewman heave on the tow-rope while a second jumped across to the following boat. Engine turning over, the cruiser approached a small space at the end of the berthing area.

Three men in overalls seemed to appear out of nowhere to reach for ropes. They soon had the cruiser efficiently moored as the Coastguard vessel turned a tight circle before docking further round the Outer Harbour, where the men had moved on to help it. When the man who had guided the cruiser jumped onto the dockside, a gaggle of people stood waiting.

'All right,' she heard DCI Hudson shout from the back. 'Let's all just hold our horses, shall we?'

She pushed forward to where Sara was waiting. Lizzie moved off, talking and listening to the radio intently. Sara waited for the boss to take charge. Hudson began to issue instructions and form teams. 'The body?' she asked.

'In the forward cabin,' said the man.

'We'll need a DNA sample to eliminate you from the scene,' said Hudson. The man nodded and was led away by one of the forensic investigators.

While Sara waited for her job to be allocated, she looked carefully at the front of the cruiser. The boat was largely white with a blue canopy above a high area where the driver sat. The hull was smooth and in good condition. Patting the side of the boat, she could feel it was made of hardened fibreglass. So, what were those other marks?

Dropping to one knee, she ran her fingers along the water line. The hull was smooth, even where it cut through the water. Leaning over the dockside, with one hand fending off the bulk of the cruiser, Sara stared along it. Leaning closer, she could definitely see several bumps. They weren't very large, but they were in a star-shaped pattern. Whatever had made these marks, it had been done inside the boat.

'Careful under there,' said Lizzie. 'It will have your arm off if it traps you between the hull and the dock, and you won't be able to stop it.'

Sara scrambled upright, shaking the water from her hand. 'Did you get anything about the boat?'

'Yep. They're emailing me over the details. It should be in Ipswich Oasis Marina. It went out on hire over the weekend and was never returned.'

'Find anything?' asked Dr Taylor.

Sara hadn't seen his car on the waste ground. He must have arrived after them. She smiled at him, glad to see he was already waiting to begin. She turned to include Lizzie in her next question as she patted the cruiser's side. 'Is the forward cabin about here?'

'On this model, I think so.'

'Then my best guess is that there are bullet holes just below the waterline.'

'Oh goodie.' Dr Taylor sighed.

CHAPTER 26

Theo Collins tied Terry the Labrador by his lead to the handle of the heavy wooden church door. Clearly used to being left here, the dog flopped onto the flagstone floor. Roger skirted past him, keeping Mu between himself and the enthusiastic younger dog. Once safely inside, he halted and glanced back at Terry, tail wagging tentatively.

'You can bring him in,' called Theo. 'The basket is over here.'

The church was even more magnificent inside than the outside suggested. There were stone arches leading to white-washed walls and a wooden vaulted roof. Upper and lower walls were lanced with plain and stained-glass windows, which flooded the building with light even on such a dull day. A pierced wooden screen separated the pews from the choir. Mu remembered the place from the one visit she had made as a child when the Brownie pack attended for Easter service. They had each been given a chocolate egg afterwards. There had been no such treats at home.

Theo Collins was at the back of the pews by a large stone font. He piled a selection of leaflets on a wooden table and lifted up a large wicker basket to replace them, which was full of tins and packets. A handwritten label said, *We welcome donations for the Marlham Food Bank.*

'Please help yourself as much as you want,' he said. 'There's a carrier bag there if you need it.'

He stepped away to sort out the leaflets, giving Mu and Roger space to come and look. To her relief, there was quite a lot of useful stuff. There was no point in taking things like bags of pasta because she had no means of cooking them. The tins were another matter. Some of them could be eaten cold. Unfortunately, there was no dog food, but she was grateful to find a packet of tampons tucked discreetly at the back.

'May I take all this?' she asked as she piled the useful stuff into the carrier.

'Of course,' said the vicar, without looking up. 'Is there any pet food?'

'No.' Mu gathered up her rations and collected Roger. 'Thank you. This is very kind.'

'If you would walk round to the vicarage with us—' Theo waved in the direction of his dog — 'I am sure Terry can spare a few tins for . . .'

'Roger.' Tears wobbled on the edge of Mu's eyes. 'His name is Roger.' She sniffed.

Theo looked up and, stepping forward, placed his hand on Mu's arm. 'Your life must be very difficult. Would a prayer help?'

Mu wasn't a religious person. Even so, she nodded. If she thought about God at all, it was in terms of abandonment. A category in which she also placed both her parents. None of them had looked after her. When Mu lost her best friend, Mighty Mark, it had been the worst moment of her life, and there had been no time to mourn for him.

As Theo began quietly with 'Our Father, who art in heaven,' Mark's anguished face swam in front of her eyes. Tears ran down her cheeks, and a sob escaped her mouth. Roger leaned against her leg, pushing his muzzle into her hand in a gesture of comfort. Mu dropped to one knee.

Pulling the dog into her arms, she wept uncontrollably, her face buried in the fur on his back.

Theo waited patiently when he had finished. Mu gained some control of herself. Hiccupping with grief, she swiped at her face to clean up the tears and snot.

'Here,' said the vicar gently. He passed her a tissue.

Mu blew her nose as her emotions began to settle back down.

'Difficult times?'

She nodded.

'What's your name?'

'Mu. It's short for Muriel.'

'I won't ask why you're in this situation, Mu. I'm not going to judge you.'

Mu smiled reluctantly. 'That makes a change. People usually do.'

'I can imagine,' Theo said. 'Will you at least allow me to give you a warm drink?'

Mu grasped her carrier bag and followed the vicar out of the church. Terry led the way, dragging Theo eagerly down the vicarage drive and round to the back of the house.

'Bring him in.' Theo pointed to Roger. 'I imagine he'd like to warm up as well.'

The kitchen was centred around an old-fashioned Aga. A scrubbed pine table stood in the centre of the room with chairs tucked neatly underneath. A woman sat at the table, a laptop open in front of her.

'This is my wife, Vicky.'

Terry was already making a fuss of Vicky, who was petting him back. She smiled at Mu, although there was a ghost of a moment when her nose wrinkled at the unusual smell. Mu knew it was herself, but what could she do?

'Shall I put the kettle on?'

'Yes, please, darling.' Theo took the carrier bag from Mu's hand. He placed it by a leg of the table. 'Take your coat off, or you won't feel the benefit, as my mother used to say.'

Shamefaced, Mu slowly undid her ragged anorak, revealing the layers of old clothes underneath. Neither the vicar nor his wife commented. They bustled about making tea and bringing tins of dog food to add to Mu's carrier bag, keeping up a cheerful stream of light conversation.

Terry had worked his way under the kitchen table. His nose was now inches away from Roger's face, each dog sniffing the other. Terry's tail wagged furiously. Roger's waved cautiously. They moved on and sniffed each other's behinds, as dogs always seem to do. Somehow this made things acceptable between them, and when Theo produced a couple of dog chew treats, both accepted them with good grace. Lying down next to each other, they guzzled away until the things were gone. Terry curled up in his basket next to the warmth of the Aga, watching as Roger slowly approached. Perhaps the young dog sensed Roger's age or saw him as a friend. Either way, when Roger lay next to the basket, Terry settled himself comfortably, and both were soon drifting to sleep.

Furnished with a cup of tea and a plate of biscuits, Mu waited until the couple sat down opposite her. Vicky returned to whatever she was doing on the laptop.

'I can explain,' she said.

'You don't have to,' said Theo. 'Unless talking helps.'

'It was my friend, Mark.' Mu looked at the vicar's kindly face. Perhaps talking *would* help. 'We met at a hostel about three years ago. Roger was his dog, and the hostels don't like pets much. So, we joined forces. It's easier if you're not on your own. Especially as a woman.'

'I imagine it is.' Theo sipped his tea. 'Especially for a young person, too.'

'Mark was a lot older than me,' said Mu. She didn't want to give the wrong impression. 'We were just friends. Looking out for each other and sharing stuff.'

'Food?'

'Partly. Finding food in London can be easy.' Mu told Theo about the Saturday gurdwara curry station.

'They regard sharing food as a tenet of being a good Sikh,' he said. 'A service to humanity.'

Mu hadn't known that. 'It was wonderful, and some food shops give out their unused sandwiches and stuff at the end of the day. Warm drinks too. It's more about safe spaces and having each other's backs.'

'Were you in London a long time?'

'Four years.'

'That must have been frightening.'

'You bet it was.' Mu pulled an angry face. 'People do the most horrible things. Shouting abuse, swearing at you, dragging your stuff about. If you try to bed down in the wrong place, then security guards are all bullies, male or female. They enjoy making you move on, preferably when the weather is crap. Then some drunks pissed on Mark one night. Oh, sorry.' Mu looked at Vicky.

'Don't mind me.' She looked up from her laptop with a smile for them both. Then she stopped pretending to work and turned in her seat to listen attentively to Mu's story. 'Do go on.'

'We were in a stage door, round the back of Shaftesbury Avenue.'

Theo raised an eyebrow. 'Posh address.'

'It's set back out of the wind. The doorman used to let us bed down there after they finished for the night. Said it was okay, so long as we were gone when he needed to open up the next morning.'

Mu fell silent, remembering that autumn night. The drunken men. The fight. Running away with Roger in tow. She tried to explain it to Theo and Vicky. 'It was the last straw. Mark just lost it. He had a knife. They were younger. It would have been all right if they had just kept running. But they didn't.'

Vicky's eyes were wide with horror. Theo stretched across the table and took Mu's hand. 'Don't tell us if you don't want to.'

'They surrounded him.' Mu could see it now as vividly as the moment it happened. 'Taunting him. He kept threatening with the knife, but they dodged it and laughed. Then one of them ran at Mark. Ran straight onto the fucking knife. Mark yelled at me. Get out. Run. Take Roger and run.'

There was a stunned silence. Eventually, Theo cleared his throat. 'What happened to Mark?'

'I don't know.' Mu watched Theo process this. 'I grabbed what I could, and we ran. The last I saw, he was being held by one of those bastards. Another of them was stabbing him over and over.'

The silence was longer this time.

'So, you came up here?'

Mu nodded. 'I lived here as a child. I thought it would be a good place to hide.'

'Perhaps it can be,' said Vicky. 'It will be if I can help you.' Her face was set angrily.

Mu shook her head. She doubted she was any safer here than in Central London. Not after what she had seen over the last couple of nights.

CHAPTER 27

The group followed Lisa London through the facility. Danni knew cannabis factories were dotted around the countryside, but she'd never been in one. Mr Smith and the guard led the way. Striker brought up the rear, sliding on his sunglasses as they went into the growing area. Danni understood why he needed them when they walked through the next room. The light intensity jazzed and jangled in front of her eyes. London walked calmly, seemingly unaffected.

For Danni, these last couple of days had been full of worrying surprises. There was obviously something odd going on at this 'facility'. It seemed that there had been some kind of fight. But the guards had taken control, and things were being tidied up. It wasn't the sort of thing London would usually bother with in person. So why was she here?

Gary was keeping his distance from Danni, which was one small mercy. He'd filled out physically since she'd last seen him. His puppy fat had turned to muscle, and his sun-tanned face was more handsome than she remembered. He must also have been toughening up under the guidance of his Camorra family in Naples. Otherwise, why was London risking him in this business? How the hell were they going to get him back out of the country? As soon as they were settled, Danni needed to complete the various bookings she had started on their wild car journey.

She couldn't help wondering what was making London's famously strong stomach and willpower break down enough to have left her vomiting at the side of the church wall. If her boss was ill in some way, what did that mean for Danni's future? She was hardly going to get a useable reference from a mafia boss.

They headed through the factory room. The workers were all male, as were the guards. While most of the guards were white, all the workers were black, and although they went steadily about their tasks, they looked frightened of the guards. Several had cuts, bruises or swellings on their faces. The guards were less damaged and swaggered arrogantly around the place, enjoying their power over the less fortunate men.

Gary caught up with Danni as they reached the canteen. He looked around with narrowed eyes. Where, she wondered, did Gary imagine all the family money came from? Or was it just the scale of the place that was as new to him as it was to her? They exchanged a glance, and Danni thought he might speak, until Striker loomed up behind them to hassle them apart.

London paused to survey the room. 'You spoil them.'

'Not really,' protested Mr Smith. He glanced at the two large-screen TVs on the wall and the well-constructed kitchen. 'They have to be fed. It's a long-term investment.'

London snorted derisively and looked pointedly at the televisions.

'The men like to watch it,' said Mr Smith. 'I mean my men, not the workers.'

'Where's their accommodation?'

'Across the yard. They eat here with the rest.'

The place had the air of 'new prison' about it. All the necessary functions were there. But there was no natural light, no sense of time passing without the constant news feed running on the televisions. In fact, there were no windows anywhere. The lives of these people were carried out entirely in artificial light. No difference in day or night, just an endless cycle of work and some time to sleep in shifts. How long could a person live like that?

'Get rid of them,' said London to Striker. She waved at the screens. 'Where do you think they got the idea from in the bloody first place?'

Striker walked swiftly to one screen and wrenched it off the wall brackets. Heaving it over his head, he smashed it to the floor. Mr Smith gasped as the bodyguard strode to the second one and did the same. The two workers watched in horrified silence. It was their only connection to the outside world.

Danni watched with an impassive face, which was calmer than her pounding heart. Her mind was racing too. These workers were surely illegal immigrants. Male, in their twenties, probably refugees, they were prime targets for the people smugglers in the camps on the European coastline, which was only a stone's throw from Norfolk by sea. The ones sheltering underground must have been extra workers. Danni knew London was big in the drugs game, having originally been forced to act as a mule for the woman. It was clever when you considered it — create her own goods to sell down her drug lines and cut out the middleman. But she hadn't the slightest suspicion that London was also in people smuggling. Danni wasn't sure how she felt about that.

Too late to develop a conscience now. There was no choice but to keep trusting her boss.

The crash of plastic ceased. With a smile of satisfaction, London walked on. Danni dumped her handbag and laptop at a table and followed the party across the canteen.

In the corridor beyond, the guard stood waiting. He unlocked the cell at a wave from Mr Smith. The waft of human waste that accompanied the door's opening made Danni want to gag. She suppressed the instinct. Gary took up station at the canteen end of the corridor, cutting off the only escape route.

Striker stepped through the cell door. The man sitting on the floor got up hurriedly. The prone man didn't respond. In a swift, expert move, Striker turned the first man to the wall, his face pinned against the rough plaster in seconds, arms up his back. London stepped carefully inside. Danni stayed in the corridor next to Mr Smith, who seemed more than content to allow others to deal with the problem. They watched through the open door.

London hunkered down next to the prone man to feel for a pulse. She tried three places and, unhappy with finding no response, grabbed the man's shoulder and shook it. The man groaned but didn't move. London's hand was covered in blood where she had touched him.

'You're right.' She glanced at Mr Smith through the open door. 'For once. He does need a doctor. Too bad.'

The other man whimpered. 'My brother.'

'Not much of a brother, are you?' asked London. 'Doing this to him.'

'Not me,' said the man breathlessly as Striker leaned hard on his back ribs. He spoke English with an easy familiarity and no trace of an accent. 'We just wanted a better life. To get away from the persecution.'

Striker rammed him harder against the wall, making the victim's head rattle on the plaster. 'Shut the fuck up.'

'Well, you've broken your deal,' said London. She folded her arms and turned her icicle stare to Mr Smith. 'So have you.'

Danni half smiled to herself. Now they were going to find out. Mr Smith shuffled, looking in embarrassment at the corridor floor, unable to meet London's gaze. There was a considerable pause.

Danni waited, knowing her boss was back in control. It was her speciality. This was why she followed the woman. Why she admired her so much.

'No doctors here,' said London. She poked at the man on the floor with her foot. 'What a shame.'

'We could dump him near a hospital or something,' suggested Mr Smith.

'Fetch Jerry,' London commanded.

Mr Smith looked up in surprise. 'The guards' team leader?'

'That's what I said,' London purred.

'How did you know?' The businessman sounded confused.

You're not nearly as smart as you think you are, thought Danni.

'Lock up the workers in the dormitory and bring all the men to the canteen,' London continued.

Smith gaped at her, still not understanding.

At a signal from London, Striker pulled the other prisoner round to face her, kicking the man in the back of his knees to force him to kneel.

'And you, Mr Not-Much-of-a-Brother,' began London. She bent over so that her face was only inches away from his. 'You're going to look after him. You'd better keep him alive because disposing of a body would be most inconvenient.'

CHAPTER 28

The team split up. DCI Hudson took DC Bowen back to their office to set up the incident board. DC Noble remained with the cruiser to relay any early findings from Dr Taylor or the forensic team. Sara joined DI Edwards, and they drove the sixty or so miles to Ipswich Oasis Marina. As they were heading into Suffolk Police's territory, Aggie rang ahead to advise their CID. No objection was raised. Not much curiosity either. Just a brisk, 'If you need any help, let us know.'

The marina was on an island in the centre of the Ipswich Waterfront development. Aggie had called ahead for them, and the manager had agreed to reserve a parking space next to the pub at the entrance. DI Edwards pulled up to work out which space was for them. A middle-aged man dressed in navy slacks and a jumper with an embroidered logo walked jauntily out of the pub door waving a piece of card.

'I take it you're our visiting detectives,' he said with a grin.

Edwards agreed that they were.

'I'm Bill, the marina manager. Pop that in your wind-screen and put her over there.'

Edwards handed the parking pass to Sara, which she plonked on the dashboard. Bill waved them into a space, moving the two parking cones that had kept it free. He rubbed his hands as if pleased with his own efficiency.

'You've had a bit of a drive,' he said. 'Would you like anything to eat or drink?'

Leading them into the pub, they ordered coffees before following Bill through a door marked *Staff Only*.

'Amy will bring them through,' said Bill. He led them down a narrow corridor, made smaller by stacked boxes and wraps of bottles waiting to be used behind the bar. 'My office is in the back.'

The offices were bigger than Sara expected, occupying the length of the pub building. Two rooms were decked out with the usual desks and equipment. Maps and boat pictures lined the walls and were draped with gaudy Christmas decorations. A miniature tree, complete with baubles and lights, sat on the desk in the first room, where Bill's secretary was diligently typing. She looked quite young. Her blonde hair was pulled into a ponytail, and she was bundled up in a fluffy jumper. There was another entrance in a small hallway with a desk between the two offices.

'Reception,' said Bill, waving at the setup as they went into his office. 'You want to know about the *Empire State*, I believe?'

Edwards nodded. 'It was towed into Great Yarmouth this morning by the Coastguard.'

'We wondered where she had got to.' Bill settled behind his desk and offered a blue flip-top folder with *Empire State* handwritten in black felt pen on the top. 'She belongs to Todd Lane. Todd berths her with us all year round.'

Sara looked through the contents. 'Mr Lane lives in London?' She pulled out a form and showed it to Edwards.

'Yes. He works in the City.'

'Doing what?' asked Edwards.

'Banker? Hedge fund manager?' Bill sounded unsure.

'So why does he keep the boat here and not there?' Sara couldn't keep the antagonism from her face. She had suffered at the hands of arrogant City men on investigations during her days in the Met.

'I don't know. You'd have to ask him. Easier to get into the countryside here, of course.'

'How often does he use the boat?' She pulled an ownership form and insurance docket from the file. *Empire State* was valued at £175,000.

'Most weekends in the summer. He brings his family down during the holidays. Not so much in between, hence the hires.'

'Hires?' Edwards looked sharply at Bill.

Sara found another form, a signed agency hire agreement. 'Sir.' She handed it to the DI, who looked it over.

'An owner who berths here can join our hire-out scheme,' explained Bill. 'They allocate dates when they don't wish to use the boat themselves, and we put them on our hiring database.'

Bill began to open tabs on his computer screen. When he found what he wanted, he swivelled the screen around for the detectives to have a look. It showed a page with pictures of the boat, inside and out, specifications and hire rates. There was a box at the bottom to check for available dates. It was expensive to take the thing out, even for a few nights.

'It's a way of making the boat earn some of its keep,' said Bill. He swung the screen back to face him. He tapped again. 'Thought so. Todd had only just joined the scheme. This was *Empire State*'s first hiring.'

Sara felt rather smug that the overpaid City banker had got his comeuppance for being able to afford a cruiser. She shook her head to clear it of the jealousy. 'Do you have records of who hired it?'

'Naturally.' Bill opened a large diary. Tracing his finger down the previous week, he stopped at an entry. 'Going out at this time of year is a little unusual. Hirer was called John Brown. Said it was a stag party. I had to clear that with Todd because not every owner will accept them. They reckoned they would go up and down the river to the various pubs.'

'Do they have to give proof of identity?' Edwards had finished reading the forms. Sara stuffed them back in the file.

'Yes, for the insurance as much as anything. Amy will have copies in the hire system. Ah, here we are.' The secretary wandered in with their drinks. 'Amy, can you get copies of the hire documents for the *Empire State* at the weekend?'

'Have you found her, then?' asked the secretary. 'Todd was ever so worried.'

'We have.' Sara nodded. 'Could you do copies of everything in this file as well?'

Amy glanced at Bill, who frowned. 'That's private information,' he prevaricated.

'Did we not mention?' asked the DI in his sweetest tone, which always threatened trouble in Sara's experience. 'We found a body on board.'

Amy gasped, turning pale under her mask of make-up. 'Murder?'

'We can't confirm that,' said Sara. 'It's being treated as suspicious, so you must keep this under wraps. No social media posts, please.'

'No one said.' Bill's eyes were wide. 'Copies of everything, Amy.'

The secretary looked stunned. She gripped the file and hurried out towards the photocopier in her own office.

'Have you spoken to the owner?' asked Edwards.

'No, not yet. I thought I would see you first.'

'Good idea. Best leave that to us.' Edwards sipped his coffee. 'This is good. Tell me more about the hire system.'

Sara drank her own coffee. Edwards was right, and she was glad of the caffeine hit. The manager launched into a lengthy explanation of how the marina worked.

'I'll collect those documents,' she said to Edwards, placing her empty cup back in its saucer.

In the other office, Amy was feeding the sheets through the copier. 'I've done copies of the hire stuff as well,' she said.

There was a pile of papers in a buff folder. Sara looked through them, stopping at a copy of a passport, which had been given as proof of identity. Although the picture was clear, she didn't recognise the man's face.

'She was hired from Sunday through Tuesday morning,' said Amy. She added more copies to the folder. 'I thought that was a bit odd, to be honest.'

'Why?'

'Normally stag dos are Friday and Saturday nights, returning late Sunday.'

'Do you get many of these stag weekends?'

'A few. Unfortunately, the boats tend to need a big clean when they get back, which is why some owners won't allow them. May I ask where you found it?'

'Drifting out at sea,' said Sara. 'Although it looks like it may have been damaged before that.'

'Oh.' Amy looked perplexed. 'Run aground, maybe? That's only happened once before. Well, to one of our boats anyway.'

'Before?'

'It was a few years back.' Amy tucked the papers back in their folder and leaned on the copier, ready for a good gossip. 'A group of three men hired an ocean-going cruiser for Easter weekend. As far as we could ever make out, they went straight across to Holland. It's not all that far from here, to be honest. They picked up a drugs consignment and sailed straight back. Abandoned the boat on the Essex marshes. Took several days before it was found. The police checked it out and found all kinds of traces, fingerprints and powder among them. But no one was ever arrested for it. That's why we introduced the system with photo ID. The insurers insisted, and we needed to cover our backs.'

'So, this is the only photo you have of the man who hired *Empire State*?'

'Oh no, there'll be CCTV as well.' Amy moved round to her desk. Sara followed her eagerly.

Clicking on an icon, Amy opened a programme that showed views from various cameras around the marina. 'This is reception.'

Pointing from a corner of the room, the live feed showed the empty reception desk with Bill's office door open beyond it.

'And you keep copies of this?' asked Sara, feeling hopeful.

Amy looked at her shyly. 'When the boat didn't come back on time, I asked Security to make a copy of everything to do with the hire and departure. I knew our insurers would demand it. Would you like a copy?'

She held up a memory stick, and it took all of Sara's discipline not to snatch it out of the woman's hand.

CHAPTER 29

It was late afternoon when Edwards and Sara returned to the office. Hudson was sitting in her office, the door closed. Aggie was doing her best mother hen impression, fussing around everyone with drinks and cake. Noble and Bowen were both there, adding things to the incident boards. One board had a blown-up copy of the Sudanese family and the Mayday report. The bigger board now held early forensic team pictures of the body on the *Empire State*. There were also photos of the damage to the hull, inside and out. Edwards headed to his own office to dump his coat.

Sara handed the memory stick to Noble. 'You're the best at all this stuff. See what you make of this.'

'Anything I can do?' Aggie placed a mug of coffee, made just how Sara liked it, in front of her. A slice of Christmas cake followed on a paper napkin. Despite her rumbling stomach, Sara didn't have the heart to tell Aggie that she didn't like the rich fruit cake and wouldn't eat it. Sara extracted several pages from the file of information that the marina had given them.

'I'm really hoping this guy is on the Police National Database.' She held up the copy of the passport. 'Unfortunately, that's an obviously false name and fake passport.'

Aggie examined the picture. 'Mmm, could be,' she replied. 'Any idea where he might be from?'

'My guess would be the Met area.'

'I'll give them a call.'

The door to Hudson's office opened slowly. The DCI squared her shoulders and took a deep breath before moving to the incident boards. 'Updates, please.' She stood facing the team, looking tired. 'Sara?'

'The owner of the recovered boat is a Mr Todd Lane from London. It was hired by a group of men claiming to be going on a stag weekend.' Sara explained all they had found out at the marina. 'Aggie has the passport picture and will call her Met counterpart.'

'Good idea,' said Hudson. 'Ian, you have the CCTV recordings?'

Noble nodded. 'Working on them now, ma'am. It was after teatime when they picked the boat up, so it's dark outside, I'm afraid.'

'See what you can find,' said Hudson. 'Good work, Sara. Can I leave you to talk with Todd Lane and break the bad news? I think a phone call would do. Then provide anything they need for the insurance claim. DI Edwards, anything to add?'

'I think the marina assumed it was a genuine hire,' replied Edwards. 'They advised the group to stay in the river system and moor up at a pub or something if the weather got bad.'

'Do we know if the cruiser seen by this fisherman was definitely the same boat?'

'It is as far as I can understand from the Coastguard,' said Sara. 'Do you want me to get a full trace on it from them?'

'I think we're going to need it. What about forensics? Noble, you stayed with the team?'

'Dr Taylor is bringing the victim back to the mortuary for a full investigation,' said Noble. 'He said the first impressions were that the victim had been shot several times. He also said that the victim had been dead for some time. The doctor will be doing the examination this evening to clear it as soon as possible.'

Dr Taylor no doubt also had Christmas plans. 'Were those bullet holes in the hull?' asked Sara.

'They think so. Forensics were having it lifted out of the harbour this afternoon and transferred to Snetterton.'

The unit at Snetterton was a new facility where large items like vehicles or pieces of furniture could be examined and stored. If there was anything to be found, this was the place to do it. The forensic department was justifiably proud of the unit, which had been built to their exact specification.

Hudson sighed. 'We'll have to wait for everyone else. Okay, this means a change of Christmas plans.'

The team grew silent.

'Obviously, this will be a murder investigation.' Hudson kept her voice level. Normally they would all be excited at the prospect. 'Equally obviously, it's Christmas Eve tomorrow. We're going to have to work, folks, and there's nothing I can do about it. I'm sorry.'

They all knew it went with the job, and their families were used to it. Only Noble groaned. His new girlfriend might be less understanding. Mike and Aggie looked at each other and shrugged while DI Edwards pursed his lips.

'Not necessarily,' he said. 'Let's face it, no one else is likely to be working on the day — or Boxing Day, come to that. We could all work tomorrow and run a skeleton team for two days in case news comes in. Then regroup on the twenty-seventh. I can cover it for you.'

'I intended to go home for a couple of days,' Hudson admitted. 'But what about the rest of you?'

'I'm happy to work,' said Sara.

Noble flashed her a grateful smile.

'I wasn't going anywhere. Just you and me, then, boss?'

'Agreed,' said DI Edwards.

It was going to be just like old times. Hudson looked between the two. For a moment, Sara watched indecision flash across the woman's face. She didn't want to miss out on anything here, nor visiting her family down in Gloucestershire. 'You'll keep me informed?'

'Of course, ma'am,' promised Sara. 'If we find anything. We all know that the labs and the rest will shut down.'

'Sounds like a plan,' said Hudson, and the office began to bubble once more. 'Let's get on with everything possible before teatime tomorrow.'

The team knuckled down to their various tasks. Sara rang the mobile number for Todd Lane. It went straight to voicemail, and she left a carefully worded message. This news was going to put a damper on his Christmas. When her extension rang a few minutes later, she expected it to be the boat owner, not the friendly tones of Sergeant Trevor Jones. Past retirement age, Jones still worked on the reception desk as he used to in the old days at Bethel Street. His friendly smile and helpful attitude meant that management had allowed him to continue working when the job should have gone to a civilian.

'Merry Christmas, lass,' said Jones. 'You have a visitor in reception.'

'Who? Why?'

'I'll leave him to tell you all about it.' Sara could hear the smile in the sergeant's voice. 'I don't think you'll be disappointed, though.'

'On my way,' she said.

Collecting the Christmas card she had for the genial guardian of the front desk, Sara walked swiftly downstairs and handed the card to Jones. 'Merry Christmas, sergeant.'

Jones reached into a pile of cards, selected one and handed it to Sara in return.

'Thank you. So where is my visitor?'

'Behind you.'

A man clutching a heavy file and a mobile phone stood up from a sofa in the guests' waiting area.

Sara almost took a step back in surprise. 'DS Mead. To what do we owe this pleasure?'

CHAPTER 30

Jerry was the biggest gorilla of them all. It was easy to see why he was in charge of the guards. He spoke to London and immediately began to put her orders into action. Danni unpacked her laptop and, having obtained the passcode from Jerry, signed into the Wi-Fi. This place and its systems were going to be as secure as the Bank of England's gold vault. She didn't need to worry about online tracking here.

Locking herself in a toilet cubicle that stank like an unemptied Portaloo, Danni lifted the panel in the bottom of her handbag and extracted three of the false passports. She gripped them for a moment, gazing at her own lying snugly between the banknotes. She could last a little while on that amount of money, but not for long now that she had expensive tastes. What had Alessandro, the 3Js café manager, said to her? Naples was a fine place in the spring. She extracted her own passport and held it with the others. Replacing the panel, she dumped her stuff in the handbag and sat at the canteen table.

As the guards collected the bewildered workers from different areas, Danni found a flight from Norwich to Amsterdam that afternoon. There was a connecting flight to Naples first thing in the morning. They would need a hotel, which was a risk. She needed more instructions.

London sat at the adjacent table, flipping through her diary. Danni sat opposite and explained the booking.

'Book both,' said London. 'Use di Maletesti passports because we won't get on it. I can't leave tonight — I'm not nearly finished here. But it's a good distraction as we're being followed. Look for what there is tomorrow at other airports and ferry terminals. Spend whatever you need, and use various names in different places. Create a smokescreen. Danni, the imperative thing is that Gary gets back to Naples.'

'Of course.' Danni nodded.

London looked straight at her. 'You're coming with us, I take it?'

'Yes, please.'

'Get my brother home safely, and you will be properly rewarded.'

By the time the guards had rounded up all the workers and dumped them in the dormitory, Danni had booked a flight in the morning from Stansted to Naples and an afternoon ferry ride from Dover.

Looking around the canteen, she did a quick headcount. There must have been at least twenty guards. Danni was no fighter, even if London could be nasty when she chose to be. Striker and the newly muscled Gary could hardly take on that many men in a fight. Whatever her boss had planned, it had better be good.

As the guards settled at the tables, Mr Smith tentatively approached London. 'What's all this about?'

'You're about to find out,' said London without looking up.

Mr Smith fiddled with his jacket for a moment, then chose bluster over common sense. 'Now look here, I'm your partner, and I demand to know what's going on.'

Danni cringed inwardly. No one spoke to Lisa London like that and got away with it. Before Mr Smith could say anything else, Striker was at his side, gripping his elbow in a painful pinch. He slapped his meaty hand on the businessman's shoulder and forced him away from the table.

Gary was sitting at a separate table from the rest. He had acquired a cup of tea from somewhere. Danni wished he'd brought her one. For a second, they locked eyes, and she glanced at the mug with a frown. He smiled and shrugged.

Lisa London stood up and walked purposefully to the serving area, Striker at her shoulder. Mr Smith trailed behind her looking worried. She banged on the countertop with a large metal spoon, making the guards turn to look at her. Gary didn't react.

'Some of you may not know me,' she said, in a voice raised just enough to be clear but not enough to become a shout. 'You will know of my family. Some of you have worked for us over the years.'

'Done time for you, too,' called a voice from the back. There were a few seconds of laughter, which quickly died away.

'For which you would have been appropriately reimbursed.' London eyeballed the guard, who dropped his gaze immediately. 'This situation is entirely salvageable, even though you men are, frankly, responsible for allowing things to get out of hand. Here's what you're going to do now. Come here, Jerry.'

The large man moved to stand behind London, shoulder to shoulder with Striker. He was taller than the Italian, though Striker would undoubtedly be the nastier fighter. Danni wouldn't like to cross either of them.

'You may not be aware, but Jerry is one of my own employees.'

Mr Smith made a choking noise. 'But I picked the guard staff. That was my part of the job.'

'It was indeed.' London turned to face the businessman. 'Along with providing and running the site. The money and the contacts were mine. Is that correct?'

Mr Smith nodded, swaying with fear as he saw the look on London's face. The room was so silent that Danni wondered if every man in the place was holding his breath. She certainly was.

'You haven't done a very good job on your side of things, have you?'

'I don't know what you mean.' Mr Smith tried to move away.

'You were supposed to pick efficient men who knew the score,' said London. Some of the guards shuffled in their seats as she turned to look at them. 'Two nights ago, while some of you were away on the latest night run, what happened?'

Jerry cleared his throat. 'I was out, Miss London.'

'I'm aware of that. What happened?' She pointed to a man sitting at a nearby table. 'You. Remind us all.'

'Some of the workers tried to get away,' he mumbled.

'They did indeed,' said London. 'You were so complacent with your widescreen televisions and nice canteen food that you allowed yourselves to be surprised by them. What the fuck were you thinking? This isn't a holiday in the countryside. It's a business.'

Danni looked round the guards. Many were looking shamefaced, while one or two looked defiant. There was a brief murmuring between some of them.

'And as for the last night run—' London had turned on Jerry this time — 'I know why the shipment was coming up short, but why is there a pregnant woman in the system?'

Danni had to give the man credit. He looked London in the eye before answering. 'She was hidden by the group. When I found out, I dealt with the idiot who had smuggled her on board.'

'Which idiot?'

'One of the new workers.'

'How did you deal with him?'

'I gave him a pasting,' said Jerry.

'And where is he now?'

'I've no idea. He fell off a cliff.'

There was a gasp. For a second, even London looked surprised. Jerry locked his legs firmly as if waiting for a blow.

London ran a hand over her face before looking at Jerry again. 'Let's hope he got washed out to sea, then.'

Mr Smith chose the moment to protest. 'Jerry is your man, you said. My men have done well. It's all his fault.'

London turned on Mr Smith, using her most sarcastic tone. 'By beating up the ringleaders? Good work! You're such a great organiser.'

'I've done my best,' said Mr Smith.

At the look on London's face, he stepped backwards, only to run into Striker. Danni had rarely seen her boss look this angry.

'What a pity you decided to try to make some money on the side,' she said.

'What?' It came out as a scream. 'What are you talking about? I've no idea what you mean.'

'It wasn't enough for you that we should create this business, was it? You took my money and used it to set yourself up nicely. But you had to take something off the top as well.'

Mr Smith had gone pale. His lips worked as he tried to find an explanation. He could only form a denial, which was as good as a confession in the di Maletesti world. 'I didn't do that.'

'My information is that you have not only been bringing workers here on your little night trips, but you have also been bringing other immigrants. Charging them for the ride and dumping them on the marshes.'

'That's not true,' yelled Mr Smith.

'In fact, that's almost more lucrative than this place, isn't it? Not only are you running this night crossing, there are others. At least three times a month.'

Once again, bluster let the man down. He puffed out his chest angrily. 'You can't prove it. Where's your evidence?'

'The trouble with you amateurs,' said London, 'is that you always get greedy. My evidence is right here in this room.'

She turned to look at the guards. Striker grabbed Mr Smith's shoulder and spun him to face the men. Picking out five individuals, the guards stood up as London named them.

'These gentlemen are my insurance policy,' said London. 'They've been with you from the start, and you didn't realise.

I've known for some time that you have been cheating on me. It just took them a while to work out how.'

The room grew silent again, holding its collective breath.

'And just to be certain, meet someone I'd trust with my life.'

There was the scrape of a chair as Gary stood up.

'He came up the refugee line from Lampedusa last month, acting as a guard. Along with two more of my cousins — oh, and a pregnant woman for some bloody reason.'

Mr Smith looked around in stunned silence.

'No one takes advantage of a di Maletesti,' stated London.

Danni began to laugh.

CHAPTER 31

Mu and Roger accepted lunch from the vicar and his wife. Hot vegetable soup and garlic bread, fresh from the Aga. When she thanked them, Mu admitted that she had run out of gas for her tiny camping stove and that warm food was hard to come by.

'I might be able to help with that,' said Theo. His face brightened as he stood up. 'If you could come and help me. Leave Roger in the warm.'

Pulling on their coats, Mu followed the vicar down the path, wondering what on earth he was doing. The garden was surrounded by a tall brick wall, which sheltered it from the worst of the weather. It looked as if neither the vicar nor his wife were keen gardeners. Behind overgrown bushes and tall weeds, a 1950s showman's caravan stood in dilapidated glory. Theo selected a key from the bunch he was carrying and climbed up a short rickety set of wooden steps to unlock the door.

It was dark and musty inside. Ivy had grown over the windows, blocking the light and turning the little that filtered through a strange green colour. The wagon was lined with fitted wooden shelves and cupboards. There was an empty fireplace that would once have housed a wood-burning stove. A grimy mirror was fastened over the dusty mantel shelf.

'This is lovely,' Mu said. 'Where did you get it from?'

'Came with the house,' said Theo. 'Been here for decades, I suspect.'

She looked around at the interior. Piles of old boxes and half-used tins of paint littered the surfaces. To their left, the old sofa, with its dining table, was swamped by cushions and blankets. To the right, an inner door was half shut. Theo pushed it wider, and Mu could see it used to be a bedroom. The old mattress was buried under a selection of camping equipment. She could see tents folded for storage in their bags, collapsible chairs and cooking equipment.

'This stuff used to belong to the Brownies,' explained Theo. 'For when they went to jamborees or on holiday.'

'Used to?'

'The local group ceased to function a few years ago.' Theo was rummaging in a damp cardboard box. 'There was no one to run it, apparently. The stuff was stored by the caravan park as a favour. When it had to close, I rescued all of this.'

'Why?'

'I thought it might come in useful. I hoped the Brownies might get restarted one day. But not so far. This place is just a dumping ground, isn't it? Ah, here we are.'

He triumphantly produced two small blue gas cylinders. They looked a little rusty on the seams. Theo turned them over in his hands, inspecting the damage.

'They look useable. Are they the right sort for you?'

Mu took one, feeling the weight of it in her hand. 'I think they are.'

'You're welcome to take them to try.'

Mu nodded sadly. 'Thank you.'

'You don't look certain.' Theo sounded concerned. 'I can take them back to the camping shop for disposal if you think they're not safe.'

'It's not that,' said Mu. 'I don't have much to cook on them anymore.'

'And no money to buy things with, I take it?'

Mu looked at Theo, expecting him to be growing cynical. Here she was, a beggar, who they had fed and trusted in

146

their home. Now she was asking for something else. Taking advantage. It was what people always ended up thinking, even when they were being kind and generous.

'The poor are always with us,' said Theo. He smiled gently. 'Or so our Lord tells us. Would teabags and milk help?'

Mu smiled in return. 'You really are very kind.'

'I hope I'm a practising Christian,' said Theo. 'Best to be in this job. "Practising" is the operative word here. I practise to be a better Christian, and charity is definitely one of our teachings. Come on.'

They went back to the kitchen. Vicky provided a small box of teabags and a new carton of milk.

'Would you like something else?' she asked as Mu added the extra items to her full carrier bag. 'Coffee, perhaps?'

'No, thank you,' she said. Patting Roger out of his snooze, she clipped his lead on and encouraged him to sit up. He moved stiffly, stretching his legs with a shudder. 'You have both been so kind.'

'Where are you staying now?' Vicky seemed reluctant to let Mu go.

'In the village,' said Mu vaguely. If she had to leave suddenly, she didn't want this kind couple to feel they had been fooled by her. Best not to tell them the danger she might be in or drag them into it. Who knew what was happening at that old bunker or the derelict caravan site? It was only a few hundred yards away, but it was a very different world from their cosy lives.

Vicky pointed at her laptop. 'I've been doing a bit of research. I think I can help you, but I'll need to be able to find you. Everyone has more or less shut down for the holidays. It may take a while.'

'Can Terry and I walk you back there?' asked Theo. He also seemed reluctant to send her back into the stormy afternoon.

'No, that's okay. If you don't object, I could visit again?' Mu zipped up her shabby coat and collected her carrier. It was heavy. 'Thank you so much for everything.'

She clicked her tongue to Roger, who followed very reluctantly. Theo accompanied her to the end of the vicarage drive.

'You could come tomorrow if you like,' he said. 'There will be mince pies and mulled wine at the church after Christmas Eve morning service. Lunch afterwards?'

Mu nodded, then began to walk. She knew that the vicar was watching them out of sight. The rain was getting heavy now. It squalled in the wind, battering Mu and her reluctant canine friend. The sky was already growing dark with storm clouds and approaching evening. It was going to be a difficult night.

Turning the corner beyond the church, they reached the front car park of the pub. It was full of vehicles and warm light from the restaurant, which sounded packed with customers, all busy celebrating the festive season, and too occupied to be watching this slim woman in her dark clothes and her companion with his makeshift coat. They skirted the shadowy edge of the car park until they reached the small road from the village's main street. She turned left down the side of the pub, keeping an eye on the backyard in case Paolo, the chef, was still about. The kitchen door was open. The wind drove gusts of delicious smells to Mu and Roger as they passed silently and, mercifully, unseen.

The old office door stood ajar. Mu checked inside before allowing Roger to step in. Paolo didn't appear to have gone into the back room where they were camping. A paper plate with a sandwich wrapped in silver foil stood next to a tin of dog food on the ruined customer counter. Double-checking their sleeping area, not least for such horrors as rats, Mu gratefully placed her heavy carrier bag next to her small store of food and personal hygiene products. A quick visit to the toilet in the next block made her comfortable, and she filled her small billy can with water at the sink.

Never willing to let anything go to waste, Mu brought in the things Paolo had left for them. The bacon sandwich was just as good cold as fresh. Roger enjoyed one of the vicar's tins of dog food. The gas cylinder slotted easily into her tiny stove, boiling the water for a cup of tea.

She rolled out their blankets and sleeping bags. It had been a good day, despite the fright Paolo had given her at the old ruin. She would be foolish to move on now with allies like the vicar, his wife and the kind old biddy she'd met at the shop. Sipping her fresh cuppa, Mu unpacked the rest of her carrier to inspect her treasured hoard of food and necessities.

'I reckon we can get away with a few more days,' she murmured to Roger, who was slurping at his water dish. 'Let's stick it out, shall we? I think I might need a bigger bag to carry all this food, don't you?'

Mu pulled the last of the tins out for inspection. Beans and sausages. That could be for her Christmas lunch. She even had the means to heat it up now.

An envelope dropped from the carrier as she shook it out to fold it for later. Mu picked it up and opened it. Inside were four five-pound notes and a slip of paper that said, *Merry Christmas*.

CHAPTER 32

DS Mead greeted Sara with a grin and introduced the young man behind him as DC Solomon. She led the pair up to the SCU office, where Mead was welcomed by the rest of the team. DC Solomon stood uncertainly in the doorway until Aggie bustled forward with a smile.

DCI Hudson looked up curiously from her desk. Sara had explained to DS Mead that they had a new boss as they'd climbed the stairs.

'How can we help you, DS Mead?' asked Hudson. 'It's good to welcome colleagues from the Met.' She held out her hand to shake with Mead.

'I came to advise you of our activities as we're from out of the area.' He took a seat at Hudson's indication. 'We've been following a suspect. Someone that the team have helped me with before.'

Hudson glanced at Sara. DI Edwards came in to listen, standing with his arms folded next to Sara.

'A county lines issue,' she explained.

'The main player is someone we've been watching for some time,' continued DS Mead. 'A woman called Lisa London.'

Hudson frowned thoughtfully, then tapped at her computer. 'I thought the name was familiar. We had dealings with one of her associates in Gloucester. There is a similar issue with county lines drug dealing down there.'

'You'll know what a slippery fish she is, then,' said Mead. 'Her Achilles heel is her younger brother. Known as Gary Barr or Barnet.'

'The family are Neapolitan Camorra,' filled in Sara.

'It's a pain getting any information from there,' Mead continued. 'The families hold a lot of power. However, we have one contact who does feed us information on the side. He advised that Gary suddenly vanished about three weeks ago.'

'Heading where?' asked Hudson.

'We watch Lisa London's house when we have the budget. But there was no sign of him there. So, I tried following her. I lost them in the Jermyn Street area.'

'Clumsy of you,' said Hudson.

Mead looked hard at her for a moment, then took the comment as banter and smiled. 'Indeed. It's been a while since I actually had to tail someone. I usually have staff for that.' Mead glanced at Solomon, who nodded back at him. 'Her car was left in a private garage near Regent Street.'

'What brings you here?'

'London had lunch with a man known as Mr Smith in certain circles. Actually, he's Neil McCarthy. After I lost her, we searched for his vehicle. It went up the M11 that afternoon.'

'Cambridge is a bigger place,' suggested Hudson.

'We traced it up here to Norwich, parked overnight at a hotel called the Gardens,' said Mead. 'McCarthy is someone else we've been keeping an eye on recently. His brother lives in Norfolk.'

Hudson looked at Sara.

'It's next to the Roman Catholic Cathedral. Posh boutique place.'

'I doubt London is up here on a shopping trip,' said Mead. 'Whatever she might claim. They left early this morning, but we lost them after leaving the city.'

'The lanes network is pretty confusing,' suggested Sara.

DS Mead nodded. He checked his watch. 'In theory, the lot of them were booked on a flight to Amsterdam from Norwich this afternoon, using di Maletesti passports. We went to wait for them, but there was no sign and the flight's gone now.'

'This is all very interesting,' said DI Edwards. 'But how would you like us to help you? We've got a murder inquiry just come in.'

'I was hoping to borrow DS Hirst,' replied Mead. 'I'm afraid it looks like Lisa London and Neil McCarthy may have business interests in your area. I can't see any other reason why the pair would be up here together.'

'DS Hirst will be working on our own case over Christmas,' said Hudson firmly. 'There is no one I can spare. However, you're welcome to use this office as a base while you're up here if that helps.'

'I can act as a liaison if that's okay with you, ma'am,' suggested Sara.

Hudson nodded.

Mead frowned. 'If that's the best you can manage.'

'It is.' Hudson stood, indicating that this was the end of the conversation. 'Thank you for informing us of your suspicions and activities.'

Sara took Mead and Solomon into the main office. They selected desks to work on, placing their laptops and mobile phones ready for use. With the excitement of seeing colleagues over, the others returned to their original tasks. Sara asked Aggie to do a search on Neil McCarthy for local connections, while she tried to contact the boat owner again without success. Mead huddled over a call on his mobile phone.

It didn't take Aggie long to get some results. She gestured to Sara to join her. 'That was easy,' she said. 'His brother Carl McCarthy owns a large farm.'

She showed Sara a website for North Elmham Estates. Pictures showed a Georgian house surrounded by farm buildings and verdant fields with a selection of crops. There were photos of the brothers. It seemed they were both involved in the business.

'He looks just like a farmer.' Aggie barely suppressed a giggle at the photo of Carl in his working clothes and flat cap, standing in front of an expensive tractor. He looked to be the older of the pair.

'I don't think his brother is hands-on, do you?' Sara pointed to the immaculately dressed Neil in a Savile Row suit, tailored shirt and silk tie. 'More of an investor, I'd say. Is this him?'

DS Mead came to join them. 'Yeah, that's the guy. You know how they often have legitimate business ventures to hide behind. The family connection is a good way to hide things too. You might want to get the forensic accountants to have a look at that lot.'

'Got a match!' DC Bowen suddenly said. He sounded pleased and grinned at DS Mead. 'On that passport photo. One of your people knew him. They've just sent the link through.'

Sara and Noble gathered excitedly to look at Bowen's computer.

'Duncan Blake,' read Sara. 'Done time for GBH. Came out of prison eight months ago. DNA is on file.'

'Is this your victim?' Mead joined them in looking at the screen.

'Not sure at the moment, but it's certainly the man who hired the boat we found the body on.'

'Well, it looks as if our cases might have something to do with each other after all,' said DS Mead. 'Duncan Blake is a known associate of Neil McCarthy. You'd better fill me in.'

CHAPTER 33

When they told DCI Hudson of the connection and Mead's identification of Duncan Blake, she groaned.

'Well, that looks like the end of any Christmas holidays,' she said. 'Although I don't suppose the farming operation is likely to go anywhere over the next few days. Let Dr Taylor know about Blake. He can match the DNA from the database. What else do you want us to do, DS Mead?'

'Given that they didn't turn up for the Amsterdam flight, I suspect there's still unfinished business here.'

'You think they may still be in the area?' asked Sara.

'It's possible,' agreed Mead. 'Or they may be heading for another route. My team are checking all airports and ferry terminals for bookings.'

'Time is running out for them. If they don't get out by mid-afternoon tomorrow, most of these avenues will be closed until at least the twenty-sixth.'

'Do you think we could check for sightings of the vehicle?' Mead asked. 'They will probably have changed their number plates by now, but we could look for the model.'

'The traffic cameras are concentrated on the main roads,' said Sara. 'It's all too easy to avoid being caught on CCTV by using the back roads.'

DS Mead looked depressed. 'I don't want to lose this bloody woman again. Especially if she's up here on business. It could be the key we've been looking for.'

'What about this boat hire? Let's see if that tells us anything.'

DC Noble had worked his way through the images on the memory stick Amy had given them at the marina. They crowded behind him, craning to get a better view. He brought up a grainy video on his computer.

'I assume they arrive by car, but unfortunately, there's no video from the car park.' He pointed to a man standing at the marina reception desk. 'This is our man. I think this is clear enough for confirmation.'

'That's him, all right,' agreed Mead.

'When Amy has done the paperwork, the boss, Bill, goes to the boat with him. Two other men are waiting by the boat.'

This image was less clear. It was dark outside, and despite the lights trained on the berths, the picture was too distant to show enough detail. The other men had pulled up the hoods on their jackets, further obscuring their faces.

'He obviously spends time showing them how the boat works.' Noble ran the video forward until he reached a point where the marina manager climbed off the boat. Bill waved a couple of sheets of paper and pointed to its information, clearly trying to emphasise something. Then he handed the sheets to Duncan Blake. 'I'm guessing that's a weather forecast. I'll check with him tomorrow morning. He'll have gone home by now.'

Sara glanced at the office clock. It was already half past six. 'Ask if the car park has any CCTV coverage as well.'

Noble clicked to run the video forward a few minutes. 'I don't know much about boats, but I'm assuming something that size takes some time to learn to drive. You might be a bit cautious with it at first. Watch this.'

As soon as Bill left the camera's range, Blake and one of the other men appeared on deck. They rapidly unmoored the boat, which slid gracefully and efficiently out of its berth. It slipped swiftly past the other vessels, which rocked uneasily in the blustering wind.

'Is that the end of it?' Edwards asked.

'Nope. Amy certainly knows her stuff,' said Noble. 'She's collected all of this from other people's cameras.'

'It's evidence they provide for the insurers,' said Sara. 'She's had to do it for claims before.'

The video changed to another view of the marina. The *Empire State* came round the bend, passing more moored boats. The footage changed again. This time they could see their target from the back as it headed to the entrance to the marina, which was a large boat lock leading down to the river.

'Now look.'

Blake and one of the other men jumped off the boat, pulling it to the side. Another man approached them from a building further along the quay, zipping up his coat. There seemed to be some sort of argument. Arms were waving, and the other man jabbed pointedly at where his wristwatch would be until Blake moved threateningly close to him. The man backed away, pointing to the building, and walked rapidly inside.

A few minutes later, the upper lock gates swung open, and the *Empire State* went in. She looked dwarfed as she waited. The lock was designed to hold several boats at a time. Blake and the other man climbed back on board as the vessel slowly sank in the retreating water. A few minutes later, obscured by the camera angle, the bottom lock gates must have opened, and their target sailed out onto the river and into the night.

'I don't think this is their first time on a boat,' said Mead. 'They also seem to know the system here. Do you think they've used this place before?'

Aggie spoke from the back of the group. 'I had a look at the waterfront development online. There are three companies you can hire these cruisers from in that basin.'

'It could have been the first time they used this particular hire company,' said Sara thoughtfully. 'If they've used one of those other places, they must have brought the boats back safely. If they'd abandoned or damaged a boat previously, surely the businesses would share that sort of information.'

'You'd think so,' agreed Mead.

'Mike, I want you to follow that up,' said Hudson. 'Go down there with our man's photo and speak to the other two companies. Let's see if they make a habit of this.'

'If they have used the place before,' said DI Edwards, 'what made them go out on a night like that? The forecast was crap, and the weather dangerous. It ended up all the way up the coast at Winterton-on-Sea the following night.'

'I'd say there are two possibilities,' began DS Mead.

'Drug smuggling,' interrupted Sara. 'When we found the RIB, the local officer told me they sometimes take part in NCA-organised take-downs on the more remote beaches.'

'That's one,' agreed Mead. 'The other is people smuggling. Either way, they might well have carried on if they had prearranged meets or collections. Whatever the risk.'

'Then things must have gone badly wrong,' said Edwards. 'We can assume that they had some kind of argument. One of them shot Blake, and they had to dump the boat.'

'So, they ran it close to the shore in the dark and escaped on the RIB?' suggested Sara. The team looked excitedly at one another. 'Or one of them escaped on the RIB, and the other ran it aground elsewhere to escape.'

'It's as good a theory as any to work with.' Edwards sounded enthusiastic.

'Whatever it is, I don't want the NCA involved in this,' snapped Hudson. 'Bad enough losing our Christmas without letting them get any credit that accrues. We'll do this ourselves.'

CHAPTER 34

Danni's laughter had brought a grin from Gary and a certain amount of chuckling from the guards. London had frowned at her to make her stop. Danni obeyed, but she still smiled. This was why she worked for London, why she trusted her absolutely. She'd known all along and put Gary into the line to find the exact leaks. Mr Smith was still spluttering his denials.

'We need to get this mess sorted out,' said London to the guards. 'To begin with, you'd best get those workers fed and put back in the dormitory. Get on with it.'

She then called an urgent and hushed meeting. Striker forced Mr Smith into a chair and sat next to him. Jerry, the guard, sat waiting for instructions. Danni picked up her laptop and joined them, but Gary remained at his table, drinking tea. London was still berating Mr Smith.

'Your extra runs have caused problems,' she told him. 'We're being followed, as you very well know.'

'Why is that my fault?' Mr Smith huffed, unwilling to accept defeat.

'Those crossings were the only link to this place. Which is the only link between us. If you hadn't been so greedy, I wouldn't have needed to find out what you were up to. Now the Met have followed us all the way to Norfolk. I'll have to shut the bloody operation down, at least for now.'

Mr Smith looked genuinely shocked. 'No, you can't.'

'Yes, I can,' replied London. 'And I will.'

Before Mr Smith could find the words to object, the guard from the cell corridor suddenly appeared.

'I think you'd better see this,' he said to Mr Smith. 'Something's wrong.'

They followed the guard to the cell. He opened the door and pointed to the men inside. Danni drew a sharp breath. The less injured of the two men was sitting cross-legged on the floor, cradling the other man in his arms, rocking him gently and crooning some sort of lullaby. The body he held was limp, and the jaw hung slack. The chest was still, the eyes stared unseeing at the ceiling.

Despite all her work with London, Danni had never actually seen a dead person before. Mr Smith hovered in the corridor as London and Striker entered.

The cross-legged man looked up at her. 'He was a doctor, but you didn't know that.' He pulled the body closer to his chest and, bowing his head, dropped a kiss on his brother's forehead.

London tried the man's wrist for a pulse. 'He's cold.' She stood up again and looked exasperated. The man's grief clearly meant nothing to her.

She turned on Mr Smith. 'Another of your bloody messes to clear up. Are there any lakes or deep rivers near here?'

He seemed caught out by the question. 'Erm, there's a fishing lake about five miles away.'

'How deep?'

'No idea.'

'Let's hope the fish enjoy their Christmas dinner.' London turned on the guard. 'You. Find chains, ropes, blocks and rocks.'

The man walked quickly away, looking grateful to have been allowed to leave. At a signal from London, Striker pulled the other prisoner round to face her.

'And you, brother.' She leaned over so that her face was only inches away from his. 'You are going to help get rid of him.'

* * *

The guards got busy organising the workers, who were brought out and fed. London was handing out instructions via Jerry, and Danni found herself at a loose end. She sat with Gary, who brought her a cup of tea. Her hands trembled a little as she sipped it. The vision of the dead man was still playing on her mind.

'You look amazing,' he said. 'Taken a leaf out of my sister's book?'

'Could anyone find a better role model?' she asked with a shaky smile. 'You look different too.'

'My cousin has taken me in hand.' Gary grinned. His face was still youthful, but the innocence was gone. 'Said it was time I stopped buggering about. I needed to be an asset to the family.'

'And you believed him?'

Gary nodded. He held up one arm and flexed his bicep. 'Fabio started taking me to the gym. Go on, feel it.'

Danni squeezed the muscle. It was rock hard. Gary would be able to pack a punch now.

'Then he started taking me on jobs with him.' Gary sounded almost excited, as if the 'jobs' were an exciting game he enjoyed. 'When Elisabeta contacted us, he said I was ready for the big one.'

'Was it Fabio who came with you up the line? All the way to England?'

'Yes. He's still at that underground place.'

Lisa London had infiltrated every section of the line, and Danni admired her for it. 'They're going to have to be dealt with,' she said cautiously. 'Especially that pregnant woman. I assume you came over on this boat that Mr Smith organised?'

'Yeah. That was a bit difficult, actually. Made me seasick for a start.'

'Difficult? How?'

'There were already three men on the thing when it arrived,' explained Gary. 'I don't think they expected Fabio and me to want to come over with them. One of Smith's men had to stay behind. He wasn't best pleased.'

'I bet.'

'It all got a bit leery when we were loading the people on. Arguments about who was going to be left. I guess that's when they smuggled the woman on board.'

Danni remembered that Gary had been prone to making mistakes when she'd first had dealings with him. He had been younger and more naive then. He hadn't understood the consequences of his actions and made mistakes. He might not be so innocent now, but it seemed that the attention to detail was still a problem.

'And then you got seasick?'

'Yeah. It was kinda cramped in there. The sea was really rough. I thought we might sink, so I went up top.' Gary looked thoughtful. Before Danni could ask him anything else, he shook his head and looked around the canteen. 'That food smells okay, doesn't it? The men have been fed. Perhaps we should have some too.'

He stood up, holding out his hand. Danni allowed him to pull her up and into an awkward hug. 'It's bloody brilliant to see you again.'

He led her to the serving hatch.

* * *

Danni's presence was not currently required. The smokescreen had been created. She and Gary had eaten, then drunk cup after cup of tea that one of the guards seemed to be in charge of making. Everyone was busy, even London. She sat issuing orders and tapping on Danni's laptop. The guards allowed Danni to walk unimpeded about the facility to stretch her legs.

Gary went with her. It was dark outside until the yard lights flicked on. They weren't very bright but provided enough light to see and walk without colliding with something.

'Is everything going to be all right?' he suddenly asked her. 'Are we going to get away?'

Checking her mobile for the time, Danni shook her head — 21:35. 'Not today. Miss London still has stuff to do. Best wait for instructions.'

Gary yawned and tapped his nose. 'I don't suppose you . . . ?'

'Not my poison.' Danni shook her head. Gary using coke to stay alert was another new aspect to him. One she would never approve of. 'I've got some caffeine tabs if you want?'

'Yes, please.'

Danni had brought her handbag outside with her, not wanting to leave the passports and money unguarded. She scrabbled in the bottom of it. Lurking down there was a packet of perk-up pills, the sort people on long shifts could get from any health food shop. She popped several into Gary's hand, put a couple into her mouth and swigged them down with a gulp from a bottle of water. She passed the bottle on.

Suddenly the yard blazed with light. Gary was so surprised he nearly dropped the bottle. Danni looked around at the facility's roof, shading her eyes with her hand. Someone must have turned on some additional high-power lights.

The door opened and several guards came out. A pair of them headed towards the ramshackle red vans parked across the yard, starting up the engines and moving two of them close to the door. Danni could hear voices inside the first room, the fake break area. One by one, the workers were forcibly escorted out, hanging on to sports bags or rucksacks, which spewed clothes as if they had been hastily packed. Each man gripped something in his fist or shoved something he had been given into a pocket. Danni moved a little nearer to watch.

'Stay away, miss,' said one of the guards. His wool hat was pulled low over his brow and neck to hide his identity. Danni stopped moving, but they didn't stop her watching.

The workers were forced into the back of one of the vans, their bags thrown in after them. She glanced at a thin wrap of twenty-pound notes in one man's hand. Another man held a printed-out train ticket. The workers were being shipped out.

The guards ensured it didn't take long to load up the workers. The back of each van was full to bursting point with men and bags. They stood crushed against one another as the rear doors were shut and locked.

The tall metal gates opened and, with three guards in the front of each vehicle, the dirty vans bounced down the cart track away from the facility. Wherever they were being taken, it would be an uncomfortable ride.

Locking up, the remaining guards went back inside. Seconds later, the extra lights went off, and the yard was plunged into semi-darkness again.

Danni checked her burner mobile. Getting rid of the workers had only taken a few minutes. She turned to Gary, who stood with the caffeine pills still in the palm of his hand. 'Looks like things are moving.'

'We'd better get back inside,' he said and swallowed several pills. He offered the water bottle back to Danni.

'Keep it.' Danni shook her head. 'Take some spare tablets. It may be a very long night.'

Rapping on the door, Danni looked at the security camera pointing down at her. There was a buzz, and she let herself in. The guard who had spoken to her outside nodded in recognition and punched in the code to allow them back into the facility.

The banks of screens flickered, two guards watching them as always. The growing room was empty, and in the processing room they found one guard selecting a large trolley normally used for moving heavy boxes. When he saw Danni, he held open the door into the canteen for her.

The remaining guards seemed to be in there. The atmosphere felt tense now that things were happening. The door to the corridor and cell opened noisily. Lisa London walked in, followed by Striker, and at the back came Mr Smith. Another guard pulled the door shut and stood in front of it.

London walked smartly to the serving area. The guards mumbled expectantly. 'Jerry will sort you out into teams,' she said. She indicated Striker. 'My personal bodyguard will choose three men for special duties. The rest will stay here and clean up. I want no trace of the workforce left inside or outside this building. Is that clear?'

The guards agreed with nods and murmurs.

'Then move.'

London turned to speak to Mr Smith, confident that her orders would be obeyed. Mr Smith flinched from her approach as if he expected her to hit him. Striker selected guards and led them down the corridor towards the cell.

Jerry organised the rest of the men into teams, who armed themselves with buckets and cleaning chemicals before vanishing to begin their tasks. Danni joined Gary at the table, slipping quietly into the chair next to him.

He looked at her. 'Did my sister explain all this to you? They have a deal, you know.'

'What sort of deal?'

'They agree to work here for six months in return for safe passage into the country.' He waved towards the cell corridor. His face grew dark with anger. 'Those men in there decided it was too long and started a riot to try and escape.'

'Reneging on their deal,' said Danni. 'Letting your sister down.'

'Bastards!' snapped Gary. 'How dare they? Think of the risk Elisabeta is taking bringing them here. They'd drown if they came on one of those dinghy things. She's their best hope.'

Before his anger could get the better of him, the door to the cell corridor smacked open. Two guards appeared carrying what could only be the dead man bundled into an old duvet wrapped in heavy chains. They dumped the corpse on the loading area trolley and manoeuvred it out of the room.

One of the guards appeared pulling the other prisoner behind him. The man's hands were tied behind his back, and an old pillowcase was over his head. He stumbled along, ankles bound by a series of white cable ties looped together to give him just enough room to take a short step and no more. Striker prodded the man in the back with the point of his knife to keep him moving.

'Let's go,' said London.

Mr Smith looked startled. 'What, me?'

'Yes, you. Time to clear up your bloody mess.'

CHAPTER 35

The team had tidied up their jobs, set up their tasks for the morning and headed home. Aggie had found rooms in a city centre hotel for their visitors. They looked over a street map of Norwich with Sara to see how far it was from their hotel to the Gardens.

'Might just keep an eye on the place between us,' said DS Mead. 'They might come back for the night. You never know.'

Sara tried the boat owner one more time as she drove home. It switched to voicemail again, and she left another message. It was after nine o'clock when she let herself into the cottage. Tilly greeted her with that chittering cry again.

'Are you winding me up?' She picked the creature up and received an affection head bump in return. 'Hasn't Gilly been round to feed you? I sent her a text.'

Her neighbour had indeed been in to check on Tilly. There were scraps of food left in her bowl to prove it. Sara put some kibble in a fresh bowl, and the cat crunched them up as if she hadn't been fed in days. There was also a plastic food container and a note. *Thought you might need something warm. G.*

Sara opened the lid. There was a generous helping of chilli and rice in the container, which she put in the microwave. It was too late to light her open fire, so Sara contented

166

herself with turning up the radiator. She flicked on the Christmas tree lights and drew her curtains. Changing into a pair of fleecy pyjamas, Sara curled up on the sofa with her food and Tilly's company.

The television was full of Christmas cheerfulness. Sara didn't feel up to joining in with it. She stretched out on the cushions and was dozing off when someone knocked at the front door. It could only be her neighbour checking up on her in her usual motherly fashion. What she hadn't expected was that Gilly had someone with her.

'Can we come in?' Gilly asked.

'Of course.' Sara stood aside to allow the pair in.

'This is Reverend Collins.' Gilly introduced the man who followed her in. 'He's in charge up at Saint Mary's.'

Unsure what to say to an actual vicar, Sara felt stupid as she said, 'Oh yes. Merry Christmas to you.'

'And to you too.' The vicar's handshake was firm and businesslike. 'I do hope you don't mind us disturbing you.'

Sara ushered them to the sofa. Tilly mewed at Gilly. 'Don't listen to her. She's just had another helping of food.'

Gilly smiled and caressed the cat. 'Who's a greedy guts, then?'

Sara settled in her armchair, waiting for them to explain their visit. Were they trying to enlist her to do something for the church over the holiday? They would be out of luck, given that she would be working.

'This isn't about Christmas, actually.' Gilly pulled Tilly onto her lap. The cat kneaded for a moment, then folded up neatly for a cuddle. 'Do you remember we spoke about the young woman at the shop?'

'The homeless one, with the dog?'

'Mu. Muriel.'

'The dog is called Roger,' said the vicar. 'I think he's quite old, poor thing. Not a good life for him on the road.'

'Or the young woman,' suggested Sara, eyeing the man.

'No, indeed.' He glanced at Gilly, who picked up the story.

'I was doing the decorations in the church this evening, and I mentioned Mu to Theo.'

The vicar pointed to himself. 'Please call me Theo. Everyone does.'

'It seems she took my advice this morning,' continued Gilly. 'Went to the church to get some supplies from the food bank basket. I told her she could.'

'Cut out the middleman, so to speak,' said the vicar cheerfully. When Sara frowned at this attempted humour at the expense of someone's poverty, the vicar blushed. 'Look, I know what I'm making myself sound like. I don't mean to. To be honest, I've never been in this situation before. If I'd spent more time doing my ministry in big cities, I would understand better.'

Sara turned to her friend. 'I'm confused, Gilly. What's going on here?'

'Theo met Mu and Roger, helped them to the supplies,' explained Gilly. 'Took them home for something to eat.'

'When we were in the church, I offered her a prayer,' said the vicar. 'She accepted, but it upset her, and I asked her if she wanted to talk. She did.'

As succinctly as possible, the vicar retold Mu's story of her friend, Mighty Mark. Sara listened with increasing despondency. Violence against homeless people was not uncommon, but she'd never heard of anything this bad.

The vicar finished with a sigh. 'I didn't know what to do about it. When Gilly suggested asking you, I was very grateful. If indeed anything can be done. She made her way up here after this happened, so I'm guessing it was some days ago, if not longer.'

'It depends on what the outcome was, I suspect.' Sara unfolded her legs and sat upright. 'If either man was killed, there would have to be an investigation. If one or other was injured, and those injuries weren't serious, this Mark may just have wandered off. If either turned up in a hospital, it may still not have reached the police as a complaint, I'm afraid. Unfortunately, it's out of my jurisdiction.'

'Of course,' said Theo glumly. 'Do you think they may come after this young woman?'

'The perpetrators? It seems unlikely. How would they know where to look? It sounds as if it was random violence, not something planned. The homeless pair were just unlucky. This is the same person you said might have been abused as a child, Gilly?'

Her neighbour nodded. 'She must have been absolutely terrified by what happened to feel that coming back here was a better option. The place where she lived when her father . . .'

'You didn't mention this.' Theo's face crumpled. 'What a life. The poor thing. My wife is looking into places that might help.'

'Most of them won't take the dog.' Sara thought for a moment. DS Mead's face grinned at her. 'There is someone I could ask as a favour, although not at the moment, as he's tied up with a big case.'

'Thank you,' said Gilly with a smile. 'I knew you'd help if you could.'

'It's too late and too dark to do much more tonight,' said Theo. 'I hate to think of them out there alone in this weather, let alone at Christmas.'

'Any idea where is this young woman staying?'

Theo looked at Gilly. 'We're not sure,' she said. 'Possibly at the old caravan park. There are some derelict offices there.'

'Or at the old gun emplacement,' added the vicar. 'Even my dog, Terry, thinks something's going on over there.'

CHAPTER 36

Nothing about this trip to Norfolk was easy to accomplish or watch. Danni's worries about Lisa London had vanished. All the same, the sight of the man hooded and bound made her stomach churn. Poked and prodded, he lumbered through the facility in the wake of the trolley with the dead man on it — a disturbing sight. It reminded Danni of torture videos of prisoners filmed in captivity before execution. She felt ready to throw up. She had occasionally witnessed London or her men beating people or strapping them to chairs and leaving cut marks on their bodies. Fear was London's way of keeping control of her supply lines. But she had never seen anything like this.

Gary was staying behind. His sister wasn't cruel enough to make him witness whatever was about to happen. One of London's loyal guards would keep him company. Danni had been summoned by London to follow her.

In the facility, guards were busy cleaning every available surface. Two were balancing on pallets raised on the prongs of forklift trucks, scrubbing as high up the walls as they could reach. Not one of them looked in the direction of the strange procession. You can't be forced to talk about what you haven't seen.

In the yard, the last of the dirty vans stood waiting by the door, its engine running. Guards wheeled the trolley to the rear doors and lifted the body inside, throwing rocks and concrete blocks in after it. The brother was forced to sit on the back ledge, his legs too tightly bound to allow him to step up. One guard grabbed his legs and tipped him backwards into the van, then jumped in and dragged the man inside next to the body. By now, the prisoner had lost any will to fight. The second guard slammed the doors and climbed into the driver's seat, followed by a third, who got in the passenger side.

'You're with us,' said London to Mr Smith. He shuddered and took a step back.

'I can't.' His face was a rictus of fear. Danni could hear the strangle in his voice. 'I really can't. What are you going to do?'

'Does your driver know where we're going?' snapped London.

Mr Smith nodded.

'Get them on their way.'

The guard from the fake rest area strode across to the gates and unlocked them. The van drove through, headlights jerking as it bumped down the muddy track.

Striker grabbed Mr Smith by both arms and dragged him roughly to the Mercedes. Danni trotted after the pair, skirting past to open the back door. Striker acknowledged her help with a grunt as he stuffed Mr Smith inside.

'Get in,' said London to Danni. 'You'll have a job to do after this.'

With Striker at the wheel, they followed the van out of the yard to the minor road they had come in on. They turned in the other direction, continuing until it met a B road, still remote but wide enough for two cars. It was very dark between the hedges on either side. Storm clouds blocked any moonlight, and street lighting was a distant dream this far from a town. Rain spattered the windscreen in heavy bursts. Reluctantly, Mr Smith gave Striker an instruction, and before long, they turned left along another very minor road. After a couple of miles, they reached a gap in the hedge with a wooden sign that said, *Billingwell Angling Club. Private. Members Only.* They hadn't seen a single car or person in the whole twenty-minute journey.

Striker pulled up in a rutted grass parking area. A chain-link fence loomed beyond the waiting van, the metal gates padlocked. One guard was already cutting it open with bolt croppers. When they swung open, he unlocked the van doors.

The two guards dragged the dead man out onto the floor. The body fell with a thump, coating the duvet wrapping in mud and water. They attached the bits of debris to the chains with some difficulty. After several sweaty, swearing minutes, they picked up one end of each of their heavy parcel with pursed lips and bumped and dragged it through the gates.

The other guard pulled the prisoner out of the van into the car park. Once balanced, the man took tiny steps through the gate after the others, slipping on the mud, the covering on his head still blocking his vision. The howling wind must have been chilling him to the bone. Danni could see the man shaking even in the dark.

Mr Smith simply refused to get out of the back of the car. He clung to the seat in front of him, arms locked around it. Striker produced his knife and dragged it along the man's neck, leaving a welt of fresh blood in its wake.

Smith shouted with shock. As his grip loosened, Striker forced the protesting businessman onto the dirty floor and escorted the whimpering man after the body.

'Got a torch on that thing?' London pointed to the mobile in Danni's hand.

She nodded.

'Come on, then. Fun time.'

The two women went after the sad parade, guided by the lights from their phones. Everyone followed a path in the grass around the lake. The water had small waves on it, driven up by the storm. Every few yards, a wooden platform led from the gently shelving bank out over the water. Danni could only assume these were where fishermen stood. After passing several of these, the party reached one where the bank plunged suddenly into deeper water.

'This will do,' said London. 'Get him as far out as you can.'

'Just a minute . . .' Striker let go of Mr Smith, who immediately turned his back on the proceedings. Stepping forward, knife in hand, Striker slashed downwards several times, cutting holes in the duvet and puncturing the body. Unless she imagined it in the windy weather, Danni heard a faint hiss of gas. 'Go.'

The two guards dragged the body to the water's edge. Wading in, one on either side, they managed three steps before the land under their feet plunged sharply, and they were up to their thighs. A few more steps brought the water up to their waists, then their chests. At first, the body floated, making it easier to manoeuvre.

One glanced back at London.

'Keep going.'

The two men went on until the water reached their shoulders. Danni trained her light across the water to help the men see. The body was getting waterlogged and much harder to handle. One gave the dead man a shove.

The cadaver turned in a circle as the water claimed it. First, it began to sink at the head end, dipping slowly downwards. With a massive gurgle, the rest of the body slipped out of sight.

The two guards waded back to the bank. They shook with cold.

'Let's hope it stays down there,' said London to Mr Smith, who turned to look at her, horrified.

'You mean it might not?'

'Depends on the build-up of gases,' said London. 'If it comes back to haunt us, you'll get fingered. Trust me. Now, what about you, Mr Brother? Fancy a swim?'

The prisoner tried to step away from them. His ankles strained against the cable ties, and he tumbled to the ground.

Unable to put out his hands to break his fall, a moan of pain escaped from him as he landed on his back, arms crushed beneath himself.

London actually laughed. Danni looked at her boss, unwilling to show any amusement.

'Can't we just let him go like the others?' Mr Smith groaned.

London turned on him sharply. 'He's not like the others, is he? He tried to shut down our business. Why should we forgive that?'

'Isn't one death enough?' Mr Smith's belly began to spasm. Any second now, he would be vomiting. 'You can't possibly expect me to watch you kill him.'

'Who said we were going to kill him?' asked London.

Smith hurried a few steps away and threw up the entire contents of his stomach. Striker looked on with vague disgust at the man while Danni stopped herself from reacting to the smell and joining in. It didn't do to show weakness.

London bent down to speak close to the prisoner's ear. 'I'm going to let you go,' she said. 'But I'm sure you understand that I can't do that until you've been punished.'

Shining her torch to guide her, London walked away along the footpath. As the guards moved in on the trussed and hooded man, Danni hurried after her. Despite the wind and sheets of rain, she could hear them beating up the prisoner, the sound of boots connecting with bone and fists with flesh. His cries followed them down the path.

One guard was only a few steps behind them, forcing the stunned businessman along too. Striker had obviously stayed to enjoy himself. Danni shivered and was glad when they reached the vehicles. Mr Smith climbed gratefully into the rear of the car. He was shaking uncontrollably.

London stood waiting for the rest of the crew. For once, the boss looked less than composed. Although her features were impassive, in the light from their torches, Danni thought she looked tired. London pinched at the bridge of her nose. Her beautiful hair was hanging in wet rats' tails.

The expensive black designer coat and jeans looked soaked through.

When Striker and the guards returned, he carried a handful of cut cable ties and the pillowcase that had been over the prisoner's head. He threw them in the back of the old van.

London looked up. 'How is our friend?'

'Unconscious.' Striker patted his own face. 'Unrecognisable. I left him money and a train ticket.'

'Let's hope they don't blow away.' London sighed. 'Right, we're going back to the facility. All except you two.'

London indicated Danni and Striker. They followed her a few steps away from the others.

'You're going back to the hotel.' She handed her room key to Danni. 'Pack all our bags, don't leave a single thing behind. Understand? Then bring them out to the facility. Oh, and bring some toiletries. We'll need them.'

'We'll be staying there?' asked Danni.

'We haven't finished tidying up this disaster yet.' London glanced angrily at Mr Smith. 'They know where we're staying and that we have a booking for tonight. The buggers will be waiting for us to return, and I can't face fencing with the police right now.'

'But won't they recognise the car?'

'That's why you two are going in the van.'

CHAPTER 37

Rain battered in gusts against the boarded-up windows and roof of the old office building. It broke through in places, the rhythmic *drip-drip* lulling Mu and Roger into a doze, that half-asleep state when you can still hear things but are not totally conscious. Wrapped warmly in their blanket cocoon, time passed. With no means to judge it, Mu couldn't tell how long she sat there with the snoozing Roger next to her, his head on her lap, eyes dreamy.

She only half recognised the crunch of footsteps on the gravel path outside. Then the front door of the building exploded into shards. Someone kicked the wood so hard it disintegrated, shattering inwards with a bang.

Roger was instantly on his feet, barking crazily. His hackles were fully up, his teeth bared. Mu struggled to get out of her sleeping bag, her legs tangling with the blankets. Her heart pounded with shock and fear. She was on her knees when the inside door flew open, slamming hard against the wall. The whole building shuddered with the force.

There were two men. It had to be men — it always was. Both had head torches on. The beams raked across the room as they looked around. The first man kicked at their tins of food and camping equipment.

Roger didn't hesitate. He flew at the man, sinking his teeth as hard as possible through the trouser leg and into the attacker's calf. The man cried out in pain. Roger meant it this time. Snarling angrily, the dog gnashed his teeth together. The man hopped sideways with a shout of pain and crashed into the door, scrabbling at it to ensure he stayed upright. He shook his leg violently, making Roger dance in the air. The dog was still hanging on.

The second man pushed past him, hands outstretched. Mu frantically tried to shake off the blanket around her legs. The man grabbed her arms and dragged her towards him.

She flung her head up, catching him under the chin. His teeth rattled together, and his torch beam skittered up the ceiling. It wasn't enough. He let go with one hand, swung it back and slapped Mu heavily across the face.

The impact made her lurch sideways. Her ears rang, and tears sprang in her eyes. Stunned, it gave the man enough time to grab her again.

What was that move Mighty Mark had taught her? *Break the hold.* That was it.

Mu shoved her fists hard up between her attacker's arms, then jerked them outwards with all the force she could. Caught unawares, the man's grip loosened. Drawing her hands down a little, she punched upwards with the heel of both palms, jamming them under the man's throat. She could feel the wool of his balaclava, not the skin of his throat. Her anger spiralled to red-eyed ferocity. 'You bastard!' she screamed. Now she was on her feet. 'Fuck off! Leave us alone!'

The man swiftly brought up his knee, catching Mu in the stomach. She gasped in pain. He lunged forward, carrying her backwards in his onslaught, until they slammed into the other office wall. The place rattled and Mu's breath left her lungs, leaving her gasping.

The man turned her to face the wall in a swift movement she could not prevent. He ground his body against her back. She could feel his erection through her layers of clothing.

So, this was it. After all these years, she was going to be raped. The one thing she had managed to avoid with Mighty Mark's protection. The act that the handful of other women warned her about during her occasional stays in homeless shelters. Memories of her father shoving his fingers inside her in her bedroom aged eleven shot into her brain. Memories of her mother bursting through the door screaming abuse, dragging her father away.

She opened her mouth to scream. To vent her fury.

There was another shout. This one came from the man that had Roger attached to his leg. 'Help me!'

Mu's attacker pinned her to the wall at arm's length and swivelled his head to his partner. 'Hit the fucking thing with something.'

It had to be Paolo, the chef. His accent and tone were unmistakable.

'I can't. I can't!' shouted the other man.

Mu slammed her head backwards. Her skull connected with Paolo's jaw. He let go of her and staggered a couple of steps back. It was enough space to allow Mu to swing round, her arms flailing wildly.

Paolo swivelled between the two points of attack while the second man clung uselessly to the office door, still shaking his leg ineffectually. Roger's jaw had locked shut. Even in this half-light, Mu could tell that the man was no fighter. Where Paolo was young, fit and strong, this man was overweight and obviously unused to violence.

Paolo made his decision and picked up a length of timber, advancing on Roger. 'Keep still.'

The second man moaned but did as he was told. Paolo raised the wooden baton to strike the dog.

Mu leaped at him, kicking and punching. 'Don't you fucking dare!' she screamed. Landing punches to the chef's kidneys, she grabbed at the swinging wood in mid-air. 'Leave my dog alone!'

Mu struggled with the weapon as Paolo kicked at her to free himself. Roger let go of the victim's leg. He turned, snarling, and launched another attack at Paolo's face. The old dog wasn't really that heavy, but the surprise was effective. His teeth reached Paolo's balaclava, his paws scratching the man's chest. The three of them collapsed in a heap. The second man had also fallen to the floor.

Paolo was the first to recover. Dropping his hold on the wooden bar, he grabbed Roger's body and heaved him away. The old dog stumbled towards the wall and fell to the floor, panting exhaustedly.

Mu scrambled up, grabbing the piece of wood and brandishing it at the men. Paolo rolled to his feet and swung to face Mu. He held up his hands in a pacifying gesture. 'All right,' he said. 'We leave the dog alone. You go now. Get out. Go on. Leave!'

His last words were a shout as he hefted an old piece of a desk. It had a sharp, jagged edge. Paolo waved it in a sawing motion at Mu. She circled around him to reach Roger, standing guard over her companion.

'You'll let us leave?' she demanded.

'Yes,' growled Paolo. 'Do it. Now.'

Mu hesitated. Paolo was panting with effort. The other man was still sitting on the floor, gripping his leg where Roger had clung on.

'Last chance.' Paolo indicated the outer door with a tilt of his head.

Mu dropped her weapon, turned to the dog and lifted him into her arms. Staggering through the remnants of her possessions, she reached the door. The second man grabbed her ankle.

'Does it have—' he stuttered. 'Does he have rabies?'

'Oh, for fuck's sake,' snarled Mu, aiming a kick at the man's injured leg. 'Of course not.'

The kick connected, and the man squealed as he let go.

Mu stumbled out into the rain. It was so dark she could barely see the ground. Storm clouds blotted out the moon. She staggered away from the building southwards, weighed down by an inert Roger. There was scrubland with bushes on that side of the site. It might provide some cover.

A crash behind her gave her an extra boost of adrenaline. She broke into an exhausted run, reaching the nearest group of bushes. Skirting around them, she found an area of crushed grass behind. Perhaps local children had made a den, or animals had hidden there. Mu collapsed gratefully, hugging Roger to her. The dog turned his face to hers and licked her cheek.

There were crashing noises from the old building. They lay there, both panting with terror and effort.

After a few minutes, Mu lay Roger on the brittle old grass, pulled off her coat, and draped it over him to protect him from the rain. Squirming down, she peered through the bush.

Paolo and the other man were destroying their shelter. As she watched, the pair ripped boards from the windows and threw the remnants of both doors out of the gaps. The place would no longer be dry or secret. Mu stifled a cry of despair as the men scattered her belongings, throwing her blankets and sleeping bag into the wind, which snatched the warmth-giving protection away. Then they lobbed her tins, packets and Roger's food around the place. They stamped on her cooking stove and billy can, scattering her very means of survival.

When they seemed happy with the destruction they had wrought, the pair slowly left. The second man limped, Paolo helping him up the path towards the pub backyard. From behind the bushes, Mu couldn't tell where they went after that.

The rain slashed down on Mu and Roger. The dog was shaking. He lay his head on the floor and closed his eyes. Despair brought Mu to tears. She was trembling with shock, her hands clenched tightly. She lay down next to the dog to comfort him. The bushes were no shelter.

'We need to get out of this weather,' she whispered. 'Give me a few minutes.'

The dog didn't acknowledge her. Mu checked the area in front of them. Then she ran out, darting here and there, collecting what she could of the damaged items. Chasing into the wind, she caught her sleeping bag and a couple of blankets. Mu checked inside the old office. Her rucksack was buried under debris from the men's rampage. Tugging at it, Mu managed to pull it free. Outside she loaded the few items she could salvage into the bag, strapping it shut and rolling the blankets under the flap. Luckily, she had put the vicar's twenty pounds in her trouser pockets earlier.

She ran back to where Roger still lay unmoving. 'Come on, my fella,' she murmured. Hefting the rucksack onto her back, she lifted the dog into her arms once more.

There was only one realistic means of escape, which led past the pub's backyard. Fear lending her one final burst of strength, Mu carried Roger up the little hill past Paolo's car. Her heart pounded in her ears, and her breathing was coarse and ragged as they crossed the front car park. It was nearly empty.

The vicar's money crinkled in her pocket, reminding Mu of the one place that might give them sanctuary. A building that had offered refuge to the persecuted for centuries. She staggered along the road to the church gate. Rain lashed her face as she carried her companion across the graveyard. Limping into the old stone porch, she realised gratefully that it faced out of the weather. With the bulk of the building behind it, the entrance was a place of quiet in the storm. The wind blustered around it but not inside.

Placing Roger on one of the ancient stone benches, Mu tried the large wooden door. It was locked. She almost shouted in frustration. What could she do now? Gazing out into the night, she assumed it must be late. Too late to disturb anyone. Even if she could wake the vicar or his wife, they would surely insist that the police be called. Mu couldn't face any of that. She slumped exhaustedly next to the dog.

He snuffled at her. At least he was awake. Mu took back her coat and zipped it up. Then she pulled out the rescued blankets and sleeping bag. Laying one on the stone floor under the bench, she placed the rucksack as a pillow and pushed Roger under the bench, curling herself around him. She wrapped the sleeping bag around them both and pulled the other blanket on top of that. They huddled together, hidden from the outside world. It was uncomfortable and insecure. But at least they could share their body heat and keep out of the storm.

Wincing at the soreness in her stomach, Mu wrapped her arms around her brave companion and settled down to protect him from the night.

CHAPTER 38

The wind had howled with increasing fury as the night had worn on. Sara wasn't sure if the weather or the thought of Lisa London being back on their patch had kept her awake. She caught the earliest local news and weather as she hurriedly sorted out Tilly for the day.

'*Storm David is set to wreak havoc along the Norfolk coast,*' said the weather lady. '*Winds are expected to reach gusts of up to eighty miles per hour, and the spring tide could bring swells of up to twenty-five feet or more. A full storm surge is now predicted between five and ten this evening.*'

Sara paused to look at the images of waves smashing onto the promenade at Cromer.

'*Coastal villages are being advised to evacuate vulnerable community members and put their sea defences in place,*' continued a local reporter. '*The police are requesting that people do not travel to the seaside to look at the spectacle as emergency services may require access at any time. The people of Great Yarmouth are filling sandbags as a last line of defence.*'

Sara pulled on her waterproofs as she left the cottage. Remembering the homeless woman and her dog, she wondered if she had access to the news. Probably not. There was no time for Sara to deal with it, so she rang Gilly and left a voicemail asking her to round up the vicar and find the pair before they got injured. Then she set off for Norwich.

There were trees down all over the place. The wind buffeted her small car across the road as she struggled to straighten the wheel. *When this is over*, Sara promised herself, *I'm going to get a bigger vehicle*. As she battled towards Wymondham HQ, the local radio exhorted everyone to stay at home if they didn't have to go out.

'*Never mind your turkey*,' the presenter suggested. '*Better to have beans on toast for Christmas dinner than to get caught out in this.*'

Sara would have smiled at this had she not been so busy weaving past a huge branch blocking the road outside Wroxham. The river was already so swollen it had broken its banks, flooded the boatyard car park and spread out over the road. She struggled to drive through it. The streets were less busy than they might have been. Perhaps people were being sensible after all.

Despite leaving early, it was after seven thirty when Sara arrived at the office. Aggie looked up with a smile when Sara gratefully pushed the door open and slumped into her chair.

Aggie brought a cup of coffee to warm Sara up. 'Thought you might not make it.'

'It's hideous,' muttered Sara. 'Never seen anything like it.'

'The last time it was this bad was back in 2013,' agreed Aggie. 'That nice young man from the Met is doing the bacon butties.'

The team gathered around the pile of bags as DC Solomon dished out their breakfast. DCI Hudson opened the morning meeting as they chewed.

'Updates, if you please.'

'We watched that hotel until after midnight,' said DS Mead. 'No sign of any known vehicle belonging to the London clan or associates. Gave up after that and went to get some kip. Better news from the rest of my team, however. The di Maletestis are booked on another flight to Naples this morning. Direct from Stansted to Naples. I have a team down there watching.'

'It'll be chaos.' Bowen picked a length of bacon rind from his roll and dropped it in the bin. 'Christmas Eve is one of the biggest getaway days, and this weather will be mucking up the flights.'

'Are you sure they're trying to get out of the country?' asked Edwards. 'If they didn't turn up yesterday in Norwich, is it to distract us? Maybe they have something else planned.'

Mead nodded. 'Or they're leaving by a less obvious route. Ferry, perhaps?'

'They're all being kept back in port,' said Aggie from her desk. 'It was on the news this morning. All sailings on the east coast are cancelled until Boxing Day.'

'This might be to our advantage,' suggested Sara. 'If the flights and ferries are obstructed by the storm surge, they'll be trapped here. You still watching her house in Ealing?'

'Of course,' said Mead. 'No sign of them there. I'm not sure Ms London is finished with her business up here. She'd feel confident enough to go home if it was tied up properly.'

'What about this farm?' asked Noble. 'The one run by Carl McCarthy out at North Elmham. Is that worth a look? Could they be staying out there?'

'Possible,' said Hudson. 'Any news from Dr Taylor?'

'I'll check my emails.' Sara moved to her computer and opened the inbox. A message from the pathologist had arrived about sixty seconds before. She scanned it quickly. 'We're in luck with that, at least. Doc says our man in the boat is a DNA match for Duncan Blake. Ah, hang on — there's another one.'

Sara paused to read it through and then whistled.

'Well?' the DCI said in frustration.

'You remember the RIB? They fast-tracked that DNA as well. Guess who?' Sara looked at DS Mead. 'Gary Barr, Lisa London's little brother.'

Mead crowed in delight. 'He must be back in the country. And he may have been on the boat when Blake was murdered.'

Sara scrolled down the email. 'Hang on. They found a bit of fabric too. That also had DNA on it. Match on the Interpol database? Surely not?'

'I'll do that.' Aggie began to rattle away on her keyboard.

'Good, that gives us enough excuse to visit the farm,' said Edwards. 'Blake is a known associate with the brother of the farm owner, and we need to find Neil McCarthy. If the man is visiting Norfolk, surely he's staying with his brother?'

'Let's sort out what we're doing for the rest of the day.' Hudson grabbed a marker pen and started a list on the whiteboard.

'Fabio Rossi,' said Aggie. 'Mean anything? Wanted by Naples Police.'

Mead scrunched up his eyes in concentration. 'Sounds familiar, but I can't bring it to mind. Part of the di Maletesti clan at a guess.'

Sara's phone rang. A tentative male voice asked if she was Detective Sergeant Hirst.

'I am,' she confirmed. 'Who is this?'

'Todd Lane,' said the man. 'I'm sorry not to have got back to you sooner, but I've been away on a family matter.'

'Mr Lane.' Sara braced herself to deliver the bad news. 'I rang you about your vessel, the *Empire State*.'

'My lovely girl,' said Lane. His voice was breathy with emotion. 'Yes, I had a call from Bill at the marina. He told me it had been damaged. Such a shock. Just one bad piece of news after the other.'

Sara felt relieved that the marina manager had taken the sting out of what she was about to say, if not all of it. 'I'm afraid there's rather more to it than that.'

'Oh no, what else can there be?'

'The boat was found drifting out at sea by the Coastguard, who towed it back to Great Yarmouth. I'm afraid there was an unwelcome passenger when it arrived.'

'Unwelcome? Not drugs!' Lane almost squealed. 'Not that.' Obviously, he'd heard the notorious story Amy had told to Sara.

'Not drugs. It's worse than that.' Sara drew a deep breath. 'I'm afraid we found a dead man in the front cabin.'

This time Lane did squeal. 'Oh my God! Who was it? Not one of those nice men who borrowed it?'

'One of which nice men?'

'A friend introduced us,' said Lane. 'He likes to go up and down the river sometimes. Takes his mates with him.'

'You know the men who hired your boat?'

'Oh yes. It was their idea to hire it out in the first place.'

'Bill at the marina gave me to understand that this was the first time you'd hired it out.'

'Officially, yes,' said Lane, who sounded more confused by the second. 'They'd borrowed her before. Privately, as it were. Then I decided it might be worthwhile doing a few more people, and Bill said he could do it all through the company.'

'So, these men had used the boat before?' Sara was aware that the office had grown silent as the rest of the team stopped to listen to her end of the conversation.

'Several times. I can check my diary to be sure. In fact, Duncan seemed rather put out when I said he had to go through Bill this time. Said he didn't like official channels. I wasn't even sure he would turn up, he got so angry about it.'

CHAPTER 39

Mu and Roger's night had been long, cold and uncomfortable. The weather had worsened by the hour and turned into a storm long before light dawned. Neither of them had moved all night.

Mu had been grateful that after the sudden attack and desperate escape, Roger had recovered as she cuddled him. Slowly his body heat had increased, and his breathing returned to normal. Mu tried to stretch her stiff limbs as she rolled out from under the stone bench in the church porch. Roger stirred in his cocoon of blankets, raising an ear to listen. It was early morning.

'Let's see what I managed to recover,' she said. The lumpy rucksack had been an uncomfortable pillow, but it had kept their heads sheltered. Mu undid the straps and inspected what was left of her possessions. There wasn't much. She selected two tins with ring-pull lids and dug around until she found a spoon lodged in an outside pocket.

'You first,' she said, encouraging the dog to sit up. Her tin plates had gone, as had the mugs and Roger's water bowl. 'At least it's food.'

She scraped some dog food onto the flag floor, mashing it and turning it so Roger could eat it easily. He tentatively picked up small mouthfuls, which he swallowed without chewing. Mu assumed his teeth ached from his heroic attack the previous evening. The more he ate, the more awake he became.

The vicar's twenty pounds were still nestled in her pocket. Mu could afford to buy him more food, so she scraped until the tin was empty. Roger wagged his tail gratefully in reply.

She wiped the spoon clean on a bit of greenery beside the porch entrance and opened the other tin. Cold baked beans weren't everyone's idea of a great meal, but Mu knew what hunger was, and this was filling. With the wind blustering around her, she took the empty tins out into the graveyard, looking for some kind of bin. There wasn't one. She looked along the church wall to see if there was a tap. There wasn't.

She stashed the empty tins at the end of the bench. 'We both need water,' she said hopelessly. 'What are we going to do?'

Roger stood and moved to the open end of the porch. Sniffing the air, he walked a few paces across the grass to the nearest gravestone, where he lifted his leg. A gust of wind almost knocked him over as he relieved himself, and he was back at Mu's side seconds later. Giving a heartfelt sigh, he snuggled under the bench again.

'Oh, Roger, I've let you down.' Mu had never felt despair like this before. She began to cry quietly, her body vibrating with cold and fear. 'I thought we'd found somewhere we could stay for a while. Instead, we're trapped.'

The wind raged at the open stone porch. She could hear the waves battering against the cliffs even this far from the beach. Where on earth could she go now?

She curled up next to her companion, distraught. With her back against the outside world, Mu drifted in and out of a heavy doze, not hearing the footsteps that approached on the gravel path across the cemetery. When the man spoke, the sound shocked her awake for the second time in a few hours.

'Well now, what have we here?'

Mu rolled away from Roger and the bench, her movement causing the dog to swivel round in alarm. Kicking off her sleeping bag, Mu sprang upright, hands outstretched. 'Don't touch him!'

'I wasn't going to,' said the vicar. 'Nor you. It's all going to be okay.'

Panic-ridden and wild-eyed, Mu stepped back against the far wall of the porch so that she was braced. It took her a moment to figure out who was blocking the light from the porch doorway. Roger was faster on the uptake. He squirmed out from under the bench, his tail wagging. With a huff of welcome, he moved forward to greet his friend from yesterday, the vicar's golden Labrador.

'Play nicely, you two.'

Mu relaxed as she recognised the vicar's friendly tone. The smile didn't reach his eyes, which were wide with concern. His face fell into worry lines as he looked around at their makeshift camp.

'I didn't know where else to go.' With deep embarrassment, Mu recalled that she'd had to go round the back of the church and change her tampon at one point last night. It had been dark, and she'd had to bury the old one among a pile of dead flowers and grass clippings. Now she felt the familiar ache that told her she needed to revisit the issue. 'I thought I'd be gone by the time anyone got here.'

'I always come here first thing in the morning.' The vicar brandished an ancient-looking key. 'I like the church to be open as much as possible.'

'Not at night?'

He looked at her bedding. 'Unfortunately, no. We have problems with vandals if we do. Have you been here all night?'

'Most of it.'

'Give me a minute.' He stepped past the two dogs doing what dogs always do, sniffing at their friend's rear. The large key turned with a clunk, and the heavy wooden door creaked open. As he clearly did most mornings, Terry trotted inside, with Roger walking more slowly behind. The vicar followed them, leaving Mu in the porch.

'I won't be long,' he called. 'Just want to switch on the heating. We have a service at eleven.'

Of course, it was Christmas Eve. How could Mu have forgotten? She began to pack up her stuff. She wouldn't be welcome in the porch when the ladies of the parish arrived for their carols and mince pies. Through the door, Mu saw the heaters inside glowing faintly red.

'You can tell me why you needed sanctuary later.' Theo Collins returned, clicking his tongue to call the dogs to follow him. 'For now, I suspect you need something to eat and somewhere warm to sit if you've been out in this all night.'

He collected the two empty tins. Mu clipped the lead onto Roger's collar and hoisted her rucksack onto her back. The wind nearly blew her off her feet as they left the porch in a little procession. At the gate, Terry looked confused as the vicar turned back towards his house.

'Walkies later,' called Theo. 'Come on.'

Unsure if he meant all of them, Mu hesitated. The vicar was already on his mobile. He waved for her to follow him. The wind whipped his words away, but as she joined him, Mu felt sure she heard him say, 'Mrs Barker? I've already found her. Plan B it is.'

CHAPTER 40

The cell stank of bleach. When Danni returned with their bags from the hotel, she found that she and Lisa were sharing it. Two camp-beds had been brought in and set up with what she hoped were clean sheets and pillows. Mr Smith was in the room next door. Gary and Striker were bunking down with the guards in the dormitory. Gary wasn't happy about this. 'Wasn't what I expected after all I've done for you,' he'd grumbled.

'For God's sake, Gary, grow up,' London had snapped. She'd rubbed her face, smearing make-up below her eyes, a sight Danni had found worrying. She had never seen her boss less than immaculate.

They passed a fitful night. Danni was tired, but her survival instincts were revving, and she dozed rather than slept. London lay motionless. Danni couldn't be certain if the woman was asleep or staring at the ceiling. Nor could she tell how much time had passed without checking her laptop or phone, both of which she had plugged in to charge at a socket out in the corridor.

The facility might not have had any windows and precious few doors, but it wasn't soundproof. The wind battered at the walls and roof with increasing intensity. When they got up the next morning in this strange otherworldly place, it felt ridiculous to Danni that it was Christmas Eve.

The showers in the dormitories looked disgusting. London and Danni risked them, drying themselves on worn and used towels. Danni felt almost as dirty afterwards as she had before. She watched as London wiped her face using the cracked mirror to guide her, failing to remove the black rings of dead mascara beneath her eyes. She'd repaired her make-up in the gloomy light of the smelly toilets, slapping on a new layer as best she could, but had only succeeded in making herself look haggard and older than her real age.

Danni knew she didn't look any better. She'd removed the protective cosmetic mask that helped mentally support her every day and left her skin bare. The resulting panda eyes and red patches on her cheeks made her look younger and far less sophisticated. The two women dressed practically for warmth and bad weather. No more high heels or designer labels.

'Cup of tea, sis?' asked Gary when they sat at a table in the canteen area.

London nodded. The other four sat around the table as Gary went off to make himself useful. Mr Smith still looked white and pasty as he fidgeted in his chair. Danni opened her laptop, ready for instructions. She checked various news and weather apps as she waited. Striker sat silent and unmoving.

The guards filtered past in pairs or small groups to get breakfast. Gary was probably getting under the cook's feet, thought Danni. But better that he was kept out of this.

'What are we going to do now?' Mr Smith's voice was taut and low.

'Carry on clearing up your bloody mess,' said London. 'We need to get the other workers from that bunker. They'd have been moved before this if you hadn't allowed this damn riot.'

'I didn't know about her. I really didn't.'

London looked at him icily. 'I left that side of things to you, and look where that's got us. We'll have to get rid of them all. Especially the pregnant one.'

'How?' Mr Smith couldn't have sounded more shocked. His face turned green. 'We can't just leave her at a remote railway station.'

'I don't know.' London sighed with frustration. She turned to look at Danni. 'A mother-and-baby hostel maybe?'

Danni began a search. It didn't take long to bring up a website for a homeless young mums' hostel. 'That's not far from here. In Colchester. A charity, of course.'

She jotted down the details on a piece of paper and handed it to London, who passed it on to Mr Smith. 'We'll take her there in one of the vans. An anonymous donation ought to be sufficient.'

'Leave her on the doorstep, like a bad Christmas present?' Mr Smith was aghast.

'What would you rather I did with her?' demanded London. 'And you can deal with the donation. Make it a decent one.'

So, even Lisa London baulked at abandoning a heavily pregnant woman. Yet another side of her that Danni had never known existed. These last few days, she'd felt the world was tilting back and forth so quickly that her head was swimming.

'Are we going to Stansted?' Danni hazarded the question, though she had already guessed the answer.

'No. It's likely to be being watched by now. What about ferries?'

Danni was prepared for this too. 'The weather's too bad for sailing. No more crossings until at least Boxing Day.'

'Trapped!' London snorted angrily and stood rapidly, scraping her chair on the concrete floor. Her body was stiff with pent-up energy. When the seat caught at the back of her legs, she spun round and kicked the thing out of her way. It smashed into the neighbouring table, scattering more chairs.

She strode round to stand over Mr Smith. 'We can't move until it's dark again. You'd better pray that we can get those people out tonight and get rid of them, whatever the weather.'

'Of course, o-o-of course,' stuttered Mr Smith.

'And you'd better find us somewhere else to stay tonight. I'm not going to sleep in that cell again.' London's voice was rising in pitch. 'What about your brother's place? Call him. Sort it.'

'Right away.' Mr Smith pulled his mobile from his pocket.

As he walked across the canteen, concentrating on the phone screen, London turned to Striker. 'Don't let that fucker out of your sight. Watch him all day, or he'll do a runner.'

Gary returned with mugs of tea balanced in his hands. Plonking them down on the table, he slumped into the chair next to Danni. London sat on the other side and pulled a mug towards her, breathing heavily.

Gary's lips began to tremble. 'I'm sorry, sis,' he said quietly. 'I didn't mean to be rude to you last night.'

He glanced at Danni. She smiled a little in return, reaching for a drink. On the laptop screen, extreme weather warnings flashed and blinked.

'It wasn't how I envisaged spending Christmas, either.' London pulled her brother into her arms for a hug.

'I think I'd like to go home now,' he murmured. 'Back to Naples.'

'So would I,' agreed London. 'And never come back.'

CHAPTER 41

Sara arranged for the local police to visit Todd Lane and take his statement. She sent through a scan of the passport photo for confirmation. 'Find out which friend introduced them,' she instructed. 'We definitely need to follow that up.'

DS Mead looked positively gleeful. 'This might be what we've been waiting for.'

'If London's in Norfolk, could she be here to pick up her brother?' suggested Sara.

DCI Hudson was allocating more tasks for the team. 'DI Edwards and DS Hirst, you will go to see Carl McCarthy at North Elmham.'

'I should go,' insisted Mead. 'This is our lead against Neil McCarthy.'

'It's our murder, with possible drugs or people smuggling onto our coast,' retorted Hudson. 'We can't let you take over our investigation.'

'And you can't poach ours,' snapped Mead. DC Solomon turned away, looking embarrassed. Sara sat back in her chair to see who would win.

'Then we'll all have to go,' put in DI Edwards. 'We need to inform our drugs team too. Powell needs to know about our suspicions. Besides, there's still Christmas to think of.'

After taking a deep breath, Hudson spoke again. 'Apart from myself, who has plans for Christmas Day? Noble, I know about you. Bowen? Aggie?'

'Aggie's son is home for the holiday,' said Bowen. Aggie tried to shush him, but he frowned at her. 'He's only here until the twenty-seventh.'

'Mead? Solomon?'

DC Solomon avoided his sergeant's eye. 'I'm supposed to be off duty from midday for four days. But I want to catch the bugger.'

'What about your mum?' asked Mead. 'I thought you told me she was rather ill.'

Solomon dropped his gaze to the carpet and didn't reply.

'So, the only ones without a social life—' Edwards sounded resigned — 'are me, DS Mead and Sara. Can the rest of you bear it if you leave for a couple of days and come back later? This could be very big indeed.'

Bowen turned red. 'I'm game. I'll stay. We can do Christmas dinner another time.'

Aggie looked at him proudly and nodded too.

Edwards knew it wasn't his decision. He turned to DCI Hudson. 'Ma'am?'

Hudson chewed her lip thoughtfully. 'I can't go. It's not fair to leave you all. But Noble, Bowen and Aggie can. You should take your leave as planned. Solomon isn't under my command.'

'You can go home, son,' said Mead. 'We thought it would only be a simple following job, didn't we? Not anymore. Let me sort it out. Take our car. I can go along with these guys.'

'Of course,' agreed Edwards.

'All right.' Hudson sighed. 'Bowen, given the conversation with the boat owner, you no longer need to go to Ipswich to speak to the other hire companies. Noble, ask about the CCTV in the car park. Hirst, you'd better inform Drugs while I call my family. Then we can get out to North Elmham Estates.'

Sara left them to make new arrangements and went to the Drugs team office along the corridor. The room was busy, but of the dozen or more desks, only two were occupied. DC Adebayo sat at one, speaking on the phone. Sara's friend DS Ellie James stood at another, arranging snacks into paper bowls. She looked up when Sara came in and flashed a friendly grin, accompanied by a roll of her eyes.

Despite the early hour, clearly the team were already getting into the Christmas spirit. Most of them were standing around a desk where DI Powell was handing out tins and bottles of booze, the officers holding a variety of half-unwrapped parcels and joining in the general bonhomie. The team must have been having a Secret Santa moment. It seemed a shame to spoil it. Sara hovered on the edge of the incipient party until she caught DI Powell's attention.

'Sorry to interrupt, sir,' she said. 'DCI Hudson asked me to update you on our current investigation.'

'If you must.' Powell laughed, and his team followed suit. 'Not a day for working, though, is it?'

'In private, sir, please.'

With a shrug of annoyance, Powell led her to a glass office, which mirrored the one Hudson occupied in SCU. Technically it belonged to DCI Chakrabarti, who was conspicuous by his absence. Probably already on his way home to visit family in Manchester. Sara explained their findings to Powell.

The DI started to take her seriously as she added more detail. 'Do you think it will come to a head over the next couple of days?' he asked.

'Can't tell, sir.' Sara shrugged. 'Christmas messes things up all over the place, doesn't it? For them, as well as for us.'

Powell looked past her to the team outside, already starting to get jolly. 'I don't want to keep them back if nothing happens. That wouldn't make me very popular.'

As far as Sara was aware, DI Powell wasn't very popular with several of his team anyway. He had a tendency to shout or belittle staff given half a chance. Perhaps this newfound consideration resulted from having a DCI on the team at last.

He reached a decision. 'I'll assign DC Adebayo to work with you. He's on shift anyway, and it might be more interesting than manning the bloody phones.'

A cold twinge ran down Sara's back. She had been doing her best to avoid DC Adebayo for weeks, ever since he had first invited her out for a drink. Sara thought of the Christmas card in her drawer. She hadn't got one for him.

Powell stalked to the door and, raising his voice above the joviality, called Adebayo to join them. The situation was soon explained, and the DC smiled at Sara.

'Yes, sir,' he agreed. 'Much better than sitting here waiting for the phone to ring.'

Ellie gave Sara the universal *call me* signal as they left. No doubt she was curious. Adebayo followed Sara to SCU, his waterproof jacket slung over his shoulder. The room was emptier than Sara expected. It was quiet after the festivities along the corridor.

'I've already sent Solomon home,' said Mead. 'Might as well get him away.'

Noble was also missing, sent on a mission to Forensics to ask about the ballistics damage to the *Empire State*, Bowen said.

Edwards welcomed Adebayo. 'Drawn the short straw? I remember your help last time. Good to have you with us.'

Someone had placed a small parcel in fancy wrapping paper by Sara's phone. A slice of Christmas cake lay on a piece of tissue.

'I didn't think we would be in the mood for Secret Santa, so I handed them out,' said Aggie quietly. She flicked her gaze sideways to Hudson's office.

The boss sat leaning on her desk with one hand in front of her face. For a second, Sara wondered if she was crying about not being able to go home for the holiday. Her face was white when Hudson looked up, but not tear-stained. Slowly, she stood up and came into the main room.

'Well, guess what?' The question was clearly rhetorical. No one tried to answer. 'We've just had another Christmas present. Another body has been found, this time at an angling club of all places.'

CHAPTER 42

'I'm sorry,' apologised Vicky Collins. 'I've tried to find a charity to help you, but everyone seems to have shut down for Christmas. At least, their offices have.'

Mu nodded tiredly. She was finding it hard to stay awake. Her nose was nearly touching the surface of the hot cup of tea on the kitchen table. She had swallowed a bowl of breakfast cereal in half a dozen stacked spoonfuls. Forcing herself to sit more upright, she tried to pay attention to the couple's words. Roger had lapped noisily at the water bowl and curled up next to his friend. Terry had cheerfully made room for the older dog in his floppy bed. Now they lay wrapped in each other's paws like some loving couple, eyes closing. The makeshift coat was drying over the rail of the Aga.

'You can't stay out in this weather tonight,' said the vicar. 'They say that there's a storm surge coming. It won't be safe, even at the old caravan site. That is where you were staying, isn't it?'

Mu agreed that it was. She told them about the previous evening, and their faces fell. Theo became angry.

'Why would they object?' he said, huffing exactly like Terry. 'Is there no Christian charity left? You couldn't be seen from the pub.'

'Perhaps they thought Mu might beg from the customers,' suggested Vicky.

'There's a cook there,' explained Mu. 'He brought me food. Tins for Roger too. I don't think it was that.'

'Then why?' Theo still hadn't settled his offended conscience. A knock at the kitchen door interrupted them. 'Ah! The cavalry, I believe.'

Armed with a bucket full of cleaning materials and a heavy handbag slung over her shoulder, the old lady from the village shop followed the vicar into the kitchen. She dropped her things on the floor and held out her hand to Mu.

'Hello, Mu,' she said, squeezing Mu's hand lightly. 'So pleased we found you.'

'You're early,' said Theo in mock offence. 'I was going to pick you up in the car. You shouldn't have carried that stuff all the way up here.'

'Glad to be of help,' said the lady. 'I'm Gilly. Remember?'

Mu's memory had indeed served her well. She looked at the woman closely. 'You used to run the Brownies, didn't you?'

Gilly smiled and nodded vigorously. 'I was right, then. You used to live here when you were young.'

'For a couple of years.'

'If you ever want to talk about it, I'd be happy to listen. I often wondered why you disappeared so suddenly.'

Mu couldn't reply and turned away.

Theo cleared his throat to break the uncomfortable silence that threatened to build. 'The thing is,' he said, 'none of us like the idea of you being out in this storm. Or at that other place, to be honest.'

'It's only a temporary offer,' said Vicky. 'Until after Christmas when we might be able to find something more appropriate.'

'I've come to help clean it out,' rushed in Gilly. 'Better an old roof than no roof. Oh, sorry.'

Theo had put a finger to his lips, and Gilly subsided. Mu watched them, hope growing inside her. The solution was obvious if this was what she thought they meant. She didn't dare to ask in case she was wrong.

'Only, it sits down there just being a junk store,' continued the vicar. 'I'm sure it's still watertight, even if it's rather old. We can clean it up a bit and get you some equipment.'

Mu looked at Vicky. The vicar's wife must have understood the mixture of confusion and hope on Mu's face.

'The old showman's van at the bottom of the garden,' she said gently. 'Would it do for a couple of weeks until we find somewhere better? I'm afraid there's no power, but we have an idea for that.'

'Well?' asked Gilly. 'Say yes?' She picked up her bucket of cleaning items and rattled it.

Relief flooded Mu. Years of looking after herself had left her ill-equipped to know how to be truly grateful for kindness. She'd known so little of it in her twenty-two years. Her face crumpled, and she nodded. 'Thank you so much,' she managed to say.

'Good,' said Gilly. 'Because I have a couple of friends on their way to give us a hand.'

'Nobody cleans like the WI,' said Theo.

He collected the key to the old caravan and headed off down the garden path with Gilly in tow. After a few minutes, Gilly welcomed another pair of older ladies and dragged them away to help. Vicky sat in silence with Mu until she felt able to look up.

'I don't know how to say thank you properly.'

'That's all right,' said Vicky. 'You can pay it forward, as they say.'

She brought a key from a rack and handed it to Mu. 'This opens the back porch door.' She pointed to the lobby, where dozens of coats hung on a row of hooks. 'Can you see those two other doors? One is a wet room. It has a toilet and a shower. You're welcome to use them. The caravan doesn't have anything like that.'

And if the inner kitchen door was usually locked, Mu wouldn't blame them. After all, what did they know about her, really?

'Do you have many clothes?'

'I did have a few spares,' said Mu.

'Until those men attacked you?'

Mu nodded.

'Okay.' Vicky went off into the main part of the vicarage.

Roger sighed contentedly in the basket next to Terry. Mu didn't want to disturb him. Digging in her rucksack, she collected a tampon and, opening both doors in the lobby, found the toilet. When she came out, Vicky was waiting for her in the kitchen.

'I suspect Gilly and her friends are having the time of their lives down there. But I have to extract the Rev in time for morning service.'

Mu looked at the kitchen clock. It was half past nine.

'Why don't you get yourself a shower,' suggested Vicky. She pointed to a pile of clean clothes and a pair of towels on the table. 'Help yourself to anything you need. After that, we can see how far the intrepid ladies have got.'

In the wet room, there was rose-scented soap on the basin and new bottles of shampoo and body gel on a shelf in the shower. Heat flooded from the radiator and warmed the fresh towels. It had been many weeks since she had last been really clean. The prospect filled her with delight. Stepping into the shower, she thought of the generosity of the vicar and his wife. No doubt they would come in for some criticism from parishioners. Or even their bosses.

Mu took a silent vow not to let this couple down if she could help it.

CHAPTER 43

Billingwell Angling Club was suspiciously close to North Elmham Estates. No more than five miles separated the two places.

'This can't be a coincidence,' said DCI Hudson, her lips pouting as she looked around the team. 'Edwards, take Sara and go to this club, find out what you can. Forensics are on their way, apparently. Mead, Adebayo, you're with me. We're going to the farmhouse. Let's see if we can track down Neil McCarthy. If he's in the county, hopefully his brother will know where he is. I want to ask what he knows about Duncan Blake.'

'Or if he knows where Lisa London and Gary Barr are,' added Mead.

'The rest of you can collate anything that comes in, then bugger off home when your shift ends.'

The two cars followed the same road towards Fakenham. Both turned off at the same junction into the lanes west of the main road. Hudson's car turned off first as tall green signs with gold lettering announced the main entrance to North Elmham Estates. Sara glanced down the immaculate gravel drive to a large, Georgian-looking farmhouse. Edwards turned twice more onto ever-narrower roads to reach the angling club.

The well-used entrance was marked by a rather less obvious sign. *Billingwell Angling Club. Private. Members Only.* The club's sizeable grass car park was full of forensic vans, Dr Taylor's car and two police vehicles.

A bewildered-looking older man in a waxed jacket and green wellies stood talking to a uniformed officer. Sara and Edwards approached, and the man introduced himself as John Middleton.

'I found him,' said the man. 'About an hour ago.' He looked as if he could throw up at any moment.

'May I ask why you were here on Christmas Eve?' asked Sara. She indicated the terrible weather with a wave of her hand.

'It was my turn on the rota to do an inspection,' said Middleton. 'With the high winds, I thought I'd better come and make sure the clubhouse was still here.'

Behind the fence and to one side of the gate stood a large log cabin. Middleton pointed to where shreds of roofing felt were flapping angrily in the wind.

'The walls look fine, but I think we're going to need a new roof.'

'How did you find the victim?'

Middleton pointed to a path through the grass. 'I thought I'd go around the lake to see if there was any tree damage. We've had them go over before in bad weather. Found him partway along there and called the police immediately.'

'Thank you, sir.' Sara fumbled in her jacket pocket for a business card, and handed one to Middleton. 'If you could give your details to the officer here, we can arrange for a formal statement to be made later.'

She handed a second card to the officer and left them, zipping up her waterproof against the squalling rain with a grimace. Edwards was waiting impatiently at the gates, where a uniformed officer stood with a clipboard in front of a barrier of rattling exclusion tape. He signed them in, and Sara led the way along a grass track that appeared to run round the perimeter of the small lake. A short walk brought them to a forensic tent, which shuddered and shivered in the gusts. Two forensic officers were kneeling on the grass, attempting a fingertip search between the flimsy tent and the waterside. They were wrapped up against the cold under their protective boiler suits.

Sara and Edwards pulled on the suits offered to them by another team member as they stepped into the tent. A white-suited woman was trying to hold the structure still, gripping one of the corner poles nearest the tent flap. Another man in a similar suit was doing the same in the opposite corner. The plastic of the tent billowed and shrieked in protest.

'Good morning,' said Dr Taylor cheerfully. He was kneeling by the victim, who was lying on his front on the floor. His head was turned to the side so that only one side of his face was visible. It was bruised and bloodied. There was an indentation to the skull, which must have bled profusely but had been washed almost clean by the rain. 'I think the sooner we get the site cleared, the better, don't you? Before we get blown away.'

'What can you tell us?' asked Edwards.

Taylor sat back on his heels. 'IC3 male. I'd estimate he is in his mid-twenties. His back is soaking. Seems a bit drier underneath him.'

'So here overnight?' asked Sara.

'Certainly been here some hours as rigor mortis is fully developed. The cold and rain will have made a difference, of course. Probably died around midnight.'

'Cause of death?' Edwards was making notes on his pad. The wind rattled the pages, despite the cover from the tent.

'My best guess in these conditions is bruising and wounds consistent with a beating. I'll have to confirm later, of course.'

'All the way out here?' Sara was astonished. 'But that sounds like drugs gang stuff to me.'

'Agreed,' said Taylor. 'We'll turn him over in a minute. You finished with the photos, Vaseem?'

Another suited forensic man, holding an expensive-looking camera with a light ring circling the lens, agreed he was.

He put down the camera and helped Dr Taylor gently roll the victim onto his back.

The man's twisted neck held rigid, bringing the other side of his face into view. It was deformed with bruises and bloody gashes. His eyes were open, and his jaw hung wide. It was a gruesome sight. Both arms had been crushed under the man's body, one across his stomach, the other under his chest. The man's hands were clutched shut. Taylor gently tried the fingers, which refused to budge. He stood to allow the photographer to carry on.

'I can't do much out here in this,' said Taylor. 'Once Vaseem's finished with the photos, I think we'll get this poor soul back to the lab. So much for my holiday.'

'We're working too,' said Sara. 'If that's any compensation.'

'Both of you? My favourite team. I'll do what I can by tonight and finish on Boxing Day. But I'm having tomorrow off, whatever happens. Just so you know.'

Edwards nodded. 'Don't blame you.'

Suddenly, the wind gusted even harder. The two officers trying to keep the tent still struggled to prevent it from flying away. Sara grabbed the corner pole nearest to her and hung on. After a moment, things settled again.

'Was the private ambulance in the car park when you came in?' asked Taylor.

Sara shook her head.

'Think I'll go and check.'

The three of them left the tent together. One of the forensic pair outside stood as they emerged.

'Dr Taylor? Detectives?' He pointed to the floor. 'I think you might want to look at this.'

'What have you got?' asked Edwards. They carefully stood to one side.

'We're doing the best we can in the circumstances,' said the officer, getting his excuses in first. 'You can see that there are lots of footprints around this area.'

'Hardly surprising,' said Edwards, 'given the nature of the place. What else?'

'We think those are drag marks.' The man pointed to a patch of mud. 'Leading straight into the water.'

Sara sucked in a breath. 'And?'

'We'd have to compare them to the boat hull.' Another gesture pointed along the waterside where a small rowing dinghy lay upside down on the bank. 'Even so, I think whoever worked over our friend on the bank may also have disposed of something in the lake.'

'Something, or someone?' Sara said.

'You mean we should be getting the divers out to drag the lake?' asked Edwards.

The officer nodded.

'Well, that's going to make us popular. You'd better be right.'

CHAPTER 44

After much argument, Mr Smith managed to arrange accommodation for London and her party at his brother's farmhouse. They packed into the Mercedes and drove less than a mile before turning down an immaculate gravel drive. It led to a three-storey Georgian house. In Danni's opinion, it was the sort of place you might see in a ghost story on the television. As soon as they were inside, the car was removed and hidden among the modern farm buildings that stood to one side of the house. The courtyard of barns and workshops looked almost identical to the facility buildings, which was undoubtedly intentional.

'I'm Mrs McCarthy,' said a dumpy woman in her fifties. She was dressed in a hand-knitted jumper, and wool trousers. 'I've put some of you on the second floor.'

She led them upstairs. Lisa London had been given a room to herself, complete with en suite. Mr Smith was next to London, and Danni was across the hall. Although her room was much smaller, it overlooked the driveway and also had its own bathroom. Gary and Striker went up another floor. Striker wouldn't be happy to be so far away from London.

Danni's room was full of old-fashioned furniture and chintz. It smelled musty from lack of use, and the bedclothes felt slightly damp. There was no hairdryer, but at least the heating had been turned on. The radiator warmed as it groaned metallically with unaccustomed use. It would have to do for a couple of days. After such a difficult twenty-four hours, Danni was glad to strip and get into a decent shower. As she massaged her hair with the toiletries she had brought from the hotel, she tried to work out why they were here. What had London said? *What about that brother of yours?*

Obviously, the farm and the facility were all on one property. The woman called herself Mrs McCarthy. Assuming she was married to the brother, it followed that he was Mr McCarthy, and so was Mr Smith. The McCarthy brothers. Danni racked her brain but couldn't recall hearing their names before. As she brushed out her hair, she searched on the laptop.

It took just seconds to find North Elmham Estates, with photos of the two men. Bingo. So, the brother was in on this too. The facility was a major investment. It couldn't have been built without the farmer's knowledge.

Still forgoing make-up, Danni pulled on warm, dark clothing and decided to go in search of Mrs McCarthy. With any luck, she could cajole some refreshments out of the old biddy.

Gary was emerging from London's room as Danni left hers. As she went downstairs, Danni watched the guard change. A freshly showered Striker, his hair plastered to his skull, waved Gary away and sat bolt upright in the chair by London's door. The two men exchanged words and glanced at Mr Smith's room. Or rather, Mr McCarthy's room. Unless the man had gone out of the window or there was a secret exit, he must still be there.

Danni opened a couple of doors before finding the kitchen. The room was well lit and a little steamy. A radio on a dresser was playing middle-of-the-road pop music. Mrs McCarthy stood by a cream-coloured cooker, poking the contents of various saucepans on the hob. She looked up as Danni entered and nodded a greeting. 'It will have to be ordinary plain cooking,' she grumbled. 'Carl didn't give me any notice that we were having guests.'

'I'm sure it will be lovely,' said Danni. Hopefully better than what they'd had at the facility anyway. 'Can I get a cup of tea?'

'Stuff's over there.' The woman pointed to the kitchen cabinet next to the sink. 'Help yourself.'

Danni got organised with a tray and mugs for their whole party. Did Gary take sugar these days? She put the bowl on the tray and let them sort themselves out. Mrs McCarthy didn't speak again as Danni boiled the kettle and dunked teabags. She glanced over when Danni left with her tray full of drinks but didn't comment.

Mr Smith was coming downstairs as she was heading back up. He also looked at the tray questioningly. Danni moved it slightly away from him, indicating he hadn't been included in the count. With a shrug, he went on. 'Well done, that girl,' he said patronisingly. Danni ignored him and headed upstairs to find the others.

Striker got in first, grabbing a mug from the tray as she passed and settling back in his chair. Danni went up to the second floor.

This corridor was less grand. An elderly chest of drawers stood partway along it. Danni dumped her tray and banged on a few doors. 'Tea up,' she called.

'Thank you,' Gary replied from one of the rooms.

Taking two mugs, Danni went back to her boss's room. With a polite knock, she partly opened the door. 'May I? I have a cup of tea for you.'

'Oh good. Come in.'

Lisa London was sitting on the double bed, which dominated the middle of the room. The décor was similar to that in Danni's room, though the place felt less unused. London had also showered and dressed. Her hair was wrapped in a towel. She grunted slightly as she bent over to pull on her socks. Danni ignored the sound. It didn't do to acknowledge anything unusual around London.

'Bring your tea,' said London. 'I need you to get on with some stuff.' She pointed to a chair.

'Of course.'

Danni had left her drink on the table in the corridor, next to where Striker was sitting. She brought a notepad from her suitcase and stopped to collect the mug as she returned. Above the howling of the wind, the crunch of gravel under car tyres sounded outside. Striker stood up, poised for action.

Dumping the stuff on the table, Danni strode back to her room. Cloaking herself behind the floor-length curtain, she scanned the drive. A fast-looking black saloon car had parked almost outside the front door. Three people climbed out.

The first was a hard-faced, smaller woman in smart trousers and a puffa jacket. She had been driving. A man followed from the back seat. Another man got out of the passenger door, and Danni's blood ran cold. She knew him. It was DS Mead, the pig she'd evaded in Jermyn Street. How the fuck had they found them here? Wide-eyed, she hurried back into the corridor.

'Get out of the line of sight,' she hissed to Striker. '*Andiamo! Polizia!*'

If Striker was surprised at her using Italian, it didn't show. Knife in hand, he had pressed himself against the wall next to Danni's door in three strides. She slipped into London's room without preamble, and her boss looked up in surprise. Danni held up a warning hand, holding the door open a fraction to listen.

Someone banged at the ornate metal knocker on the front door. The sound echoed across the hallway. When no one answered immediately, the sound came again. London was beside Danni in one fluid movement. Danni heard footsteps crossing the tiled floor, and the front door opening. From outside, they could just hear the woman's voice.

'Good morning. I'm DCI Hudson. These are my colleagues.'

There was some mumbling from beyond the door. Presumably, warrant cards were being shown.

'The bastard's shopped us,' breathed London into Danni's ear.

212

They could do nothing but wait.

'Oh, yes?' The second voice belonged to Mrs McCarthy.

'We're trying to find Neil McCarthy. I believe he may be associated with North Elmham Estates?'

'Oh him,' grunted Mrs McCarthy. 'He's in the kitchen. You'd better come in.'

Were they after Mr Smith? Danni looked at London. The woman was frozen still, her face a mask of anger. With luck, the police didn't even know they were all here. *Please let us be lucky*, prayed Danni silently.

The kitchen door flapped open, wafting moments of music from the radio.

'Good morning,' said Mr Smith. 'What can I do for you?'

'Is there somewhere we can talk?' asked DCI Hudson.

'If you tell me what you want.'

'I believe you know a man called Duncan Blake.' It wasn't a question.

Mr Smith didn't bother to deny it. 'And?'

'Are you aware that Mr Blake has died?'

When Mr Smith didn't reply, the woman carried on. 'Do you know that he has been murdered?'

'I'm not aware of Duncan's whereabouts,' Mr Smith said warily. 'He's just an acquaintance.'

'Where were you on the night of Monday the twenty-first of December?'

'Er . . . erm, I can't remember.'

'We have several questions about your relationship with Mr Blake,' said a man's voice. 'Would you prefer to answer them here or at the station?'

'I'm not going anywhere,' said Mr Smith. 'I don't have to answer your questions.' Danni could hear the panic in his voice.

'In which case, you leave me no choice,' said the woman. 'Neil McCarthy, I am arresting you on suspicion of the murder of Duncan Blake.' She began to intone the rights statement.

Next to Danni, London hissed, 'Stay quiet, you stupid fuck.'

There was the sound of a scuffle in the hallway. Mr Smith shouted out, 'Carl! Carl!'

The kitchen door slapped open again. More voices joined in the argument as Mr Smith was escorted firmly but without delay through the front door. Danni scooted across the corridor to look out of her window, watching Mr Smith be placed into the back seat of the dark car, which then turned in the drive and sped towards the road.

Danni waited until it had gone out of sight before she turned and walked straight into Striker. He had come up behind her, and she hadn't even noticed. With a nod, he stepped aside as Danni hurried to her boss. London was slumped on her bed again.

'They've gone.'

'For now.' London clenched her jaw. 'It seems our man in Norfolk is as thick as shit. Why do we have another body to account for? And who the fuck is Duncan Blake?'

CHAPTER 45

Both Sara and Edwards were glad to get back to the office. Standing outside at the angling club had left the pair frozen. Most of the other offices were already deserted, and the DI's bad mood only increased when they realised that Bowen, Noble and Aggie had all left for the day as instructed. He picked up his Secret Santa present, which was waiting on his desk, and waved it at Sara.

'Bet it's bloody socks,' he said. Sara didn't need him to rip open the paper to know he was right. It had all the size and consistency of a pack of socks. She slid her own package to one side. It could wait until tomorrow.

'Do you want me to contact the diving team?' she asked.

'You can try,' said Edwards. 'Bet they've already knocked off, though.'

He was right about that too. An answerphone message told Sara that the team would not be back until the twenty-seventh of December.

DS Mead joined them. 'This place is like the *Mary Celeste*.'

'You back already? How did it go?' asked Sara.

'I think your boss has a warped sense of humour.'

Sara wasn't sure that DCI Hudson had much of a sense of humour at all. 'Why?'

'We got lucky. Neil McCarthy was visiting his brother.'

'He was at the farm?' Edwards came out of his office, brandishing a pair of navy-blue socks. He waggled them at Sara with a grimace. She smiled.

'Yup. Got very cagey when we asked about Blake. So, your boss arrested him.'

'Never!' Edwards sounded shocked. 'On what grounds?'

'Suspected murder.' Mead sat down heavily. 'She'll never make it stick.'

'I assume you've brought him in?'

'Left him downstairs in an interview room,' said Mead with a nod. 'I came up to find your admin and get the duty solicitor here.'

'Doesn't he have one of his own?'

'He says so, but the man isn't answering the phone.'

'I'll sort it.' Sara moved over to Aggie's desk and lifted a black notebook from a set of filing trays. 'Aggie keeps a record of contacts. It will be in here.' Finding the right page, Sara rang the holder of the duty rota.

'They won't thank you,' said the man who answered. He gave Sara a name and number.

Then they shouldn't be in the system, she thought as she dialled again.

The duty solicitor didn't sound as grumpy as the clerk had and agreed to come out immediately. 'I'll be there in half an hour.'

Mead took off to inform DCI Hudson and their suspect. Sara picked up the piece of Christmas cake on its tissue.

'Do you like this stuff?' she asked Edwards.

'Love it. Don't you want yours?'

Sara dropped it on his desk with a heavy thump next to the socks. Her phone rang, and she hurried back to her chair. 'DS Sara Hirst.'

'Good morning,' said an efficient male voice. 'Or should I say good afternoon? I'm DC Cruttwell, Met Police. You requested a formal interview with Mr Todd Lane?'

'Yes. How did you get on?'

'I'll do the paperwork in a couple of days if you don't mind,' said Cruttwell. 'I thought you might like the headline stuff. You asked about a man called Duncan Blake, who hired a boat called the *Empire State*.'

'The boat belonging to Todd Lane.'

'Indeed. Mr Lane stated that Mr Blake had borrowed the boat on several previous occasions over the last few months. He gave me diary dates. Do they matter?'

'Not so much at the moment. Put them in the report.'

'Okay.' He sounded as though he was turning over some paper. 'The boat had been taken out for three days each time, and there had been no problem on either occasion. The only issue to comment on was that they'd used rather a lot of fuel.'

'And the last time?'

'Mr Lane advised Blake that he had to hire it officially through the marina, which he didn't like. The other times had been on a casual basis.'

'So how did they meet?'

'They were introduced. Mr Lane is a tax advisor to the seriously rich.' Cruttwell paused. 'Well, to be honest, I suspect he's more of a tax evasion advisor by the sound of it. Creative accounting, perhaps? I don't understand it myself. Anyway, a regular client introduced him to Blake.'

'Why would a seriously rich person know a scumbag like Duncan Blake?'

'I wondered that myself. Mr Lane also suggested that, in hindsight, the meeting had not been casual.'

'How so?'

'The client had been withdrawing large sums from his investments. Hold on.' Cruttwell added up some figures under his breath. 'About five million in total over twelve months. Todd Lane said he asked the client why. His investments were doing well and he saw no need to move them about. Especially when Lane wasn't doing the transactions.'

'Missing his fees?'

'Without doubt. In February this year, the client invited Lane for drinks at a private club. Something he hadn't done before.'

'And that's where he was introduced to Duncan Blake?'

'Exactly.'

'Who just happened to want to borrow a boat for the weekend? How would this client even know Lane had a boat?'

'There are pictures of it everywhere, all over the house,' said Cruttwell. 'Said he had photos of it on his desk at work, where he saw the client.'

'Let me stab a guess at this client's name,' said Sara. 'Would it be Neil McCarthy?'

'It would indeed.'

CHAPTER 46

The WI ladies had worked wonders in the hour available to them. They had cleared part of the seating area and the table by stacking the junk precariously on the opposite sofa. The old Brownies' camping equipment had been pushed onto the floor on the far side of the bed, which was now clear for use. There was a pile of blankets with two pillows waiting for Mu. They had swept and mopped all the floors, and brought down the cobwebs. In the kitchen area, they had emptied and scrubbed clean the main cupboard, sink and worktop.

At half past ten, Theo took Mu down to inspect her new quarters. 'Will it do for now?'

The freshly clean Mu began to cry. 'It's wonderful.'

'Here, none of that,' said one of the WI ladies, pulling her roughly into a hug. The other lady and Gilly queued up to hug Mu in their turn.

Outside on the path, they heard a clanking noise. When the vicar opened the van door, an older man was struggling towards them with large blue camping gas bottles. Clucking like the delightful mother hens that they were, the women went out to help. Piece by piece, elderly but serviceable equipment was brought in and set up. Inside a cardboard box were a kettle and cooking pans.

'I made sure the gas bottles were full,' said the man. He plonked a large box of matches on the worktop and looked at Mu, clearly unsure of her. Unlike the women, who had enjoyed practising their Christian principles on behalf of a poor person, this man was more cynical. Nonetheless, he was prepared to join in. He showed Mu how to operate the lantern with its little canister. There was a heater that ran on a big blue bottle and a two-ring camping stove with a grill for toast. It was all luxury to Mu.

'This stuff is old,' he warned her. 'I sometimes use it in the summer if I go camping, so I think it's still okay. Make sure you turn everything off at the tap before you sleep, or you could end up gassing yourself.'

When Mu tried to thank him, he put up his hands to ward her off. With a gruff, 'Going to church,' he strode off up the garden.

'Will you come to church?' asked Gilly.

It seemed the least she could do to thank them. Especially when Theo said she could bring both dogs and look after them for him. Mu wasn't in any sense religious. There was no time for that kind of thing on the streets. Although sometimes, she and Mighty Mark would be approached by people like the Salvation Army, who would feed them in return for a little prayer. It didn't feel any different to the gurdwara and their curry stall near the Strand on a Saturday. They were grateful for all of it.

She hovered in the graveyard, watching the congregation going in, keeping an eye on the lane from the pub. There was no sign of Paolo. No doubt he would be busy today. Mu didn't want him to find out that she was still in the area. Let him think he had driven her away. Her stomach still ached from his attack last night.

When Mu thought the worshippers were settled, she slipped in at the back, settling the two dogs next to her on the pew. With a long-suffering sigh, Terry rested his chin on his paws. Roger surveyed the goings-on for a few minutes before lying next to Mu. Neither dog lowered their vigilance enough to sleep.

Perhaps it was the kindness she had been shown or the atmosphere of the Christmas service, but in the end, Mu found herself on her knees praying with everyone else. She repeated her vow not to let these people down, hoping that saying it in church somehow made her oath stronger. Afterwards, there was mulled wine or coffee and mince pies all round. Mu hovered in her back-row pew, accepting the paper cup and pastry on a napkin.

'Can I pop round in an hour to see how you're settling in?' asked the indefatigable Gilly.

'Of course,' said Mu. 'You can be my first visitor.'

Gilly smiled at that and bustled off to make more drinks for the parishioners gathered at the back of the church.

* * *

Gilly came down the garden path bearing two carrier bags of food. Theo followed her within seconds.

'I thought you might need some supplies before the shop shuts,' she said.

Mu unpacked the food into a cupboard next to her handful of tins rescued from the night before. She offered the pair a cup of tea, which they accepted, sitting together on the sofa. Mu proudly busied herself in her new kitchen. It was almost like having her own home. Outside, the wind was roaring, angrily shaking the small trees and plants in the garden, despite its high wall. Rain spattered on the roof, but Mu could afford to ignore it for once. Roger snored happily on the bed, buried in a pile of blankets.

'Mu, there's something we'd like to ask you about,' said Theo. 'About last night and that old caravan park.'

Gilly had carefully put herself between Mu and the vicar. 'Theo has told me about them attacking you,' she said. She shuddered. 'To think that something like that can happen in our lovely village.'

'You said you didn't think it was about you being near the pub,' continued Theo. 'Is there another reason?'

'Apart from hating homeless people,' said Mu wearily. 'I told you about Mark.'

'Yes. It was shocking. We'll get back to that later.'

Mu gazed out of the window. 'I can't be sure, but I think it's something to do with that old gun emplacement.'

Gilly frowned. Theo sat up straight, giving her his full attention. 'Go on.'

'I've been staying in the old office block since I arrived on Monday evening.'

'Oh, you poor thing,' murmured Gilly.

'On Tuesday night, I saw Paolo going there. It must have been late because the pub was shut.'

'Who's Paolo?'

'He's the chef at the pub. He left me a meal and a tin for Roger. Offered to take me to the homeless shelter in Norwich. I thought he was befriending me.'

'It must have been well after midnight if the pub was closed,' suggested Theo.

'I have no way of knowing. I don't have a watch or a phone.'

'And what was he doing?'

'He took a big bag over to the emplacement. The sort of thing bike couriers use for keeping food warm. It was hard to see that far away. But he waved a torch, and another one answered. Then he vanished.'

'Vanished?'

'Yup. I'd swear he was taking food over there. Like the meal he had given me.'

'Where could he have gone?'

'Underground,' said Gilly firmly. 'My grandson showed me these pictures. Some people like to go into these abandoned places and take photos. Like secret archaeology. There are rooms under there, dating back to the war. Some even still have old metal bedsteads in them.'

Theo looked at Gilly in surprise. Mu looked at her with respect. Not only did she listen to her grandson, she paid attention to what he showed her. Lucky boy.

'Go on,' Theo said.

'There was what looked like a tunnel or a corridor,' Mu continued. 'It was blocked at one end with big bits of rubble. But they must have been able to get in at the other end to explore it.'

Theo frowned. 'Terry showed an interest in the place the other day on our walk. Do you think he could smell something?'

'Probably,' agreed Mu. 'The next day, Roger and I walked past the place. Rog kept trying to get down a blocked set of stairs in the corner. Guess who turned up to warn me off?'

'The chef?'

Mu nodded. 'Got quite agitated, which upset Roger.'

'So, there are rooms down there, and someone appears to be taking food into the place. Are we suggesting that there may be people living down there?'

Mu looked at the other two, who looked back at her. 'I suppose we are.'

'But who? And why would the pub be involved? Do you think the landlord even knows?'

'Is this landlord quite tall and overweight?' asked Mu. 'And maybe a bit soft around the edges?'

Theo smiled briefly. 'That's a good description.'

'Then I'd say he knows perfectly well.' Mu thought about the previous night. 'Paolo was definitely one of the people who attacked me. I recognised his voice. The other was older and didn't seem to be into the violence. Roger bit him. Hard. Hung onto his calf.' Roger shuffled in his sleep on the bed as if he knew they were talking about him. 'He just screamed for Paolo to rescue him. Didn't seem to know how to defend himself at all.'

Gilly blew out her cheeks in exasperation. 'What has Tim got himself into now?'

'I don't know,' said Theo. 'But I think we need to find out. Do you fancy a drink?'

'No,' said Gilly. 'We can take the collection boxes for the food bank. That should tweak their consciences.'

* * *

They took the dogs with them. Mu hovered in the lane, just out of sight of the car park, while Theo and Gilly went inside. The pub was heaving. Voices echoed loudly as the door opened and closed again. People were obviously out having a celebratory drink or meal.

Mu had acquired another anorak from Vicky. She turned up the collar and pulled up the hood. Terry and Roger huddled at her legs, all three sheltering in the lee of the hedge. She hoped the intrepid duo wouldn't take long. Her story was bizarre, and so was their conclusion. But it felt like it was right. Although she had no desire to go to the police herself, Mu couldn't help thinking that the vicar could do so and be believed. There didn't seem any need for them to have come over all Miss Marple.

The rain was just beginning to get through to her skin when the vicar and Gilly re-emerged. The collection boxes rattled heavily, and Gilly was clutching about fifty pounds in notes.

'Told you it would get to them today,' she said with satisfaction. She rolled and stuffed the notes into the collection tub. 'Shall I take this lot home for safekeeping?'

'Good idea,' said Theo. 'Then you should stay there.'

'And Tim, the landlord, was limping. I wonder why?' Gilly patted Roger's head. He wagged his tail at her. 'Right, I'm off home. And then I'm going to phone a friend.'

Theo smiled knowingly at his helper.

Mu wanted to yell that this wasn't a gameshow. She had kept the information of what she had seen on her first night in the derelict office to herself. It wasn't safe for these two kindly people to know about it. It didn't take much to put two and two together and realise that the people hiding under the gun emplacement were almost certainly the people who had climbed the rickety old steps from the beach that night. If so, the people who organised this were far more dangerous than the vicar and well-meaning Gilly could understand.

'Are you fixed for tomorrow?' asked Theo.

'Going to my daughter's for lunch,' Gilly assured him.

They waited until she had walked out of sight down the little hill to the village street.

'Would it distress you to walk the dogs over there?' asked Theo.

'I think you should call the police,' said Mu.

'Let's see what we can find first.' Taking Terry's lead from her hand, he whistled softly to the dogs. 'Come on, time for walkies.'

CHAPTER 47

The duty solicitor had arrived as promised, and Sara escorted him to meet Neil McCarthy. DCI Hudson agreed to allow DS Mead to be the second interviewer. Sara and Edwards were reduced to watching from the observation room, while DC Adebayo had been left to man the office, still guarding the phones despite his change of team.

DS Mead was in a buoyant mood. 'They didn't turn up at Stansted.'

'Lisa London and her brother?' asked Sara. 'Were the flights still going?'

'Apparently so.' He shrugged. 'Let's see what this idiot has to say for himself.'

McCarthy folded his arms and looked determined when Hudson and Mead arrived to start the interview. Armed with the information from Todd Lane, Hudson started the recorder with the usual advice statement, then launched straight in. 'Mr McCarthy, I'd like to talk to you about your associate, Duncan Blake.'

McCarthy looked at the solicitor, then nodded. 'I don't deny that I knew Blake slightly.'

'Slightly? What do you mean by that?'

'He was a casual acquaintance.'

'Were you aware that Mr Blake had a criminal record?'

'No. Why should I be?'

'Friends sometimes talk to one another,' suggested Hudson.

'He wasn't a friend,' replied McCarthy. 'I didn't know him that well.'

'How did you meet him?' asked DS Mead.

'I can't remember.' McCarthy smiled insolently. 'How did you know I knew him in the first place?'

'DS Mead is a member of the Metropolitan Police,' said Hudson.

'My special remit is drug gangs,' said Mead. He looked at McCarthy without blinking, who looked away, unable to hold Mead's stare. Watching through the two-way window, Sara thought he looked shifty.

'As I have already informed you,' continued Hudson, 'Duncan Blake has been found dead. We believe him to have been murdered.'

'Nothing to do with me.' McCarthy folded his arms even more tightly.

'Do you like boats, Mr McCarthy?' asked Mead. Even the duty solicitor looked surprised at this change of subject.

McCarthy frowned at the table. 'Not especially.'

'Do you know a Mr Todd Lane?' asked Hudson.

Behind the window, Edwards turned to look at Sara. He nodded his approval of the interview. 'Good technique.' She agreed.

'Yes,' McCarthy replied.

'What connection does he have to you?'

McCarthy leaned over to whisper to the solicitor. The man made a note on his pad and whispered back.

'He's my financial advisor,' said McCarthy. 'Looks after my investments.'

'So we understand,' said Hudson. 'We've already spoken to him.'

McCarthy shrugged. 'I have large sums in investments. It would be foolish not to have them looked after by a specialist.'

'Indeed. Would you call him a friend?'

'No. He's a business advisor, nothing more.'

'Did Lane advise you to invest in your brother's farm? North Elmham Estates?'

'That was personal. I wanted to help Carl out when things got tough a couple of years ago. No shame in that.'

'Why were you at the farm today?' asked Hudson.

'I'm visiting for Christmas. It's nice to get out of London at this time of—'

'Mr Lane also owns a boat called the *Empire State*,' interrupted Mead. 'I repeat my question. Are you interested in boats?'

McCarthy glanced at the solicitor, who advised him he didn't have to answer.

'Did you introduce Duncan Blake to Todd Lane?' asked Mead.

McCarthy shrugged.

'Mr Lane tells us that you did. Blake began to hire Mr Lane's boat for short trips a few months ago,' continued Mead. 'Why do you think that was?'

'How should I know?'

'Why would you introduce two strangers like that? One a casual acquaintance, the other a business colleague. Neither of them are close friends with you.'

'It was a casual meeting at my club,' snapped McCarthy.

'Interesting,' said Mead. 'Which club?'

'That's nothing to do with you.'

'I can understand a businessman like yourself would want somewhere private to meet,' persisted Mead. 'An exclusive, private members' club, like the one in Hereford Street, for example. Is that your club, Mr McCarthy?'

'No comment.'

'Mr Lane says that's where you took him,' said Mead.

'Expensive, is it?' asked Hudson. She sounded genuinely curious.

'Fees start at about £2,000 a year, and you don't want to ask the price of a bottle of wine.' Mead smiled at McCarthy.

'Not expensive for a successful businessman like you, of course. Can you tell me how someone like Duncan Blake could have got in a place like that unless he was signed in?'

'No comment.'

'I can only assume that you did that for him.'

'Assume away.' McCarthy smirked. 'But I won't be taking you there for dinner.'

'Did you introduce Duncan Blake to Todd Lane?' demanded Hudson.

'All right,' said McCarthy. 'Yes, I did. But that's as far as it went.'

'Why? Why did you do that?'

'No comment.'

'Not long after this introduction, Blake first hired the *Empire State*. The last time he hired it was on Sunday, supposedly returning on Tuesday the twenty-second. He collected the boat with two other men. Who would they be?'

'No idea.' McCarthy sat back in his chair. 'Why would I know?'

'Could you identify them from the camera footage we have?'

'I doubt it.'

'Mr McCarthy,' said Hudson, 'I don't think you understand the seriousness of your position. When the *Empire State* failed to return, it was tracked by the Coastguard. When they brought it back to shore, Duncan Blake was found dead inside the cabin. He had been shot four times.'

McCarthy gasped. The duty solicitor sent a warning glance at his client.

'Do you own a gun?'

'No, absolutely not.'

'Were you one of the men on the boat?'

'No. I was in London all weekend. I can prove—'

'Until a couple of days ago,' interrupted Mead, 'when I followed a suspect's vehicle up here to Norwich. Did you stay at the Garden Hotel?'

'Where? I haven't stayed in a hotel in Norwich.'

'Your car has,' said Mead. 'ANPR tells me it did. Why would it be there if you weren't?'

'No idea.' McCarthy looked sullen but resigned now. His bravado was leaking away.

'Do you know a woman called Lisa London?' asked DS Mead.

In the observation room, Sara sucked in a breath and waited.

McCarthy looked to the solicitor for confirmation. 'No comment.'

'Have you met her brother, Gary Barr?'

'No comment.'

'We believe both may be in Norfolk.' Mead went on without pause.

'So?'

'Did you bring them up here in your car?'

McCarthy frowned, then tightened his lips to stop himself from replying.

'Where is she, Mr McCarthy?' demanded Mead.

'You are playing a dangerous game if you know this woman,' said Hudson. 'Remember, you have been cautioned, and anything you say can be used in evidence. Even if it proves to be untrue later on.'

'Well, I don't know her,' snapped McCarthy, his patience obviously wearing thin. 'What has this to do with Duncan Blake? You said I was supposed to have murdered him. And I haven't. I don't see what some random woman has to do with all this.'

'You're lying,' hissed Mead. 'You're lying, and if you think I won't find out the truth, think again. I'll charge you with everything I can and it won't be just your rosy little business that you lose. Understand me?'

McCarthy sneered at DS Mead. 'No. Comment.'

CHAPTER 48

The pallor of Carl McCarthy's face suggested that he knew more than he was admitting. London had given her party twenty minutes to change and repack any bags. Danni had finished her own and her boss's suitcases, which stood ready at the top of the stairs.

They were gathered in the steamy kitchen. Striker had Carl McCarthy pinned on a kitchen chair, pushing firmly on the man's shoulders to keep him still. His favourite knife poked out of one hand and glistened against the farmer's cheek. Danni was positioned in front of the back door to prevent anyone from leaving. Gary held Mrs McCarthy's arm with a light grip. The woman was leaning against the front of her cooker.

Danni hoped the couple would cooperate. Then Gary wouldn't have to witness his sister at her worst.

London was incandescent with rage. 'Tell me what's going on, Carl.' She stood across the table from McCarthy as if she had to keep her distance to prevent herself from attacking him. 'Why have the police been here? Why have they arrested your brother?'

'Don't hurt me,' snivelled Mrs McCarthy. 'And don't hurt him. We didn't mean no harm.'

'Well?'

'Neil said it would all be easy.' The farmer's voice rattled with fear. 'Told me it was an investment in the farm, that I'd never know it was there. I'd got into trouble, see?'

'Trouble?'

'Bad harvests, expensive new equipment.' Carl ran out the words as fast as his breath would allow. 'Said he would put up the money himself. Never mentioned a partner.'

'No?' London's tone became silky. The kind of silk that cuts. 'Buildings cost money. So do staff. Rich as your brother may be, he needed my help to build and people our little enterprise. What about the workers there?'

'Who?'

'Do you know where they came from?'

'Not sure.' The knife trembled closer to his cheek, and he raced on. 'Neil said he'd met some chap in a club in London, told him he could provide workers for a price.'

'Name?'

'Mr Orange.'

Gary snickered. '*Reservoir Dogs*.'

London laughed with him. She didn't sound amused. 'You're a real pair of amateurs, aren't you? Your brother can talk the talk, but walking the walk isn't his forte, is it?'

Carl shuddered. 'Sorry.'

'If only you'd asked, I could have cut out that middleman as well. "Mr Orange" is one of the most notorious gangsters in the country. "Signor Arancia" is my cousin, for fuck's sake.'

'We have a lot of cousins,' said Gary. When Mrs McCarthy looked at him with a puzzled expression, he added, 'It's the Italian way.'

'Some by blood,' added London, waving at Striker. She turned a tight smile on Danni. 'Some by loyalty.' She suddenly snarled at Carl. 'Don't think you're likely to become family, do you?'

He shook his head, catching Striker's knife against his cheek. Mrs McCarthy cried out weakly. No one acknowledged her, but the blade dug in a little deeper.

'And if your brother says anything about me at all, to anyone—' London's voice had dropped almost to a whisper — '*anyone*, not only is he dead meat, but so are you. Do you understand?'

Mrs McCarthy began to cry. Carl spluttered, 'Yes, yes. He won't. I promise.'

London's tone changed to businesslike in a millisecond. 'Were you making any profit out of this at all?'

'Barely broke even.'

London, however, was clearly getting a cut of the profits from both the facility and the drug sales. Danni had to admire her.

'Who the fuck is Duncan Blake?'

'He was foisted on Neil by this bloke.'

'Go on.'

'Said they needed to hire boats to bring the immigrants over regularly. Blake could skipper it. Did it every few weeks. Blake and two other men went with him.'

'Only this time, obviously something went wrong,' mused London. 'Why have the police come here?'

'They said that Blake turned up dead in the boat earlier in the week. Somehow, they must have worked out that Neil knew him.'

'Fucking idiot.' London chewed her lip for a moment. She was going into planning mode. Danni felt a surge of pride. 'How did these people end up in this underground place?'

'Neil saw some pictures on the internet,' replied Carl. 'Said the beach was an ideal place to bring people ashore without being seen. Normally they're only there for a few hours before he brings them up here one vanload at a time. Neil said it looked suspect if they went with more than one.'

'Only this time, there was a riot at the facility and a pregnant woman among the shipment.'

'What?' Mrs McCarthy screeched. 'Only men. You said it was only going to be men. No women. I insisted.'

'Did you now?' London swung to look at the farmer's wife. 'Well, as it happens, I agree with you. I may be many things, but a Madam isn't one of them. What else do you know?'

'We were only trying to save our farm,' sobbed Mrs McCarthy. 'Carl asked Neil for a loan, and he came back with this suggestion. It seemed like the only way to get the money. The bank was going to foreclose on us. We've been here for four generations, and our boy will follow us. We couldn't be the ones to lose it.'

'You see,' said London expansively, 'it never pays to be too greedy. Sure, make a profit. Little and often. Spread your risk.'

Danni almost felt sorry for the couple. They had obviously been duped into this by Neil McCarthy. It was equally obvious that his brother was considerably out of his depth.

'Now, you see, my problem is this.' London's face clouded over again, and the rage returned. 'You bumbling, greedy fuckers have put my entire business at risk. Do you think I like that?'

The older couple shook their heads miserably.

'And are you going to help me put it all straight?'

They nodded.

'Here's what we're going to do . . .'

CHAPTER 49

Mu really didn't want to go near to the gun emplacement. It was out in the open, and she knew full well that it was possible to see figures there from a distance. Someone in the pub's backyard could spot them. She had tried to object because Roger was tired. 'He needs to go back to the van,' she said to Theo. 'Poor thing has had a terrible time.'

'Will he be all right on his own?' asked the vicar. Terry tugged at his lead as they stood debating outside the vicarage drive.

Mu said she was also too tired, but Theo looked hurt, so she gave in and took Roger back down the garden. He settled immediately on the bed, showing no signs of distress when Mu went out the door. Reasoning that she had different clothes on and, against expectation, would be with someone else, Mu gave in. She was glad she could hide under the hood of her jacket all the same.

They set off down the lane, the wind ripping into the hedges. It was mid-afternoon, but it might as well have been dusk. The sky was crowded with dark clouds and it was hard to see clearly, a small comfort Mu was happy to accept. When they left the shelter of the hedges, a massive gust of wind nearly swept her off her feet. Years of living on handouts meant that Mu was underweight, making her easy prey to the storm.

'I don't think we should be out in this,' she said, but the wind swept her words away. Theo looked at her with a smile and carried on along the farm track towards the emplacement. Mu's feet skidded in the mud. Theo was taller and solidly built, and although he could hardly be described as overweight, he seemed to have little trouble with the conditions.

At the end of the track, they reached the giant pile of farm manure. Chunks were being ripped away from the top of the stack by savage gusts. The stinking straw spread across the field behind them and along the footpath. Some of it even whirled over the cliff edge.

As they rounded the derelict building, Mu could hear the sea pounding against the loose sandy cliffs and felt the spray mixed in with the spattering rain. The vicar walked inside the three walls and pointed to the corner, where rubble was jammed down the old set of stairs.

'Was that where Roger wanted to go?' he asked.

Mu nodded.

'Let's go then, Terry.'

He tugged gently at the dog's lead. Terry refused to budge. His tail was clamped between his legs, and his ears were sagging. Whether it was the weather upsetting him or the place, Terry wanted to go no further.

'Isn't that what he was interested in before?' asked Mu. She raised her voice over the noise of the storm and the crashing of the waves below.

'It was,' said Theo.

'I think he just wants to go home,' suggested Mu. *And so do I.*

Theo led them back out to the muck stack. He walked around the edge of it, Terry and Mu reluctantly following. Both of them had their shoulders hunched against the weather. Theo seemed unaffected, although the wind whipped his trim grey hair into points. There was some protection behind the stack, which meant that the stink previously blown away now came back in full force.

'If what Gilly said was correct,' Theo said loudly, 'then there must be another end to the tunnel.'

'It could go in any direction.' Mu looked pointedly at the sky. 'It's getting dark. We'll never see anything in this.'

'I think it must come this way.' Theo pointed to the ground the muck stack stood on.

'Why?'

'Look at the floor.' He kicked at a pile of muck with the edge of his shoe. 'It's no accident that this lot is piled here.'

Mu bent over a little to inspect the gap he'd made. Underneath the piles of rotting straw, the ground was covered in concrete. 'Isn't that something the farmer might have done?'

'That's possible,' agreed Theo. 'You see, I'm interested in how the coastline moves over time, so I've studied old maps of the village. There were other buildings around here during the war. Mostly wooden ones. Perhaps the concrete was put down for them to stand on.'

Mu looked around the field behind them. She couldn't see any other signs of old buildings. She held up her hands with an expressive shrug to indicate the lack of evidence.

'There were guns at either end of the battery,' Theo shouted over the wind. 'The missing end was over there.'

He dragged Mu and Terry away from the shelter of the dung heap to face the cliff edge. He shouted again, pointing about thirty yards along the footpath to an old cliff fall. 'It fell into the sea in the 1990s. The council had to smash it up on the beach and bring it out on lorries.' Theo pointed excitedly to the remaining structure. 'The rooms Gilly talked about must be under the old emplacement. This underground corridor must have run between sections of the battery.'

Mu shrugged. Her anxiety was rocketing. Why couldn't the vicar just let them go home?

'I didn't know it was even there.' He began to walk up and down, staring at the floor. 'But it makes sense that there must be an entrance somewhere else to get down inside.'

Mu stood with her hands stuffed into her pockets out of the wind, praying that no one was watching them.

'Aha!' called Theo in triumph. 'Look here.'

Under a thin layer of mud and straw, he had found a large manhole cover. Bending over, he tried to lift it.

Mu ran to stop him. She grabbed his hands, ripping them off the metal handles with unexpected force. 'You mustn't,' she hissed in terror. 'We don't know if anyone is down there.'

'If there is, they'll need help.' Theo's face crinkled with earnest Christian zeal.

'If there is, they're being guarded,' snapped Mu. 'Otherwise, why was I thrown out of the old office? Leave it alone.'

She turned and ran along the farm track as fast as she could, leaving the vicar as far behind as possible.

CHAPTER 50

'I know,' snapped DS Mead. 'I'm sorry.'

'Not good enough.' DCI Hudson was not in a forgiving mood. 'Here we all are, giving up our Christmas leave, and you threaten a suspect.'

DI Edwards perched on the edge of Sara's desk. Mercifully, she could barely see the confrontation as he was blocking her view. Even Edwards was shuffling uncomfortably. DC Adebayo had wandered off to fill the coffee pot to avoid the impending fight.

Edwards cleared his throat. 'It's not so bad,' he suggested. 'The duty solicitor shut down the interview, as you would expect. You might have to apologise, though. No doubt the man has some high-flying London lawyer who will be rushing to his side the day after tomorrow.'

DS Mead threw his notepad and pen angrily onto the spare desk. 'I know, I know. It was all that shit about the posh clubs. The arrogance of the man.'

'The rich are ever with us,' said Edwards jauntily.

'And ever getting away with it,' said Sara from her seat.

'If you can't control yourself, you can go back to London,' said Hudson. 'We'll update you when we have more information.'

'No, I can't,' replied Mead. 'Not unless the trains are still running or one of you is prepared to drive me back.'

'Not in this.' Edwards looked out the office window. Night had closed in. Street lamps highlighted the trees bending in the howling wind. Rubbish whirled in mini-cyclones along the pavements. There wasn't a single person to be seen.

'We'll be lucky if everyone left on shift doesn't end up called out tonight,' sighed Hudson. 'Look at it.'

Sara checked her computer before turning it off for the night. The system showed a message had been left for her from her neighbour Gilly. She had no idea what could be so important that she would try to contact her at work. Unwilling to talk to Gilly while driving home, Sara picked up the office phone and dialled the number.

'391768,' said Gilly.

'What have I told you about saying that? Just say hello. It's safer.'

'Ah, Sara. Thank goodness you've called. I've been trying your mobile all afternoon.'

'I had it switched off. We were interviewing.' Sara wasn't going to admit that she had left it on her desk and forgotten about it.

'Right. Didn't know you had to do that.'

'What's so important?'

'It's about this homeless woman. Mu.'

'Didn't you find her?'

'Yes, we did, or at least the vicar did. We've moved her into the old van at the bottom of the vicarage garden.'

'Oh good.' Sara was even more puzzled. 'So?'

'She told us this story,' said Gilly. 'Have you got time to listen now? I think it might be important.'

Sara thought about Neil McCarthy, sat downstairs in the holding cell, looking forward to his Christmas dinner courtesy of the prison system. She thought about DS Mead, angry with himself for pushing too hard. Looking at her boss sitting rigidly in her office, Sara knew she was missing her family. Edwards had retreated to his own room and was gloomily fiddling with his computer. Was Dr Taylor still at the hospital working on the post-mortem of that morning's victim from the angling club? Everyone was at a standstill. 'Yes, Gilly. I have time. What is this about?'

Gilly drew in a breath and launched into her story. Sara listened with increasing incredulity. When Gilly finally stopped, Sara was stunned for a moment. 'Hold on, what did you say this website was?'

'The one my grandson showed me? I think it was called UrbForum, or something like that.'

Sara tapped it into the search engine. It soon threw up the site. She tapped on an article headlined 'Happisburgh Underground Gun Emplacement', with several flash-lit photos showing three mud-filled rooms with blackened brick walls. One contained several rusting metal frame bunk beds, which the author claimed had been used during the war. Another showed smashed-up tables and chairs, the wood green with slime. The third was empty, though the remains of what might have been fireplaces formed part of one wall. Other pictures showed a corridor, one end of which had a set of stairs now blocked by large blocks of concrete and rubble.

'That's amazing,' said Sara. 'How do you reckon these photographers got in?'

'The vicar says he's found a big manhole with a cover. Near where the farmer dumps the muck out of his stables.'

'And you think people are actually living down there now?' Sara was inclined to be sceptical. The underground rooms clearly existed when the urban explorer had been down there three years ago, according to the date of the article. Whether it was still accessible or even existed was another matter.

'It's not just us,' said Gilly. She sounded slightly offended. 'Mu saw that man from the pub going down there with the food bag.'

'That's the weirdest thing, for sure.' Sara didn't want to disrespect the homeless woman or doubt her word. But experience taught her that homelessness often led to drinking or drug-taking. Mu could simply have been pissed or high or just plain imagined it. Especially given the incident she had run away from in the West End. 'I think I need to talk to this woman, if she's willing.'

'I haven't told her about you.' Gilly hesitated. 'She doesn't know we've spoken to you about that other man.'

'Okay,' said Sara. 'That could be difficult. All the same, I think I ought to try. Will you come with me?'

'Of course.'

'I'll call on you when I get home, then.'

Sara put down the phone and surveyed the despondent office. Mead sat tapping a pen angrily on the desk. Hudson was on the telephone and had swung her chair round to face away from them. DC Adebayo had returned with the water-filled coffee jug. He stood looking round. 'Does anyone actually want any coffee?'

There was no reply. He dumped the jug on its stand and sat at a spare desk.

Sara headed for DI Edwards's room to tell him what Gilly had said. He listened impassively, as did Mead and Adebayo.

'Do you think it's important?' Edwards asked.

'Yes, I do, boss,' she admitted. 'It might just be kids mucking about or homeless people falling out. But it sounds suspicious. Why did the pub landlord and chef attack this young woman and drive her away? Something's going on.'

'Could it be connected to all the rest of it?'

'It would make sense,' insisted Sara. 'I know the RIB and the *Empire State* turned up further round the coast, but what if this is where they put Gary ashore?'

'You don't think he got off the boat in Yarmouth?'

'He might have, but we're part of the "dark coast" at Happisburgh. Far fewer people to witness anything.'

'London's into drug trafficking,' said Mead.

'People smuggling is very lucrative, isn't it?' Sara asked him. 'She likes to make money.'

'All right,' said Edwards. 'Don't go alone, though.'

'I'll come with you,' volunteered Adebayo.

Just what I need, thought Sara. 'I doubt I'll be coming back to the city tonight,' she said, trying to sound grateful. She didn't want to be stuck with him as a visitor. Not just the two of them alone in her house.

'Or I can come,' offered Mead.

'You have a perfectly good hotel room to go to,' said Sara. 'Why would you want to end up in my spare bedroom? It's rammed with junk.'

'It would take my mind off this afternoon,' said Mead.

'I can sleep on the sofa,' Adebayo suggested.

'We can't all descend on this poor woman mob-handed,' said Sara in exasperation.

'I'll talk to the vicar,' offered Mead.

'And I'll talk to the pub landlord,' added Adebayo.

'For God's sake, take them both,' said Edwards. 'Just bring them back in the morning unharmed by this storm.'

CHAPTER 51

It was getting dark outside, and the storm was becoming intense. Two guards had come over from the facility to protect the farmhouse's driveway. They were covertly armed. Mrs McCarthy had served up the meal she'd been cooking, although no one was interested in it. After clearing away the plates, they put all the bags into the back of the Mercedes.

Danni had checked the weather forecast closely. The storm surge was due soon and would last three to four hours. After that, Storm David would begin to transit off to the near continent. The worst would be over by tomorrow evening. There were predictions of power lines down, especially across East Anglia. She had taken it upon herself to warn Striker, who had busily gathered all the torches and batteries he could find.

London pulled Danni to one side. 'Book us on the first available ferry from the nearest port as soon as they're sailing again,' she demanded.

Danni found one running from Felixstowe to Calais on Boxing Day morning, subject to the weather. She booked the car under its current false plates. There were four passengers. London was leaving Mr and Mrs Strong behind.

She confirmed the booking with her boss, who murmured, 'You've stayed at this "safe house" in Norwich, haven't you? How safe would you say it is?'

London didn't often ask for Danni's opinion, and she was flattered. 'Nick's just a user who got drawn into small-time dealing. I suspect he prefers to be a safe house than a middleman. He talks too easily. One night might be okay. I doubt he could cope with more.'

'We need two,' muttered London. 'Call him. For tonight, at any rate.'

Danni did as she was told. Mr Chatty sounded almost pleased to hear from her. When she told him that he might have guests that evening, he readily agreed to be at home waiting for them.

'Actually, it will be nice to have some company at Christmas,' he said. 'I'll nip down the shops for the extra food before they all shut.'

'Don't tell anyone that you're expecting guests,' warned Danni. 'I mean it. One slip-up, and I can't be responsible for the consequences.'

'No problem.'

Danni was perturbed to see a police car go past the end of the drive as they prepared to leave. London didn't appear until the guard on the gate told them it had gone out of sight.

Mr and Mrs McCarthy were astonished to be forced into the back of Neil's car. Striker drove their Land Rover while a guard chauffeured the Mercedes. The final guard followed in one of the beat-up red vans from the facility. The farmhouse was now deserted.

'She doesn't need to see this,' begged Carl McCarthy as the couple were dragged out into the yard at the facility.

'Everyone involved needs to see this.' London's face was set solid, her tone verging on ballistic. 'Get them inside.'

Mrs McCarthy was pulled through the CCTV room with its dozens of screens, her eyes wide. They widened further when she saw the growing room. Danni thought they would leave her head when the older woman walked through the laboratory and packing area.

'I never knew,' she muttered to her husband. 'My God, Carl. What has Neil got us into?'

There were guards on duty as usual. Those with less to do were gathered in the canteen area. The McCarthys seemed shocked to see how many men were inside the buildings. Danni wondered how they would have reacted if there had been the usual complement of workers there as well.

London told Jerry to gather as many guards as he could. 'Those in the observation room should also listen,' she said. 'Get everyone sitting down.'

Their party gathered at the back of the men to listen. Danni placed herself next to Gary at one table. The McCarthys sat at the adjacent one, with Striker standing behind their seats. London sat making notes in her ever-present Filofax until the guards had been gathered. Then she stood at the front of the room.

'You all know what's been happening here over the last few days,' she began. 'I can't say I feel some of you have handled the situation very well, but we are where we are.'

Some of the guards looked at the floor.

'However, that is nothing compared to the incompetency of the McCarthy family.'

Mrs McCarthy looked round in bewilderment. Her husband bristled angrily.

'I am left with no option but to close this facility entirely,' continued London.

A shocked murmur ran through the room. Carl McCarthy spoke loudly. 'You can't do that. What about my brother? What about us?'

Several of the guards laughed at this. Striker stepped forward and placed one hand on the man's neck and shoulder and squeezed, making the farmer grunt in pain.

When the room calmed down, London continued. 'I know it's Christmas, but this must be done over the next twenty-four hours. If you complete it in time, there will be a good bonus for every man in this room. You will also be provided with travel back to where you came from.'

This was met with approval.

'As soon as this meeting is finished, Mr McCarthy over there—' London pointed at the farmer — 'will provide you with additional vehicles. He will also advise where to dump the growing room contents. We can hardly burn it.'

'People around here would be high for days,' said a voice from the group.

Even London managed a smile at this. 'The equipment can be smashed and left,' she continued. 'The observation suite must be cleared. Find somewhere to dump it all and break it all up. Now, onto the last batch of workers. We can't leave them where they are.'

'Why not?' shouted another voice.

This fell into a silence.

'Because even I won't leave a pregnant woman under-ground with a bunch of strangers.'

A hiss ran round the men. London allowed them to settle again.

'Don't think I'm turning soft,' she said in that menacing low tone Danni recognised. 'I'm not.' She glared around the room.

No one challenged her.

'There's a storm over the country right now. This is our best advantage. People will not only be at home preparing for the holiday but they will also be frightened of going out in it. There will be few people to see us, and the police will be busy elsewhere with emergencies.'

As if to prove the point, the wind battered the facility roof, and rain shattered down like broken glass.

'We will take three vans, each with three men. Decide between yourselves who is going on which job. You will take the workers to designated places and let them go. You will not bring them back here. Afterwards, you will return here to help with the shutdown. If you all do as you are told, this facility should be closed before tomorrow morning, when you can disperse. Your bonus money will, of course, be in cash. The vans can be used for transport and burned wherever you deem convenient outside the county. Oh, and I want videos to prove it. Don't think you can take them away as an additional payment. Nothing should be traceable back to this operation. Any questions?'

There weren't.

London placed her diary on the table before her and looked around the assembled guards. 'Anyone who fucks this up can expect a visit from the family within forty-eight hours.'

CHAPTER 52

It was after seven o'clock when Sara finally arrived at the vicarage with Gilly in tow. The journey had been tetchy, with the two men curled up in her Fiat 500 grumbling about lack of space. The wind had tugged at the car constantly and Sara had gripped the wheel until her knuckles were white.

They had collected Sara's neighbour after popping in to feed Tilly, who had hidden under the sofa spitting at the two strange men. Fortunately, it was only a few hundred yards to the Hall House. The pub had looked packed from the outside. Sara had wondered what kind of welcome Adebayo would get on such a busy evening.

Leaving Sara's little car in the pub car park, they had struggled up the small lane past the church to the vicar's house. Gilly had warned Theo and Vicky that they were calling. No one had dared to broach the visit with Mu, who remained in her caravan, oblivious to the impending police presence.

'If you're from the Met,' said the vicar, 'would you be here about Mu's friend Mark?'

'Not officially,' said Mead. 'I'm here to help DS Hirst. But I'll be happy to check it when I get back. There should be CCTV, if nothing else. Could you tell me what you've heard about it?'

'I can do that,' agreed Vicky. 'I think Theo should go down to the caravan with DS Hirst. It's a matter of trust.'

If the woman trusted anyone, Sara suspected it would be Gilly. She smiled and agreed with the couple, ensuring that Gilly went with them anyway.

The garden was as sheltered as anywhere was likely to be in the current weather conditions. They were still buffeted and pummelled by the gusts. Theo knocked loudly on the door, and a dog's bark answered. The door wasn't opened. Instead, a woman's voice called, 'Who's there?'

The dog barked more vigorously.

'It's me, Theo,' said the vicar. 'I'll go to the window.'

He moved to one side, where ivy almost obscured a grubby old window and waved. A figure moved beyond the ivy curtain. After a moment, the door opened slightly. From the back of the trio, Sara could see a young woman's fearful face peering out of the gap.

Gilly moved forward so that she could be seen fully in the light that came from inside. 'This is my friend and neighbour,' she said. 'Please don't shut us out. Sara is a police detective. She's come about what you've told us. Please talk to her.'

The woman considered her options. Then turning to calm the barking dog, she opened the door wider.

Luckily, Mu had spent some of the evening stuffing more unused items into unused cupboards. She had unearthed all the sofa space around the dining table in the process. Three visitors along with an unsettled Roger made the little caravan feel packed. The police detective was taller than the vicar, who Mu thought was tall in the first place. Roger would not be completely consoled, and stood grumbling softly, hackles raised.

'I'm Detective Sergeant Sara Hirst.' The woman offered her warrant card. 'Please call me Sara. Are we upsetting your dog?'

'It's hardly surprising.' Mu rubbed his back to comfort him. 'Given that we were both attacked last night.'

'Let's start with that, shall we?' asked the detective.

'All right,' agreed Mu. 'You'd better sit down.'

The three arranged themselves around the table. Mu continued to stand and caress her protector. It also gave her easy access to the door if she needed it.

'I was so worried for you,' explained Gilly. 'That's what made me speak to Sara.'

'Do you know what happened?' Mu was surprised the police would even be interested in what happened to a homeless woman.

Sara nodded and repeated all she knew. 'Does that sound about right?'

Mu agreed that it did. Feeling more secure, she perched on the end of the sofa next to Gilly.

'I have a colleague here with me,' said the detective. 'He's from the Met. I left him talking to Mrs Collins. He has promised to look into what happened to your friend when he returns to London in a few days.'

'He's dead,' said Mu flatly.

'Perhaps. But we can find what evidence there is, if you would like.'

Roger sat down next to Mu and put his muzzle on her knee. She patted his head. 'I think we'd both like to know for sure.'

'About this underground place—'

'There's something else,' said Mu. 'Something I haven't told anyone else.'

'Can you tell me?'

'It happened on Monday night when I first arrived.'

'Why did you come back here?' interrupted Gilly.

The detective shot the older lady a frown.

Mu turned to answer her first. 'You know I needed to get away from London. I reckoned that if we could get back up here, no one would know where I was. I thought the caravan park would still be there. Maybe I could break into a caravan and live there for a while.'

'But it had gone,' said Theo. 'Three years ago, the cliff collapsed on that section, and the owners gave up.'

'Monday night?' asked the detective, trying to steer the conversation back to Mu.

'It was late. We'd settled for the night. It was the light that disturbed me.'

'Light?'

'From some torches. At first, I thought we'd been seen and were about to be evicted. So, I hid behind the outside door with Roger. That's when I saw them.'

'Who?'

'I couldn't see exactly. There must have been at least twenty people. They climbed up the stairs from the beach.'

Theo let out a gasp. 'That's insanely dangerous. The council should have ripped it down ages ago.'

The detective nodded. 'Indeed, they should. People were coming up the stairs from the beach?'

'Yes. The moon was out, and I could see them clearly. Then there was an argument and a fight between two of them. One got hit so hard that he fell off the edge of the cliff.'

Gilly gasped. They all fell silent as Mu continued. 'There was another argument between the people who seemed to be in charge. Then the whole lot went off along the path towards Walton.'

'Towards the old gun emplacement?' asked the detective.

'Yes. I didn't dare go outside to see where they went after that.'

* * *

Danni settled in for the drive up to the coast. Gary sat in the back with her, and jammed between them was a whimpering Mrs McCarthy, taken as surety of her husband's behaviour. The three red vans had left at the same time. Each of them was taking a different route to avoid looking suspicious. They had been travelling for over half an hour, and Mrs McCarthy hadn't stopped crying yet.

'For God's sake,' snapped London at the woman from the front seat. Striker looked at Danni in the rear-view mirror and rolled his eyes. 'Do what you're told, and you won't get hurt.'

Danni found the woman's noise deeply annoying. She felt her sympathy for the older couple seeping away as she gazed at the dark countryside flashing by.

* * *

'I like the sound of this less and less,' Sara admitted to Mead. She had collected him from the vicarage kitchen, and guided by Theo, they were tramping down the lane between the hedges.

'Sounds like people smuggling to me,' agreed Mead. 'Do you get a lot of that up here?'

'Not as much as Kent or Essex,' said Sara, raising her voice above the howl of the storm.

They were forced to lean into the wind as they walked up the farm track towards the gun emplacement. There were few street lamps in Happisburgh or further away in Walton, not enough to make any difference in the deep countryside darkness surrounding them. Each trained a torch to the floor to guide their steps, and all occasionally stumbled in the slimy mud or over tussocks of grass. The sound of the waves beating on the cliffs could be heard from the vicarage. Now they approached the cliff, the volume became deafening.

'Where is this manhole cover, then?' shouted Mead. 'Can you find it in this?'

Theo didn't waste his time trying to reply. He walked to the front of the giant muck heap and scanned the ground methodically with his torch. Piles of dirty straw danced and scurried across the floor, impeding his progress. After a couple of passes, he stopped and waggled his torch. The two detectives hurried over.

Despite her height and weight, Sara could feel the wind trying to tug her legs from under her, pulling her towards the edge.

'This,' said the vicar pointing to the ground. The manhole cover was steel. It glinted in their torch beams.

'That's new,' said Mead. 'Or recent, at any rate. This thing is from World War Two, yes?'

'It is,' agreed Theo excitedly. 'I knew something was wrong with it. If it was from the period, it would be cast iron.'

'Can we lift it?' asked Sara.

Mead took one side, and she took the other. After straining at it, they managed to lever the lid up.

A waft of stinking warm air came out of the space beneath. For a moment, Sara thought she saw shadows in the underground space. And for that to happen, there had to be lights somewhere. Then the impression was gone. The beam from their torches glinted on rusty metal rungs.

'Oh my,' said the vicar bending forwards. 'They *do* look from the period.'

Mead grabbed the man and pulled him away from the hole. 'Leave it to us now, Sidney Chambers.'

'My name's not—' began Theo. Then he held up his hands. 'Oh yes. I get it. *Grantchester*. Sorry.'

'You should go home now,' Sara called. 'It's dangerous up here on the cliffs tonight.'

'What if there's someone down there?' he demanded.

'What if it's just full of spiders and mud?' said Sara. She pointed to the farm track. 'Go home, and take care of Mu for us until we can get more help.'

Reluctantly, the vicar nodded. He turned and plodded off through the gloom. They lost sight of him as he turned around the end of the muck heap.

'Right,' shouted Mead above the wind. 'I'm going in.'

'No, you're not,' replied Sara. 'I am. It's my jurisdiction if there is anyone down there. Give me five minutes — if I don't come out, send for backup.'

Sara stepped carefully onto the first metal rung and climbed down.

* * *

254

Once Gilly had gone to the kitchen to find Vicky, Mu zipped up her anorak and put Roger's lead on. She waited in the garden while the dog relieved himself and Theo and the detectives set off to the gun emplacement. Then Mu dragged the reluctant Roger after them. She didn't need to worry about being heard. The storm was making an enormous racket. She stopped at the end of the lane, sheltering behind the hedges, and watched as the three torch beams wobbled across the farmer's field.

The detective had listened carefully to her story. Mu wasn't convinced that the woman believed her, although the vicar and Gilly obviously did. Mu hoped she was wrong, that the people had already gone. That Paolo only evicted her from the old office block to cover his activities. If she wasn't wrong, then Mu's experience of the depths of human cruelty told her that what might be happening under that gun emplacement would be grim. In which case, the three of them were heading into serious danger.

The police detectives were only doing their job. Risk often came with that. But Theo had been more kind to Mu and Roger than anyone since Mighty Mark. She was going to do her best to protect him if she could.

* * *

Sara took the rungs carefully, steadying herself on both feet before feeling for the one below. Mead stepped closer to the hole with each motion so that he remained in her eyeline until the last moment. When her feet found the floor, she looked up. She could just make out the outline of his head and shoulders against the storm-riven sky. The wind whistled in the manhole entrance, but there was hardly any air movement underground.

She turned and shone her torch in an arc. The steps had descended to one end of the tunnel. Ahead she could see the passageway looking exactly as it had in the website photos. The floor was slick with a layer of slimy mud. Compared to the outside, the air felt warm. Walking slowly and cautiously, Sara made her way along the brick-lined corridor. She estimated that the roof was nine or ten feet high and rounded like a barrel. Water dripped down in places. Sara guessed that she was heading towards the old lookout spot.

The corridor must have been forty or fifty feet long. Sara was well beyond where Mead could see her from the open manhole cover. The torch was doing a decent job of lighting things up, and to her left, Sara saw three doorways. The beam almost reached the end of the corridor, where the photos had shown an old staircase blocked by large pieces of rubble and concrete. Now she could see that some kind of curtain was rigged in front of the area, which seemed odd. It fluttered in the wind.

There was a peculiar creaking sound, which seemed to be coming from the walls themselves. It rose and fell as if the ground was snoring in its sleep. Otherwise, the sound of the storm had receded, and the place was silent. Or was it?

The hairs on the back of her neck sprang up, and her heart began to race. Was that a human sound? That moan? Surely it was the storm outside. *Please, let it be the storm outside.*

Sara approached the first doorway. She was convinced she could see a dim orange light inside the first room. Her eyes were adjusting to being underground. Cautiously she turned to look, flashing the beam into the space, hoping to see nothing but old broken furniture.

Instead, it reflected in human eyes, gazing at her in terror. Paralysed with disbelief, Sara could only swing her torch to view the scene. Its beam illuminated eighteen to twenty men. They all looked to be young adults. Sara didn't doubt they had been selected from some refugee camp on the French or Belgian coast. Some of them looked at her, and some hid their faces. Most of them crouched near the floor, cowering in fear.

Sara had been right about the light. Its tiny warm glow lit the corner of the room, where a woman lay on a filthy mattress. A man sat on the floor holding her hand. The woman moaned in pain. This was where the noise had come from. The homeless woman had been right, but even she hadn't noticed this. Sara could see the woman was heavily pregnant. She lifted her head from the makeshift pillow, stared at Sara and began to speak. Sara couldn't understand what she was saying. The man sitting next to her looked up, hope on his face.

'You help us?' he asked anxiously. 'Baby coming.'

As she opened her mouth to scream at Mead to call for aid, Sara felt a hand grab her free arm and twist it up her back. She grunted as another hand slammed over her mouth. There was a brief moment of pain in her head. Stars danced in front of her eyes. Then she felt herself falling forward.

* * *

From where Mu stood at the end of the lane, she could see one torch beam weaving its way back down the farm track. Three had gone out. She waited until whoever it was reached the lane. Now she could vaguely see a figure. Unsure who it would be, she drew Roger close to her and pressed them both into the darkness of the hedge.

Puffing and panting, it was the vicar who approached them a few minutes later. When he was almost level with her, Mu spoke.

'Where are the others?'

Theo yelled with shock. 'Who on earth? Oh, it's you! What are you doing here?'

'Waiting for you. Where are the other two?'

'They're going down the tunnel.'

'No!' Mu shouted. 'It's too dangerous.'

'I wasn't sure myself,' said the vicar. 'Can you see any sign of their torches?'

Mu stepped to the end of the hedge and scanned what she could see of the fields. From the left, headlights appeared, weaving their way slowly along the lane towards the unlit farmhouse.

'What's that?' she asked.

Theo spun around and watched with her. At the corner, the lane turned up to the church. The vehicle didn't. It turned onto the farm track and began to jolt up and down towards the cliffs.

'My God!' breathed Theo. 'It's heading for the gun emplacement.'

As they watched in horror, another pair of headlights approached down the narrow lane. It also turned onto the farm track.

'We need help!' Mu shouted at Theo. 'Do you have a mobile?'

'The signal doesn't work here,' he moaned. 'Let's get back to the vicarage.'

He set off at a loping run. Mu followed, scooping up the weary Roger and running as fast as possible.

* * *

All hell had broken loose underground. As the stars in Sara's vision began to clear, noise exploded in their place. Torches were lighting the space, dancing crazily up and down the walls. She found herself sitting in the mud, leaning against the wall.

There seemed to be three men dressed in black outfits and wearing balaclavas. They looked like guards of some sort. The twenty men crouched in the darkness had suddenly been galvanised into action. They had encircled the guards, and the men seemed to be taking turns to try and attack them, yelling and screaming. The room was too small for easy manoeuvre. It had been one of the attackers kicking Sara's legs that had brought her to senses. Each sortie was beaten back. The guards were armed with knives and stick batons, which they waved in front of them, indiscriminately slashing or hitting their foes.

'Stop!' Sara tried to say. Her words were swallowed up in the shouting and mayhem.

In the corner, the woman had pulled herself up. She stood bent over, propping herself up with one hand on the wall. Her companion had not deserted her. He stood in front of the woman, trying to protect her. Sara levered herself upright, head spinning. Skirting the fight with difficulty, she reached the woman. Now all three of them were caught in the corner.

'More help is coming!' she shouted at the man, who appeared to understand her. She prayed that she was right. Surely Mead must have heard this racket and rung for backup. God knew how long it would take to get all the way out here.

Sara leaned on the wall and wrapped her free arm around the woman to support her. Under her hand, she could feel the bricks shifting. The sensation was peculiar, as if the wall was made of jelly. The gentle groaning she had heard in the corridor suddenly amplified. Sara knew what was happening in a flash and spun around to shout at the fighting men.

'Get out!' she screamed. 'Get out! The cliff is going. Everyone must get out.'

Her words were lost as one of the guards suddenly pulled out a handgun and fired two shots into the roof.

* * *

The vicar flew into the kitchen and ran to the phone. Vicky and Gilly stood in amazement as Mu staggered in behind him with Roger in her arms. She placed him next to Terry in his bed.

'Those police people have gone down the emplacement,' she panted. 'Now two vehicles are heading out there. We need help.'

For a moment, the three women looked at one another helplessly. Gilly was the first to pull herself together. 'The pub!' she said, leaping up. 'There's another police officer at the pub. We dropped him off on our way here. He must still be there.'

Then Mu was running again, this time behind Gilly, who was rather sprightlier than she appeared. Ignoring the risk to herself, Mu barged through the pub door and into the crowded interior, dragging Gilly in her wake.

'Which one?' she shouted above the din. Panting with effort, Gilly scanned the busy taproom. It was mostly full of men, all of a similar age. Several of them were wearing rugby jumpers. Perhaps it was some sort of club do, Mu guessed quickly. Then Gilly pointed. 'That one. DC Adebayo.'

Mu elbowed without apology through the crowd. The men hooted and cheered her as she reached her target.

'Are you a police officer?' she demanded. 'Did you come with Detective Hirst?'

The man looked at her in surprise. 'I did. Why?'

Mu tugged at his arm. 'You must come now. They're in trouble. They need help.'

Adebayo looked at Mu's panic-filled face and grabbed her arm. He steered her back outside, with Gilly following, still panting. Three or four of the drunken men followed them out to watch the fun.

'They've gone underground at the emplacement,' yelled Mu. 'Now cars are coming. You must get backup.'

Gilly nodded in confirmation and Adebayo punched a number into his mobile. There was no response. He shook his phone in frustration.

'No signal,' said Gilly. 'It's bad up here.'

Adebayo might have run inside to use the pub phone. The drunken men might have laughed at the scene in front of them. Mu might have stopped dancing up and down in frustration, or Gilly regained her breath. But there was no time for any of it.

Their ears were split by a sound that reached them on the wind of the storm. A rending and groaning. The scream of a building being torn to shreds. The sliding of huge amounts of earth. The noise echoed up past the church and around the car park. It headbutted the pub's walls and echoed up the little lane that ran down to the old caravan park.

'Fuck me!' shouted one of the drunken men. 'The cliff's gone.'

260

'Taken someone's house with it an' all,' yelled another. Their pints were poised in their hands.

'No! No! No!' screamed Mu. 'It's the old gun emplacement, and there are people down there.'

Everyone looked at her for a second as if she was insane. Then everyone was running, except Gilly. Adebayo aimed for the pub and the landline. Mu raced down the caravan park lane, followed by the drunken men. By the time she had got to the old office building, the number of men had increased. They were faster than her. Some held their phones in front of them, torch beams trained at the floor. Most just ran, trusting to luck.

Mu hurtled down the little hill, her legs gathering unstoppable speed as the members of the local rugby club streamed past her.

* * *

The Mercedes jolted along the farm track. It was difficult to see far out of the window, the light was so poor. Danni only realised they had reached their destination when she spotted the huge muck pile in the vehicle's headlights. Mrs McCarthy sat rigidly between her and Gary, still quietly weeping.

Ever cautious, Striker turned the car in a circle to face in the right position for a getaway. As he turned off the engine, they were all rocked in the violence of the wind.

'Will this wind never stop?' asked Gary.

'You be careful on that clifftop,' replied his sister. 'Or you might get swept over, and it's one hell of a drop.'

A couple of minutes behind them, Danni spotted the first of the red vans bumping toward them. London and Striker got out to meet it. Three guards climbed out of the front, stretching and readying themselves for action. It was pointless trying to speak in the noise of the storm. London beckoned them to follow her, and Danni watched from the car as they headed round the muck stack.

'I'm going too,' said Gary. 'Come on.'

They hadn't gone more than ten steps, bending against the force of the wind, before a man suddenly appeared from behind the stack, running as fast as he could. Gary grabbed Danni, pulling her out of the man's way and into his arms. Striker and one of the guards appeared in full pursuit. The man might have got away if he'd been fitter or luckier. Striker was gaining on him. His foot caught on a tall, heavy tussock of grass. He sprawled full length among the dirty straw and mud. When Striker picked him up, his front was foul with the stuff.

Danni gasped when she saw his face in the car headlights. She yelled to Striker, 'That's the pig that's been following us.'

Striker threw the man against the car bonnet and smacked his fist into his jaw. His head banged onto the metal and didn't come up. Striker had knocked the man out. Hooking one arm over his shoulder and yelling at the guard to take the other arm, Striker dragged the unconscious man back to where London waited by the open manhole cover. Danni and Gary joined her. When she glanced back at the car, Danni saw Mrs McCarthy climbing out of the back door. The terrified farmer's wife looked at Danni. Then she turned away and hurried down the dark farm track. In the scheme of things, she'd served her purpose. Danni ignored her. Let her go. Who cared?

'Tie him up and dump him.' London pointed to the muck heap. 'In that.'

Striker pulled cable ties from his pocket and the guard helped him restrain the detective. The other two guards stood waiting for orders. One had his head cocked, listening to something underground.

'Think it's kicking off in there,' he shouted.

'Go help them,' said London. 'Sort it out.'

The two men climbed swiftly down the metal rungs. Barely had the second man's head vanished when a sound came that Danni had never heard before.

It began with a rumble. The ground beneath their feet shook. Danni had never felt an earthquake, but living in

Naples, Gary had. He grabbed her and London, dragging them back towards the vehicle.

They could hear screaming from the underground tunnel, which was soon drowned out by a slithering, scraping noise that hurtled through the violence of the wind. As the noise grew louder, there came a rending of concrete. A groaning crash sent shards of metal and concrete from the derelict lookout post flying like shrapnel. Danni felt the debris whizzing past her as she ran next to her boss.

The ground shook several more times as three huge chunks of the cliff fell away. The land here was over a hundred feet above the beach. The cliff slid towards the storm-ravaged shore, dragging the remnants of the old gun emplacement after it. Ton after ton of material crashed into the surging waves below in a series of explosive splashes. There was a momentary silence, the sort that always followed a large accident. Then Danni heard a second rumble, this time from the underground tunnel. Part of the roof had collapsed.

* * *

Sara was deafened by the groaning sound. It came from the far end of the corridor, where the stairs were blocked off with rubble. The ground bucked under her feet, and the people inside the room were shouting and screaming. Never the quickest-thinking people in the world, the guards stood in the doorway, blocking off the exit. One of them fired his gun again. This time a man staggered backwards, clutching his arm. Blood spurted through his fingers onto the men standing next to him.

It was the final straw for the rest. They charged at the guards as one, running headlong into them. There was a brief struggle, but the mob soon had the upper hand and burst into the corridor. Sara lifted the pregnant woman bodily, ignoring her groans and the protests of the last man standing.

'Help me,' she demanded. They weaved their shoulders under her arms, then swept under the back of her legs to carry the woman as if she was in a chair. Her head hung forward as her body juddered with a contraction. They staggered through the doorway. The corridor was frantic with escaping men. Sara and the woman could go no further. They stood her down, and she promptly vomited into the mud.

There was an almighty cracking noise. The ground rumbled and shook. Sara turned to stare at the far end of the corridor. Then with a noise like a steam train passing at speed, sections of the cliff collapsed. Concrete and metal screamed as they parted company with the land. The rubble blocking the stairs sprayed outwards and backwards, ripping the curtain and the toilet bucket behind it to shreds. Sara flung herself to the floor, pulling the pregnant woman with her. Shrapnel from the collapsing building flew up the corridor, ricocheting off the bricks. Several of the fleeing men were hit by it, crying in agony as it buried itself into their flesh. Sara gritted her teeth as one piece embedded itself in her thigh, burning and stinging.

As the noise travelled towards the beach, there was another, closer rumble. Bricks fell from the roof and exploded from the wall. Glancing over her shoulder, Sara watched helplessly as the tunnel roof folded downwards, foot after foot collapsing to the floor, tons of earth following from above.

A blast of wind blew dust and broken bricks towards Sara and the stricken woman, her male companion by her side, staying with her to the bitter end.

Sara lay waiting to die. There was nothing else she could do.

CHAPTER 53

Mu stopped her headlong rush by crashing into the back of the halted rugby players. One turned and grabbed her to prevent them both from hurtling forward. The men were standing in a line, looking at the edge of the cliff.

Those who had torches on their mobiles shone them around. Where the footpath had entered the derelict caravan site, there was now one end of a semi-circular void. The cliff had fallen in a series of slides, the centre part losing the most land. Parts of the old gun emplacement walls and concrete pad could be seen hanging in mid-air.

The sea pounded the base of the cliffs hungrily. The footpath was now just a few feet away from the edge. The farmer's muck heap had also advanced many yards as the land had collapsed. Above the crashing waves and the howling storm, voices shouted and screamed. The beams from the mobiles picked up men who seemed to be climbing out of the ground, while other men tried to catch them. People were running everywhere. The rugby players stood paralysed, unsure what to do next.

Heavy footsteps clattered up behind Mu. The police officer from the pub had caught up with the group. He pushed through the line and surveyed the damage.

'Right,' he yelled above the noise and held up his warrant card. 'DC Adebayo, Norfolk Police. I want them all caught if we can. Use brute strength if you have to. We need everyone detained.'

He shone his own mobile light up the old fence line until he spotted a big gap. 'We can get through there. Let's get 'em, lads!'

The rugby players surged forward with glee. It wasn't often they were asked to help the authorities by having a punch-up. Pushing one another through the gap, they launched themselves along the path towards the struggling men.

Mu brought up the rear, grabbing Adebayo by the arm before he could vanish. 'Is help coming?'

'Yes, thank God,' he shouted. 'There are two ambulances and two police cars near Walton. They thought the sea defences there might be breached. They're on their way. More to come from the nearest station.'

He struggled through the gap and ran after the rugby players. Mu followed more slowly, searching for the female detective.

* * *

Bizarrely, it was the farmer's muck heap that sheltered them. Gary had dragged all three of them behind the twenty-foot-high stack. Striker was inches behind them. Blocks of rubble and concrete leaped into the air, rattling into the dirty straw like machine-gun bullets. Above the noise, they could hear panic-filled voices as both guards and captives emerged from the manhole.

Behind them, another set of headlights was bumping up the track. It was the second of their old red vans. Skidding to a halt in the mud, three more guards jumped out.

'Catch the bastards,' London ordered. 'Don't let them get away. We need to leave them where we want, not where they are traceable to us.'

Striker raced off with the extra guards.

'We should get in the car,' shouted Danni. 'We need to be ready to get out of here.'

London shook her head. Three men, fighting in a tangled heap, fell round the corner. Two were guards, and one a luckless captive. They wrestled him to the ground, binding his ankles and wrists. He was abandoned where he lay as the two guards returned to find more victims.

'This is chaos,' yelled London. Suddenly, she turned away and vomited into the muck heap. Danni watched in horror as her boss heaved her guts out.

'Please get in the car,' yelled Gary. 'Think of the baby.'

Danni's head began to spin. *Baby?* London clutched at her brother's arm until the spasm passed. Then she stood upright and firm. 'Let's get this sorted.'

She led them back towards the fighting.

* * *

Dust and chunks of brick sprayed past Sara where she lay using her body as a shield for the pregnant woman. The debris bounced off her back, caught the woman on her legs and covered her companion in dust. But the roof-fall stopped by the entrance to the second room about fifteen feet away, the noise echoing along what was left of the corridor.

Sara scrabbled up, pulling the woman after her. 'Come on. Move!'

What light there was barely illuminated the floor. The woman's companion clambered up using the wall. He helped get the woman up, and they propelled her along the corridor between them. Captives and guards were struggling around the rungs to the manhole exit.

Sara couldn't cope with them all on her own. She propped the woman against the wall and waited impatiently as the men climbed up one at a time.

'Get on with it!' she shouted. 'Get out before more of the cliff goes!'

* * *

The rugby players launched themselves into the fight with a roar. Adebayo was swinging left and right with his fists. From where she was, Mu couldn't really make out if anyone was winning. She skirted the worst of it, heading for the comparative safety of the muck heap. She could see vehicles beyond, near the cart track. Staggering to avoid two men pummelling each other, one a guard, the other an enthusiastic rugby player, she tripped and slapped onto the dirty straw.

It was disgusting. This close, the stink was horrible. The straw was also groaning. Startled, Mu shot upright. It wasn't the storm that was making the straw buck and writhe. Mu could see that someone was lying half-buried under the muck.

'Help me, for fuck's sake!' shouted an aggrieved voice.

Mu bent down to examine more closely. It was the Met police officer who had promised to find out about Mighty Mark.

Mu gritted her teeth and pulled the foul mess off him. He tried to sit up but flopped backwards again, his wrists tied behind his back and his legs bound at the ankles. Mu examined them helplessly. She had nothing that would cut plastic.

'Hang on,' she shouted. In the middle of the melee, Adebayo had got a man to the floor and was hastily fastening handcuffs on him. Mu rushed at him, tugging at his arm. 'You need to come with me.'

Adebayo didn't argue. He pulled Mead upright, then looked equally helpless at the cable ties. 'Fuck it! I haven't got anything to cut this.'

Mead snarled in frustration. He shook his head to clear the straw that was blocking his vision. From Mu's left, two women and a young man appeared from behind the heap.

Mead spotted them as well. 'Get her!' he screamed at Adebayo. 'That's Lisa fucking London! My cuffs are in my pocket. Get her!'

* * *

The scene was absolute chaos. Men were fighting everywhere. More men were climbing out of the manhole, some

268

joining in, others trying to run away, only to be rugby-tack-led to the floor. London was shouting abuse, trying to gain some kind, any kind, of control. Through the storm, Danni heard the sound she least wanted to hear. Emergency service sirens.

'Listen—' she grabbed at London — 'we have to go.'

A man suddenly ran at London. Too distracted by the scene in front of them, her boss didn't see him. Danni was shoved heavily out of the way. The man grabbed London and spun her around. A pair of handcuffs were on her wrists before Danni or Gary could begin to intervene. London howled in frustration.

Striker whipped around at the sound, dropping the captive he was hitting. He ran, roaring at the man. They collided, falling to the floor, punching and kicking. London staggered sideways.

Danni caught her. 'Come on!' she screamed.

London dropped to her knees. 'I can't.'

'We'll carry you,' yelled Gary, joining them at a run.

'No,' said London. She looked at Danni. 'Get him home. Get Gary back to Naples for me.'

'We can manage you too!' shouted Danni.

'You'll be faster and safer if they already have me.' London's head hung down. Danni knelt down beside her to catch her words. 'Take Striker. Go abroad.'

She looked into Danni's eyes. Danni nodded, beginning to cry. London was the one person who had helped her in all her life. 'All right. You can trust me.'

'I hope so,' said London. 'Besides, I'm pregnant. It's my get-out-of-jail-free card. Now get the fuck out of here before the reinforcements arrive.'

Striker and the officer had fought each other off. Before they could start again, Danni yanked Striker away and tried to drag him towards the car. He ran to where London was kneeling. She yelled instructions at him in Italian.

Then they were running. Striker, Gary and Danni. They scrambled into the Mercedes, and Striker gunned the engine.

Danni had no time to put on a seat belt as they bounced down the track at an insane speed.

Blue flashing lights streamed down the lane from Walton as they reached the farmhouse. Striker swung the wheel, and their vehicle shot up past the church. Spraying gravel everywhere, he drove through the pub car park, pulled the steering wheel hard and shot down a narrow track. When they reached the country lane, he turned in the opposite direction to Walton without caring where it led, and accelerated.

* * *

It looked to Mu as if the fight was losing momentum. Despite the amount they had drunk at the pub, the rugby men appeared to be gaining the upper hand. Which was lucky for the new arrivals, as a handful of coppers were not going to be able to restore order on their own. Two police cars were the first to reach them. An ambulance wasn't far behind. The four officers scrambled out and were immediately waylaid by Adebayo brandishing his warrant card. He made two officers take Lisa London away and lock her in their car. Then he ran to where Mu still stood helplessly next to Mead.

'Where's Sara?' he yelled.

'She went underground.' Mead had a faraway look on his face. 'She was down there when the cliff went.'

Adebayo sprinted away. Mu followed him. The manhole was now less than twenty yards from the cliff edge, where before it had been more like a hundred yards inland. The stream of men escaping had stopped. The detective flung himself to his knees and shone his phone light into the tunnel.

Mu dropped beside him. 'Hello? Hello?' she called. 'Can you hear us?'

A voice called after them. 'We need help down here. Who've you got?'

* * *

The last captives had scrambled up the ladder rungs, and the stormy sky showed through the manhole. It didn't bring much extra light. Sara could feel warm liquid trickling down her leg beneath her jeans. Her head was still woozy from the blow it had received.

The pregnant woman leaned against the wall and moaned and doubled up as another contraction came. The man stood beyond them, looking fear-stricken. Sara shook her head to clear it and was about to summon the energy for the last climb when she heard the homeless woman's voice. What was she doing here?

'Hello? Hello? Can you hear us?'

'We need help down here. Who've you got?' she called. The young woman was very slight. How could she help get this other woman up the ladder? Gratefully, she saw someone else look down at them.

'I'm here too,' called DC Adebayo. 'You need to get out.'

'I know,' said Sara. 'I have two people here with me. One is a woman in labour. Can you help me get her up top?'

Adebayo vanished, and Sara heard the two having a short, sharp conversation. Then he came back, leaning into the gap with both arms outstretched. Sara and her helper waited until the contraction ended, then pushed the woman to the ladder.

At first, she stood helplessly shaking her head. Then the man said something in a language Sara didn't understand, making the woman glance behind them. Wincing and groaning, she began to climb. Adebayo grabbed her wrists and pulled. Sara and the man stood under her, pushing at the woman's backside with little dignity. Slowly she made progress, her baby bump barely squeezing through the gap and up into the light.

Sara waved at the man to go next. He almost ran up the rungs. She felt a sharp pain run up and down her leg when she started to climb. With a muffled curse, she persevered. By the time her head reached the air, Adebayo was there to help pull her up the last few rungs.

The wind still battered at them, nearly knocking Sara from her feet. The stars were returning in her vision. She felt at the back of her left thigh with a shaky hand. A shard of metal was embedded there.

'Don't touch it,' shouted Adebayo. 'Look.'

To her amazement, two paramedics were running towards them. One had already reached the pregnant woman, who was almost by the muck heap. Adebayo waved frantically, and the second one headed towards them.

'This place is like a war zone,' muttered Sara. 'What the hell is going on?'

In the distance, they heard more sirens approaching.

'We need to get them further back,' said Adebayo to the paramedic. The man nodded.

They guided a limping Sara away from the manhole. Before taking more than half a dozen steps, there came a rumbling sound. Debris and dust shot out of the manhole and was blasted away in the wind. The last of the tunnel had collapsed.

'Fucking hell,' breathed Sara. Then she started to laugh.

CHAPTER 54

It had taken several more police cars, two transport vans and another ambulance to move everyone from the field. A fire engine had also arrived, and their powerful lights trained across the area had made life easier for everyone. The pregnant woman and her faithful helper had gone to the hospital in the first ambulance. The officers had rounded up and arrested everyone they could find. At one point, they also arrested a rugby player until Adebayo extricated him from the mistake. The players returned to the pub, where their names and addresses were taken. Celebrations ensued. The arrested men were taken off to various holding cells until they could be processed.

'Trust you lot to create all this extra work for us on Christmas Eve,' said one officer, but his tone and grin gave him away. 'Nice one.'

Sara had been whisked away in the second ambulance, Adebayo refusing to let her go alone. Mead, stinking of manure, had been offered a lift back to Norwich and his hotel room. He'd gratefully accepted.

A&E was full when they arrived. DI Edwards was waiting for them in the reception area.

'I heard,' he said, holding up his hands to fend off her objections. 'I wasn't going to leave you here alone.'

'I'm not alone.' Sara pointed to Adebayo.

'All right, I confess,' said Edwards. 'I can't wait to hear what's been going on.'

The paramedic hadn't attempted to remove the shard, and Sara was fast-tracked into a cubicle in case it had done serious damage. When the doctor had removed the object, cleaned and stitched the wound, he declared it to be 'not so bad'.

'In that case, I want to go home,' said Sara.

'To be honest, I might not be able to find you a bed anyway,' the doctor admitted. 'Will you be on your own?'

'Yes, but I have a wonderful friend next door who will keep an eye on me.'

'Did I mention you should get some rest?' asked the doctor. 'Give the wound time to heal.'

'I'll try,' said Sara, knowing she wouldn't.

When Adebayo objected to the plan, she pointed out that the pair of them were filthy. 'You should go home, get clean and have a rest. Like I'm going to do.'

'And how will you manage that?' he asked.

'I'll take her,' said Edwards. 'I know the way.'

Sara spent most of the journey telling Edwards as much as she knew between yawns. They speculated on what was going on. When they arrived, he watched until she let herself in, and then to Sara's relief, his car vanished. All she wanted was a shower and a cuddle from Tilly.

* * *

The next morning was, of course, Christmas Day. Sara took her time getting up. She fed the cat and wrapped up warm before collecting her car from the pub and limping into the office.

The mood there was jovial. DCI Hudson had brought in mince pies while Edwards made coffee for once in his life. Without fussing, they made sure that Sara stayed at her desk. Her leg was propped up on a spare chair. She told Hudson the story, with Edwards seeming to enjoy hearing it all again. DS Mead sat grumpily at the spare desk.

'Don't tell anyone where you found me,' he begged. 'I'll never live it down if it gets round my nick that I was trussed up and thrown in a dung heap.'

They promised to keep it in Norfolk, though Sara didn't doubt his colleagues would find out about it before long.

'Where is Lisa London?' she asked in an attempt to move them on.

'In the cells downstairs,' said Hudson. 'Refusing to say anything until her lawyer arrives.'

'Will we get to keep her? Or will she go back with you to the Met?'

'To be honest, at the moment, I don't know what I'm going to charge her with,' admitted Hudson. 'She was at the scene all right, but why? She might claim to be just a bystander trying to help.'

'That legal man of hers is pretty nifty,' said Mead. 'We'll need to find exactly what was happening. And God knows where that brother of hers is.'

'And Neil McCarthy?'

'Still saying very little,' admitted Hudson. 'We can tie him into the boat hire, but I'm not sure what else. We're running DNA tests on all the men we arrested last night. Perhaps that will break the wall for us.'

Things could have got gloomy by lunchtime. Their emails remained conspicuously silent. The phones never rang. The canteen hot meal was pasta bake and not an ounce of turkey in sight. Sara had a sandwich. But time was ticking. They'd have to let London and McCarthy go soon.

It was only two o'clock, and she had been wondering how long they would wait it out when Sara heard Aggie say, 'Don't they look glum?'

Standing in the doorway were Aggie and Bowen. He was carrying a food bag, while she had a large shopping bag full of crockery.

'Thought you might be,' said Aggie. 'As you couldn't have a proper Christmas today, I decided we should bring it to you.'

'Merry Christmas,' said Bowen. He laid out plastic boxes full of hot food. Aggie decanted plates and cutlery, encouraging the four who had been left behind to help themselves. The food was, of course, homemade. They piled the plates high, thanking their admin with genuine gratitude.

'I'm sorry, it will have to be instant gravy,' she apologised, boiling the kettle.

Hudson tucked into her turkey. 'You're a national treasure, Aggie.'

'Well, perhaps a local one,' said Bowen, pecking Aggie on the cheek. She blushed with pleasure. He turned to Sara. 'And as for you! What can we say? Are you putting her up for a bravery medal, boss?'

Edwards winked knowingly. So, they had already heard all about it, Sara accepted as she patted her belly comfortably. It was a good day, after all.

Hudson's desk phone ringing made them all jump. When the call was put through, they listened avidly. It was rare to see DCI Hudson smile, but she did now as she silently punched the air.

'Perhaps we won't have to wait after all,' she said when she rejoined them. She helped herself to another mince pie. 'That was Carl McCarthy. He and his wife want us to go out to the farm tomorrow. They have something to show us.'

CHAPTER 55

Striker had driven the Mercedes like a rally car through the lanes until they came to a place where they had to make a choice. It was clear that they were not being followed. The roads were effectively abandoned, some cut off by fallen trees or deep flooding. Danni got out her mobile and worked out a route back to Norwich that was less likely to have traffic cameras. They arrived at Mr Chatty's flat after midnight.

The men allowed Danni to have the spare bedroom to herself. Despite Mr Chatty's attempts to ply them with hot drinks, all had fallen asleep rapidly. On Christmas morning, Danni was woken by the tantalising smell of roasting meat.

'It's not a turkey,' apologised Nick, basting a large chicken. 'But I'm sure it will do for the four of us.'

Danni spent much of the day pacing the floor of the living room. She kept her mobile turned off and made sure that the other two did the same. They were hiding in Norwich, and the police would still be looking for them. It was all too close for comfort. Gary was subdued and anxious. Striker went off in the car for over an hour. When he returned, Danni went down to check on him. He'd changed the number plates again. It was a wise move, but it cost her an anxious half-hour as she went through the ferry company's website to make the alteration. When she'd done that, she made another booking for a pair of foot passengers on the Holyhead ferry to Dublin the next day.

Nick served them a tasty Christmas lunch. Danni and Striker tucked in on the army principle that you never know where your next meal might come from when you are on manoeuvres. Gary picked at it, eventually confessing that he was worried about his sister.

'I'm sure Mr Gray will be with her already,' said Danni. 'He's the best in the business. We have to do what she asked of us. You don't want to add to her worries, do you?'

Apart from Gary, they took turns to keep watch that night in case the police had worked out where they were. Danni was on the last shift, and she shook the others awake at five o'clock.

'Time to get up,' she told them. 'The ferries are running again. Get your clothes on.'

Nick had donated some clean clothes to the men but couldn't do much for Danni. She'd put her own things through his washing machine and accepted an overlarge navy-blue sweatshirt to cover her up. She pulled her hair back in an elastic band, making herself look as plain as possible.

Emptying her handbag onto the bed, Danni pulled up the base section and checked the emergency cash. She took three hundred pounds out of it and pressed the money into Mr Chatty's hand as they headed to the car.

'Listen, Nick,' she whispered. 'Things are very difficult right now. I would stay out of it if I were you.'

He nodded as he scrunched up the money and pushed it into his pocket. As they left the most hidden part of the block car park, she wondered if he would actually take notice of her warning. It was up to him.

The roads were largely empty. For once, Striker stuck to the motorways. It was quicker, and time was their enemy this morning as much as the police. When they reached the port at Felixstowe, the queue was short. It mostly consisted of lorries, with the occasional private car.

Worrying that they stuck out in the traffic, there was nothing Danni could do except hope that whoever had made the fake passports knew their stuff.

The man in the Passport Control window looked at the booking form on Danni's mobile phone. Then he made a show of checking over their passports. Danni's heart raced. She could feel it pounding in her rib cage as the man looked at each picture and stared at each passenger. He particularly paid attention to Striker. Wildly, she began to work out if she and Gary could get on board on foot if they arrested their driver. There was still plenty of cash in the bottom of her bag. Enough to find a hotel and give Gary time to contact the family in Naples for help.

'Says four on the booking,' said the man.

Danni leaned past Striker so the man could hear her. 'The other one couldn't come after all.'

The man shrugged. Then subduing a yawn, he handed their passports back to Striker and waved them through.

Danni's legs were still wobbling when they got up on deck. Striker volunteered to watch the dockside until they sailed if they wanted to go into the café. Danni sent a final text to Mrs Strong. *Have booked you both on this.* She added details of the Holyhead ferry.

After a few minutes, the reply arrived. *Thank you. We are needed in London.*

She turned the phone off again and checked that the others had done the same.

The ferry pulled away from the dockside, clanking and groaning. All they could do now was wait. The weather was calmer this morning than the previous few days, but the crossing was still rough. Its usual six hours extended to seven. Only Striker seemed unaffected by the rolling of the vessel. He lay on a sofa dozing. Danni and Gary sat in the café, nursing cold cups of tea.

'Gary, can I ask you something?' She kept her voice low. 'Two things, really.'

'I guess. What?'

'Who was Duncan Blake? He was on the boat with you all, wasn't he?'

Gary nodded. 'When I felt seasick, I went up top. Blake was driving. We chatted a bit to keep my mind off the waves. Then he began to stare at me. Like he recognised me.'

'And did he?'

'I must have met him before,' said Gary. 'Back in the old days.'

'Before you went to Naples?'

'Yeah.' Gary shrugged. 'I didn't recognise him. He started to laugh at me and say I was his golden ticket. Said that he was going to get money out of my sister to keep quiet about me being in the line. I panicked and yelled for Fabio.'

'And he shot him?'

'Yeah, he did. Not straightaway. We got the people off first. Then Fabio took him down in the cabin and shot him. We took the *Empire State* a few hundred yards off the shore and left it to drift. Thought it would sink, but obviously it got found. We pulled the RIB down and got back to the beach. That's how I got this.'

Gary held up his hand. The plaster he'd been wearing was gone, revealing a livid red scar.

'What happened to the RIB?'

'Dunno,' said Gary. 'We just threw it out to sea.'

And there it was, Danni knew. The lack of attention to detail or understanding of consequences. Gary may have toughened up, but he was always going to be a liability. She doubted the family would let him loose on something important again.

'You knew your sister was expecting a baby, didn't you?' she asked.

'That's the other reason I came over,' he said.

'Can you tell me who the father is?' Danni knew she was treading on thin ice. The family guarded their privacy intensely. After two years of working for Lisa London, Danni had no idea that her boss had become pregnant. There had been no indication that she'd even had a boyfriend. She had assumed that the discipline of London's lifestyle excluded messy ideas like romance.

Gary looked up at her. 'There isn't one. Not in the usual way. She went to a clinic.'

Was London desperate enough to do that? Did she want a baby that badly? 'I see.'

'No, you don't,' said Gary. He smiled sadly. 'You know our uncle?'

The one who owned the 3Js in Soho, who had brought them up after their father had been stabbed in a fight. Danni nodded.

'He's really old now. He wanted to see the next generation. Lisa felt she was the only one who could give him that in time. So, she paid for one.'

That was why they had gone there on Monday morning. To tell him the news. It seemed so damned long ago to Danni now. 'What about you?'

'I don't have a girlfriend.' Gary took her hand and pressed it. 'Do I?'

Danni shook her head.

'My sister said I should tell you that you're family now,' he assured her. 'We'll take care of you. Welcome, cousin, to the di Maletesti clan.'

So long as I get you home safely to Naples, thought Danni.

She bought food and water from the café, which she stuffed into the side pockets in the car doors when they returned to disembark. As they were waved down the car deck ramp, her wildly fluttering heart lodged somewhere up her throat. But the French passport checks were even more cursory than the British ones, especially as two of the fake passports were Italian. Only her UK one received a brief glance.

As they hit the first motorway, Striker glanced at her. 'You leave it to me now,' he said.

'We won't be safe until we reach Naples,' she replied.

'Three days or less. No problem.'

Danni settled back in her seat for a nap, knowing she could do no more.

CHAPTER 56

From the outside, the buildings belonging to North Elmham Estates looked like dozens of the other collections of farm buildings dotted around the Norfolk countryside. The only difference was that this set looked new and must all have been built at the same time. Farmyard junk, broken pieces of equipment, tarpaulin and wooden pallets littered the yard.

Sara shivered in her winter waterproof. Her leg ached, and the wound had bled again that morning when she'd changed the dressing. What a way to spend Boxing Day. The weather was improving, but it was still cold and windy. She stood next to DI Edwards while Carl McCarthy handed DCI Hudson a set of keys. DS Mead was wandering about the yard taking photos of the lights and very evident security cameras on his mobile.

'What did you want to show us?' asked Hudson.

'You'll see,' said the farmer. 'Not going back in there.'

His wife stood next to him. She had a black eye and a bruise on her neck. 'We'll wait here.'

Hudson went to the only visible door and tried several keys to find the correct combination. Sara, Edwards and Mead followed her inside. Using her torch, Sara located an electric board behind a reception desk. She flicked on the main power switch, and the buildings blinked into life. A large grey cupboard on the wall behind the desk clicked and whirred. Sara pulled at the door to reveal a large power input board.

'This place is eating up juice,' she commented.

After some trial and error, they got through the door behind the counter. Inside, the building was like Aladdin's cave. The first room must have been some kind of observation room. Ranks of metal shelves had probably housed screens. A row of desks stood underneath, their surfaces pitted with dirt and bare clean patches that showed where computer equipment must have stood. Cables hung from the walls, running off into rooms they could only guess at. More cables littered the shelves, the desks and the floor. But the equipment itself had gone. The next door led to a large room with day-simulation lighting. Row after row of bare tables, smothered in soil, stood empty.

'Cannabis-growing factory,' muttered Hudson. 'I've seen one before.'

'The plants have all gone,' replied Edwards.

'Forensics will have a field day in here,' said Hudson. 'They'll be able to prove it easily.'

Sara opened the door to the next room. It looked as if it had been a laboratory and packing area. 'Not just cannabis. Looks like they made pills of various sorts here.'

There were a dozen or more work areas and machines, all of which had been smashed beyond repair. Against the furthest wall, racks held chemicals in plastic containers, packing supplies and other paraphernalia.

'They must have run out of time,' said Mead. 'Or been warned about the fight at the coast. I doubt they would have left this lot otherwise.'

Another door led them to what seemed to be a canteen area. Cramped dormitories and washroom facilities were located behind that. A final door led to a narrow corridor. There were two small rooms at the end, their doors thick and solid.

'Fucking cells.' Edwards sounded horrified. 'They had cells.'

They went back outside. Sara had never seen anything quite like this place before. The cannabis operations she had been involved in rooting out before had been smaller. Often in lock-up garages or back rooms of workshops on run-down industrial estates. This purpose-built factory was way outside her experience.

Mr and Mrs McCarthy waited for them in the farmyard.

'You knew about this place?' asked Hudson.

'Sort of,' admitted Mr McCarthy. 'They paid me a lot of money to let them build it here.' He pointed to the scrub-land at the rear of the buildings. 'It was useless for farming anyway.'

'Did you know they kept workers here? Like prisoners?'

The couple looked at each other in embarrassment.

'What did you think was going on?'

'No women,' burst out Mrs McCarthy. 'They promised. Men only. Said they would work for a few weeks and then be paid off.'

'Where on earth did you think these men would come from?' asked Edwards.

Neither McCarthy answered him. The farmer reached out and gripped his wife's hand.

'Where did you get those bruises, Mrs McCarthy?' asked Sara.

The woman drew herself up proudly but didn't reply.

'They did that to her,' said her husband. He turned angrily to face Sara. 'Last night. They took her hostage. When she resisted, that man hit her. Dragged her off with his hand round her throat.'

Violence to others was acceptable, mused Sara. Violence to themselves was not. 'Is that why you contacted us? Can you tell us what man?'

'She called him Striker,' said Mrs McCarthy.

'She?'

'Lisa London.'

'Yes!' DS Mead hissed. 'Got her at last.'

'Neil told us that she was an investor. Said we had to put her up in our home. Then they threatened us and took my wife away with them. As security, they said.'

'What happened after that, Mrs McCarthy?' Sara kept her voice calm.

'We went somewhere in the dark,' said Mrs McCarthy. 'Another farm. At least an hour away. I could hear the sea. Then all hell broke out. People fighting everywhere.'

Sara felt the wound in the back of her leg. 'Go on.'

'They'd left me alone in their car,' the woman continued. 'In all the fuss, no one noticed I got out and ran off.'

'She got to the local pub and rang me from there.' Her husband finished the story for her. 'I drove out to pick her up.'

'Hall House pub in Happisburgh?' asked Sara.

'That's right. How did you know?'

'I was there. Most of us were.'

'Mr McCarthy, do you understand that you will also be in trouble over this?' asked Hudson.

The farmer nodded glumly.

'So why did you agree to show us all this?'

'They hurt my Eileen,' he said. 'I couldn't let them get away with that.'

'Not even for your brother's sake?'

'Especially him. Neil dragged us into this, and he will pay for it.'

CHAPTER 57

DCI Hudson declared that they all deserved a day off on Sunday.

'We all need some rest,' she said. 'Let's start afresh on Monday. The whole team will be here again by then. We can hold Neil McCarthy on the current charges.'

DS Mead arranged for Lisa London to be transferred to a holding facility in the Met jurisdiction on Monday.

'Her fancy lawyer is complaining,' said Mead. 'I hope we have sufficient to charge her with suspected people trafficking and drug production. I want to use it as a lever to get into the distribution network. You'll be able to come down and interview her with us.'

Hudson hadn't been very happy about that. 'This factory is on our patch. I don't want her taken away from us. The drugs team will need to be involved too.'

They had phoned ACC Miller to arbitrate the row. He'd agreed to allow London to be moved, at which point Hudson had sent everyone home.

Sara spent Sunday dozing on the sofa, collecting her energy for the tsunami of paperwork that was bound to be needed for such a difficult case. She went to work on Monday morning with less enthusiasm than usual. The storm had passed completely over the weekend, and as she parked in the HQ car park, it was hard to believe how bad the weather had been just two days previously.

London had left in the prison transport van early that morning. According to Mead, her lawyer, Mr Gray, whom Sara remembered from their previous encounter, had followed the van to its destination.

'He's not going to let her get caught up in this if he can help it,' admitted Mead when he called Sara to tell the team that their joint suspect had arrived safely. 'We'll need all the forensics we can get. A spell in prison won't harm her, though. Might make her think about her position.'

The forensic teams had called all available staff back from leave. They were now fully occupied at the farm buildings, collecting and collating evidence. A small group at the McCarthys' farmhouse even took samples to prove Lisa London and her cronies had been there.

Aggie was chasing mobile phone records for all concerned. Bowen and Noble were piecing together DNA samples and statements from the men arrested on Happisburgh clifftop. Adebayo was writing his own witness statement about the events. There were still lots of other statements to be gathered and the pub landlord and chef to be interviewed.

'Can I leave all the Happisburgh end to you?' Hudson asked Sara. 'Think of it as working from home for a couple of days. Take a uniform with you from the local station.'

'Of course,' said Sara. 'And can I observe your interview with Neil McCarthy?'

'You certainly can,' agreed Hudson. Edwards was going with her to do the interview. 'We still have our body on the boat to solve. Perhaps Mr McCarthy will explain that to us now.'

'I might be able to help with that,' called DC Noble. 'There's a match on the DNA database. One of the men we arrested at the gun emplacement was Fabio Rossi, whose DNA was on the RIB.'

'Let's get him over here, then,' said Hudson. 'Between them, let's see if we can work this out.'

* * *

Neil McCarthy's expensive lawyer sat beside him in the interview room. The businessman looked angry. His arms were folded as they had been before. Whatever his legal man said, he didn't look prepared to cooperate. With the preliminaries done and the recorder running, Hudson gave Neil McCarthy the bad news.

'We've had a long talk with your brother. He and his wife have given us statements about the factory at North Elmham Estates.'

She paused while the information sunk in. McCarthy looked at his lawyer in alarm but remained silent.

'We have forensic teams in there at the moment. Can you explain your connection to the place?'

McCarthy shook his head.

'What about an old gun emplacement next to the village of Happisburgh?'

'No idea,' snapped McCarthy.

'Were you aware that people were being kept there?'

'No comment.'

'It's the connections, you see,' explained Hudson.

Her tone was that of a schoolteacher talking to a sullen six-year-old. In the observation room, Sara was watching Edwards rather than the DCI. He could barely keep the smile from his face, and Sara was having the same difficulty. Hudson was going just the right way to make the man feel patronised, something he was likely to react badly to.

'We have spoken about your associate, Duncan Blake,' she continued. 'That you introduced Mr Blake to the owner of the *Empire State* and that Mr Blake subsequently turned up dead on the same boat.'

'Yeah, yeah,' said McCarthy. 'Nothing to do with me.'

'Four nights ago, we became involved in a mass evacuation at the old gun emplacement in Happisburgh.' Hudson changed tack abruptly. 'Several men were arrested and a pregnant woman rescued from a tunnel collapse.'

McCarthy looked uncomfortably at his lawyer. The man bent over to whisper to him.

'Yeah, so what?'

'One of the men arrested had also been on the *Empire State*. We're bringing him in for questioning. Perhaps he will prove to be the murderer. Or perhaps he will tell us who the murderer is.'

The lid blew off Neil McCarthy's temper. 'You're trying to fit me up. Just because I knew this Duncan Blake doesn't mean I had anything to do with his death.'

'We know you are involved in the drugs factory on your brother's farm.'

'I was just an investor,' snapped Neil. 'Carl said he needed some money and I could help him, so I did. I had no idea what he used it for.'

Charming, thought Sara. *What a pair. Both brothers putting the blame on the other. Glad I'm an only child.*

'Was Lisa London just an investor too?' Hudson pushed on.

'I've no idea. Ask Carl.'

'We did.'

Neil McCarthy turned puce. 'He's turned me over, hasn't he? Useless bugger. After everything I've done for him.'

'Then we have another body to worry about. A man was found at the Billingwell Angling Club lakes. He appeared to have been subjected to a punishing beating. Do you know anything about that?'

McCarthy's face was so red that Sara thought he might have a fit. He shot out of his chair, slapped his hands down on the table and leaned over, snarling in DI Edwards's face.

'That was all her. Lisa London. All of this is her fault. Her goons did that and forced me to watch. All right, I'll tell you about the facility. But I had absolutely nothing to do with any of these murders. You can't pin them on me.'

'*Any* of these murders, Mr McCarthy?' asked Edwards. He rose from his seat and went nose to nose with the businessman. 'There are more than two? Three perhaps? Is there someone in the lake as well? We did wonder.'

Suddenly McCarthy slumped back into his seat. He grasped his lawyer's arm to stop himself from falling to the floor. It looked as if the enormity of his situation had just sunk in.

'Let's start at the beginning, shall we?' suggested Edwards. 'Where does all your money come from, Mr McCarthy?'

Sara let herself out of the observation room and went to ring the diving team. They were not going to be happy.

CHAPTER 58

Their evening briefing became like a game of pass the parcel for the next few days. The sort you do with young children where there is a prize beneath each layer to prevent arguments. DCI Hudson convened the SCU team at about five, and they would vie with one another as to who had the day's best score. It started that first Monday evening when Dr Taylor arrived unexpectedly.

'I thought I'd pop by for some Christmas cake,' he said as Aggie pampered him. 'I finished the post-mortem on our friend at the angling club. He was given quite the beating, but it was two blows to the head that actually killed him. The really good news is from the stuff he was holding. Tests show not only his own DNA but also that of Luca Sinagra, bodyguard to Lisa London.'

DS Mead had been ecstatic at the news. London was refusing to answer any questions at all.

'It only places him at the scene,' said Sara. 'Not her. On the other hand, Neil McCarthy says they were both there.'

In terms of evidence, that meant one person's word against another. There was a lot of that to contend with in this case.

Sara had been unsurprised when she'd called at the Hall House and spoken to the landlord, Tim, only to find that his chef, Paolo, had vanished on Christmas Eve. His rather dilapidated car was found abandoned at the Birchanger service station on the M11. He was undoubtedly hidden among the London branch of the di Maletesti family. They let Tim off with a warning, as his main crime seemed to have been being stupid enough to allow himself to get sucked in via the chef. That and attacking Mu. She had declined to place any charges.

'He never touched me,' she said. 'It was all Paolo.'

Aggie had her moment of glory on the mobile phone front. Lisa London's personal phone had not been recovered, but the records showed it had been switched off on 23 December, the day that DS Mead had followed them out of Norwich. Well aware of the possibility of being traced that way, all the party must have switched to burners. The one person who had made a mistake was London's personal assistant Danni Jordan. If indeed it had been an error. Her phone had been turned on once on Boxing Day. It had pinged a mast at the ferry terminal in Felixstowe to send a text to a burner number. Sara suspected it would have gone overboard as soon as they were out at sea.

DS Mead had a good old-fashioned swear-fest when he heard about that. 'She got that damn brother abroad again, didn't she?'

'I suspect you're right,' agreed Sara. 'He's small fry anyway, isn't he?'

Fabio Rossi had his arm in a sling when they interviewed him. He also had one of Lisa London's expensive lawyers by his side. All they got was a prepared statement. Yes, he'd been on the *Empire State* along with Gary Barr and a third person, who he claimed had pulled the trigger on Duncan Blake. Subsequently, Rossi unhitched the RIB and escaped to shore with Barr, despite the heavy weather. The third man had carried on in the *Empire State*. He had no idea where the murderer had gone. No, he didn't know what his name was. No, he couldn't identify him. No, he had no idea where Barr had ended up or who Lisa London was. He was just a poor bit-part player in a wider scam. After that, it was professional 'No comments' all the way.

Who knew? It might even be true.

'No doubt the weapon is now decorating the sea floor,' sighed DCI Hudson after the interview. 'We can charge him with human trafficking, though.'

Sara's favourite interviews had been with Miss Marple and Sidney Chambers, as she had nicknamed Gilly and the vicar. She had spent a genial morning at the vicarage kitchen table taking statements from all three intrepid amateur sleuths. The homeless woman, Mu, looked clean and comfortable. Her dog sat dreamily next to the Aga with his chum Terry.

When they took a break for a fresh round of tea and cake, Sara took the opportunity to speak to Mu.

'How are you getting on in the caravan?'

'It's lovely, thanks.' Mu smiled at Theo and Vicky. 'We're being looked after really well.'

'When you look at it, that old van is rather nice,' said the vicar.

'I thought I might do it up a bit in the spring,' said Mu. She looked at Theo for confirmation. 'Paint it, make some curtains, stuff like that.'

'Can you stay here for a while? I'll need you to be a witness at the trial.'

'Mu can stay as long as she likes,' said Theo.

'I understand they might need some help at the pub,' said Gilly, a twinkle in her eye. 'In the kitchen, maybe?'

'I've done that before,' said Mu. 'Bar work and stuff. Mind you, the landlord might not be keen to see me. Or Roger, come to that.'

'I'm sure something else will come up,' said Gilly. 'Vicky has found a rural homeless charity that might have some accommodation in time,' said the vicar. 'Depends on availability, of course. We've set up a Just Donating site to help Mu get back on her feet.'

'I've offered to do things in return. It's not just begging,' said Mu. 'Like babysitting or cleaning.'

In Sara's experience, it was rare to find real Christian charity like this in action. She was pleased that Mu seemed to be sorting herself out. When she went home that night, Sara added an anonymous donation of £100 to Mu's page.

It was the pregnant woman who filled in some of the remaining gaps in the investigation. She gave Sara a statement, speaking through the man who had helped get her out of the tunnel as she cradled her new baby girl.

'They were in a camp on the Belgian coast,' Sara explained to the team. 'Moussa was with her husband and brother-in-law. A gang of men came around recruiting workers to go to the UK. Safe passage would be arranged in return for six months' work in a factory. A proper boat, not an inflatable. They refused to take a pregnant woman, though.'

'This was McCarthy's gang?' asked Edwards.

'It would seem so,' said Sara. 'On the prearranged night, they turned up and made the recruits wade out to the boat from a spit of land. Moussa was hidden inside the group. It was dark. The men were arguing and didn't notice that she'd got on board until they reached Norfolk. When they got off the boat, there was a fight between one of the men and Moussa's husband. He got knocked off the cliff.'

'At Happisburgh?'

'I assume so, because she says they only walked a short way before they were made to go underground. That must have been what Mu saw on her first night in the old office. It was her brother-in-law who was trying to look after her at the gun emplacement.'

'This wasn't the man on the beach with the seals, then?' asked Hudson. She pointed to the picture of the Sudanese family on the incident board.

'Unfortunately not,' said Aggie. 'DNA has confirmed it was the missing man from the container ship. I feel so sorry for his family.'

Sara agreed. 'By the way, they've called the baby Mariama Sara. Which, by chance, is my name reversed.'

'No chance about it,' muttered Bowen. Sara could have sworn he sounded proud.

Once Neil McCarthy had found other people to blame, he had revealed more details. In his opinion, was all Lisa London's fault. In Sara's, it was his own greed. Piecing it all together, the team finally worked out their routine of importing illegal immigrants to work at the drugs factory, keeping them locked up for six months and then dumping them elsewhere.

'So, who was the poor sod at the angling club?' asked Hudson at one meeting.

'McCarthy says there was some kind of riot at the factory, led by this bloke and his mate. He claims that London provided the guards, and they got too heavy-handed. The workers got beaten up and dumped.'

The diving team had spent more time in the water than they enjoyed in the cold December weather. Their reward was to find another body dumped about twenty yards from the bank, as the forensic team thought they might do.

They had difficulty getting any of the men they arrested that night on the cliff to talk about anything. Some were immigrants and were taken off to a resettlement centre. Sara knew their chances of being allowed to stay in the UK were slim. The rest appeared to be guards employed by Lisa London, if McCarthy was to be believed. Their only reply to any question was, 'No comment.' The forensic evidence turned up myriad prints and DNA traces, which showed that the men had been at the factory. But there was no way of proving which of them had done what. Their charges would be minor, and their sentences would be light.

It was DS Mead who delivered the final piece of news. 'I don't know how she's done it,' he growled over the phone to Sara. 'Bloody woman is pregnant, and consequently, they've persuaded a judge that she shouldn't be kept in prison while we sort out the charges. She's back at home in Ealing.'

'You're watching her, I assume.'

'Damn right we are. Tag on and everything.'

Three days later, Lisa London was gone.

When DS Mead told her, Sara knew she'd had enough of the stress. She needed a break and time to heal. That night she went home and booked herself a cheap two-week holiday in the Canary Islands.

* * *

Adebayo must have been waiting for Sara when she came back from Lanzarote. He intercepted her in the corridor as she returned to work.

'Did you have a good time?' he asked.

'I slept for most of it, but the sunshine was welcome.'

'Can I interest you in that drink soon?'

It was one of the things Sara had considered while she was away. 'Yes, that would be nice. Just let me get settled back in first.'

Aggie was the only one there to greet her when she reached the office. The desks were covered in piles of paper.

'Did you miss me?' Sara surveyed the mess.

'Of course. The others are out or in meetings. I brought a cake to welcome you back.'

Naturally. Aggie had news too. 'Do you remember Moussa said her husband got knocked off the cliff at Happisburgh?'

Sara nodded. 'How is she getting on?'

'At an immigration detention centre, I'm afraid. But they found him.'

'The husband?'

'Yes,' said Aggie. 'Washed up on the marshes in Essex, on a nature reserve. There wasn't much left of the poor man. They identified him through DNA.'

'Any sign of Lisa London?'

'DS Mead is still steaming about that. No official sightings.'

'Unofficially?'

'Flaunting herself and her baby bump around posh restaurants in Naples, I believe, along with that brother of hers.

296

Her PA, Danni Jordan, also seems to have moved over there. DS Mead said can you call him when you get back.'

Sara fired up her computer and then rang Mead's direct line. She allowed him to vent about Lisa London before asking, 'Was there something special you wanted to talk to me about?'

Mead paused to think. 'Is that homeless woman still staying in your village?'

'I believe so.' Sara had only had a brief catch-up with Gilly on her return.

'Then I have some news for her. I tracked down the CCTV of the fight she spoke about. It's unlikely that we will be able to bring any charges because we don't know who the attackers are. Despite running onto the knife, they never took their injured friend to a hospital. It could only have been a small wound.'

'That's a shame. At least we know it was true.'

'We also know where her friend is. He was injured, but he didn't die. I traced the ambulance that picked him up. They took him to St Thomas's and patched him up. Got the Street Army involved. He's recovering at one of their hostels.'

'Thank you so much,' she said to Mead. 'You're a star.'

Sara smiled as she wrote down the details. Their job was frustrating and difficult much of the time. It would be nice to break some good news for once. Maybe Mu would be able to settle down now and start a new life in Happisburgh. Just as Sara had.

THE END

ACKNOWLEDGEMENTS

I would like to thank Antony Dunford for his beta readings and notes. Your opinion is always spot on, and I am grateful for your time and energy on my manuscripts.

I'd also like to thank Clive Forbes, a former DI, for his police procedural advice and thoughts on whodunnit. Also, for his guidance and support, Burtie Welland, formerly a DS in the Met. Any incorrect procedures are there because I made an executive author's decision (or a mistake!).

My gratitude goes to Jasper Joffe for welcoming me to Joffe Books. It means more than I can say to belong to this fantastic publishing house. I am grateful to all the other authors and the staff who are so supportive and generous with their time. My especial thanks to Emma Grundy Haigh, Cat Phipps and Matthew Grundy Haigh, who have helped me improve the novel with their edits and weeding out of random punctuation. My grateful thanks to the rest of the Joffe Books team for all your work, from organising blog tours to spending time on reviews. I am proud to be a member of this wonderful band.

Last but not least, my family. My husband, Rhett, and my daughters, Gwyn and Ellie. Your support and understanding are crucial to me.

THE JOFFE BOOKS STORY

We began in 2014 when Jasper agreed to publish his mum's much-rejected romance novel and it became a bestseller.

Since then we've grown into the largest independent publisher in the UK. We're extremely proud to publish some of the very best writers in the world, including Joy Ellis, Faith Martin, Caro Ramsay, Helen Forrester, Simon Brett and Robert Goddard. Everyone at Joffe Books loves reading and we never forget that it all begins with the magic of an author telling a story.

We are proud to publish talented first-time authors, as well as established writers whose books we love introducing to a new generation of readers.

We have been shortlisted for Independent Publisher of the Year at the British Book Awards three times, in 2020, 2021 and 2022, and for the Diversity and Inclusivity Award at the Independent Publishing Awards in 2022.

We built this company with your help, and we love to hear from you, so please email us about absolutely anything bookish at: feedback@joffebooks.com.

If you want to receive free books every Friday and hear about all our new releases, join our mailing list: www.joffebooks.com/contact

And when you tell your friends about us, just remember: it's pronounced Joffe as in coffee or toffee!

ALSO BY JUDI DAYKIN

DETECTIVE SARA HIRST SERIES
Book 1: UNDER VIOLENT SKIES
Book 2: INTO DEADLY STORMS
Book 3: A BRUTAL SEASON
Book 4: AN ARTFUL MURDER
Book 5: THE NORFOLK BEACH MURDERS

Ingram Content Group UK Ltd.
Milton Keynes UK
UKHW011501180523
421969UK00004B/302

9 781804 058596